P9-CQZ-479

WALK ON THE WILD SIDE

"A seductive tale with strong chemistry, roiling emotions, steamy romance, and supernatural action. The fast-moving plot in *Walk on the Wild Side* will keep the readers' attention riveted through every page, and have them eagerly watching for the next installment." —*Darque Reviews*

HOWL AT THE MOON

"*Howl at the Moon* will tug at a wide range of emotions from beginning to end . . . [E]ngaging banter, a strong emotional connection, and steamy love scenes. This talented author delivers real emotion which results in delightful interactions . . . and the realistic dialogue is stimulating. Christine Warren knows how to write a winner!" —*Romance Junkies*

THE DEMON YOU KNOW

"Explodes with sexy, devilish fun, exploring the further adventures of The Others. With a number of the gang from previous books back, there's an immediate familiarity about this world that makes it easy to dive right into. Warren's storytelling style makes these books remarkably entertaining." —*Romantic Times BOOKreviews* (4½ stars)

SHE'S NO FAERIE PRINCESS

"Christine Warren has penned a story rich in fantastic characters and spellbinding plots." —*Fallen Angel Reviews*

WOLF AT THE DOOR

"This book is a fire-starter . . . a fast-paced, adrenaline- and hormonally-charged tale. The writing is fluid and fun, and makes the characters all take on life-like characteristics." —*Romance Reader at Heart*

Also by
Christine Warren

On the
PROWL

CHRISTINE WARREN

St. Martin's Paperbacks

ON THE PROWL

Copyright © 2012 by Christine Warren.

For information address St. Martin's Press, 175 Fifth Avenue, New York, NY 10010.

ISBN: 978-0-312-35721-4

Printed in the United States of America

St. Martin's Paperbacks edition / May 2012

St. Martin's Paperbacks are published by St. Martin's Press, 175 Fifth Avenue, New York, NY 10010.

10 9 8 7 6 5 4 3 2 1

For Mom, on the firm understanding that you'll stay healthy from now on. Agreed?

One

Her feet hurt, but not half as much as her face.

Saskia Arcos stood in front of the elegant marble fireplace, flanked by three imposing male figures, and wished desperately that this quote-unquote happiest moment of her life had included a couple of aspirin. Or maybe a morphine drip.

"We would like to thank all of you for joining us tonight for this wonderful occasion," her father boomed over the low buzz of conversation and curiosity, holding his champagne glass up in front of him like he'd just seized the banner in a well-fought round of Capture the Flag. Though not a large man, her father knew how to command a room. Imposing, after all, had relatively little to do with size, as two out of the three demonstrated clearly. "Joy like this is meant to be shared with friends and community. We are grateful to have each and every one of you with us tonight to bear witness as we join our families and our futures. To the happy couple!"

"The happy couple!"

The toast echoed through the high-ceilinged ballroom, the rumble of hundreds of voices nearly knocking Saskia back into the fire. Her own champagne sloshed in her glass as she swayed precariously. A hard-muscled arm slipped around her waist to steady her.

"Careful."

The quiet murmur drifted down to her, and Saskia looked up reflexively, straight into the gaze she'd been avoiding all evening. Green eyes stared down at her, their expression unreadable in spite of the flecks of molten gold sparkling in their depths. Even in the well-lit ballroom, Nicolas Preda's face gave away none of his feelings. Assuming, of course, that he had any.

"I can only echo Gregor's words and hope that this union proves to be a long and fruitful one." Stefan Preda's deep voice had hoarsened slightly with age, but the steel in it matched the resolve Saskia could see behind his son's calm mask. Neither man was one to trifle with. The son stood a head taller than the father, his shoulders wider and chest broader, but the pattern card shone through in the set of the jaw, the tilt of the head, and the glitter in the deep green eyes.

She suppressed a shiver.

"To Nicolas and Saskia!" Stefan proclaimed.

Once again, the room repeated the words and raised their glasses to the couple in front of them.

"I think that's our cue."

Confused as she was, Saskia knew better than to frown in front of her father's five hundred guests, but she felt her smile freeze when the towering figure beside her shifted. His words penetrated her social fog a split second before warm male lips settled firmly over hers.

Nicolas was kissing her.

The stunning thought took longer than the kiss itself. Before she had time to register the shock, the pressure eased and Nicolas lifted his head, leaving only a shadow of warmth behind. He turned back to face the assembled company with a grin of cocky male satisfaction. The arm he'd used to steady Saskia remained curved possessively around her back. To the guests, she supposed they looked exactly like a young, happy, newly engaged couple ought to look—him, tall and handsome in his custom tailored tuxedo, with his shiny Italian shoes and his playboy good looks; her, petite and delicate, in her apricot and gold gown with topazes dangling from her ears and an enormous diamond glinting on her finger. Tomorrow morning, she had no doubt she would see their photo on page one of the society section. She could picture the caption now: *Nicolas Preda (center), CEO of Preda Industries, Inc., and Saskia Arcos, daughter of wealthy European financier Gregor Arcos (l), pose with their fathers, Arcos and Stefan Preda (r), at their engagement party at the Royal Hotel, Preda's newly acquired Manhattan property.*

Readers across the city would ooh and ah over the details of the extravagant party and the famous and infamous guests. Everyone who was anyone in Manhattan had been invited to the festivities, from the mayor, to the heads of numerous Fortune 500 companies, to the leaders of Other society. The head of the Council of Others had dined at the head table along with the guests of honor and their families. Saskia had barely managed a bite of tender lobster, too distracted by the tension flowing just beneath the veneer of good-natured civility. She knew exactly what her father and Mr. Preda had hoped to achieve tonight, but that hadn't done much to calm her nervous stomach. All it had really done was make her hyper-aware of her own part in the performance, one in which she smiled constantly, nodded gracefully, laughed becomingly, and tried desperately to look comfortable beside the fiancé she hadn't seen in approximately eighteen years. After all, her job tonight was to convince everyone who saw her that two of the oldest and most powerful of the aristocratic Tiguri families had been firmly and permanently united as they moved into the future from their new foothold in North America. And she had to do it without uttering a word about the families' relocation from Europe, without looking anything other than bowled over by love and good fortune, and without so much as breaking a sweat.

Next to all that, the challenge of keeping a roomful of humans mixing in blissful ignorance with a company teeming with supernatural Others felt like a piece of cake. That part Saskia could have handled in her sleep. It was Nicolas she couldn't handle. She couldn't even think of where she could start that little project, and she *refused* to think about the fact that it was one she'd be stuck working on for the next seventy or eighty years. Thoughts like that were not going to help settle her stomach.

Neither was the feel of Nicolas's hand sliding from

her waist to the small of her back as he turned her toward the enormous double doors at the end of the ballroom floor.

"Come on," he murmured, leaning close to her ear, his breath stirring the strands of strawberry blonde hair that had managed to escape their elegant French twist. "We've got to make nice with everyone leaving. Almost done."

Saskia let him steer her through the crowd to take up their positions close to the exit. He deposited their drinks with a waiter along the way, and she found herself simply drifting along in Nicolas's wake as he stationed himself alongside the flow of traffic and began to share chuckles and hearty handshakes with their departing guests. The man looked like a politician, all charm and smooth words and wide smiles. With his expertly cut clothes and stylishly cut hair—a mix of browns and golds that defied a color label— Saskia couldn't decide if that image frightened or reassured her.

Most of the guests seemed content to let Saskia get away with an exhausted smile and a murmured "thank you for coming," and she felt grateful for that. She probably looked about as tired as she felt. They left her with a press of the hand and another round of congratulations, telling her what a lucky man Nicolas was to have her, or how she must be delighted to have landed such a catch as him. Of course, she always nodded and agreed, no matter how ridiculous they sounded. What was she supposed to do? Tell them that it was actually her father who had landed her fiancé, not her? That would go over nicely. So she continued to smile and nod and murmur and promised herself that when she finally crawled into bed tonight she would do it accompanied by a dose of painkillers so large, her liver would be begging for mercy all night long.

"Thank you very much for inviting me to join the festivities," a voice rumbled, jerking Saskia's mind back into focus. "The Council, of course, was pleased to be included, but I myself would have regretted had I missed being here."

Saskia blinked and lifted her chin until she could look up into a pair of startlingly golden eyes fixed in a dark, handsome face. The eyes surprised her. She'd never expected to see them so close to her own, let alone feel them burning into her with such focused intensity. After all, she might recognize the face of Rafael De Santos on sight, but considering how warily the Council of Others viewed those of her kind, she hadn't exactly pictured having a one-on-one conversation with him.

"Ah, y-y-es," she stammered, searching blindly for the poise she'd had hammered into her by tutors and nannies practically since birth. "Of course we're delighted you could come, Mr. De Santos. I hope this is only the first of many occasions when we will have the chance to get to know each other."

She offered the tall, sinfully handsome man a warm smile, the kind she'd been instructed to practice in her mirror until it looked completely natural and unstudied, and blinked when he returned it with one that glinted with feral power. Instinctively she shifted backward, and her shoulders brushed against her fiancé's jacket.

Nicolas looked down at her, his hand shifting to her hip to steady her. His glance flicked from her face to the man standing in front of her and Saskia could see his gaze harden.

"De Santos."

The Felix head of the Council nodded briefly. "Preda. I was just telling your lovely fiancée how delighted I am to have gotten the chance to meet her like this." His golden eyes sparked as he ran them over her creamy bare shoulders and the swell of her breasts at her neckline. "However sadly late it might be."

Saskia gave a start. Was Rafael De Santos flirting with her?

The hand on her hip tightened.

"We're glad you came to wish us well," Nicolas growled. There was no other word for the low warning that rumbled through the words. "My mate and I appreciate the support of the Council, especially considering we're both new to the city."

That last part wasn't precisely true. Both the Arcos and Preda families had kept houses in Manhattan for years and had visited the city frequently; they just hadn't made their primary homes in New York. Now, however, things were changing. Saskia and Nicolas's engagement was just one more symbol of that shifting dynamic. His terse tone symbolized that other things, however, never changed.

De Santos shifted his gaze to Nicolas, and the

liquid gold cooled and hardened. "The Council has never made a habit of coming between couples intent on marriage. Of course we support any decision that brings you both personal happiness."

And there it was. Saskia sighed inwardly. Without saying anything but the most polite of truths, her fiancé and the head of the Council had managed to each draw a line in the sand. The heaviness of the subtext weighed down on her like Atlas's globe. Maybe she should check exactly how much aspirin constituted an overdose.

"You're very kind," she jumped in, feeling the hand at her hip tighten and Nicolas's body draw up with tension. This was not the place for a scene, and since she'd been well trained to prevent such awkwardness, Saskia stepped in to soothe and deflect. It was reflex. Or maybe instinct. "Nicolas and I are delighted to have been able to share our big night with such gracious company."

She could see the awareness of her tactic in De Santos's eyes, could feel the way her fiancé's stiff carriage indicated a struggle over whether or not to call her on her interference, but damn it, she would not be intimidated. Not tonight. This was a party. It was not the time to rehash old enmity or to lay the foundation for future generations of mistrust and hostility. They could get back to all that in the morning.

Offering a determinedly steady hand, Saskia smiled up at the head of the Council and wordlessly dared him to contradict her implied dismissal. She saw a flash of amusement behind his bland expression and held her breath for a moment.

De Santos enveloped her hand in his much larger one and raised it to his lips. "I find myself unexpectedly delighted as well, my dear. I would not have missed this evening for the world."

His lips brushed the backs of her fingers, and Saskia blinked. In spite of years of instruction in etiquette and social rituals, in spite of finishing school in Switzerland and one memorable tea at Windsor Castle, she'd never had any man kiss her hand before. It should have looked and felt ridiculous, but Rafael De Santos carried it off as if the custom hadn't died a century before. On him, the courtly act seemed completely natural, even expected.

Before Saskia could decide how to respond, the Felix had released her hand with a gentle squeeze, nodded briefly to Nicolas, and blended back into the crowd moving through the exit. Blowing out a discreet breath, she struggled to regain her equilibrium. Rafael De Santos was a force of nature. She'd heard stories about his potent charm and seductive wiles, but she'd never expected to experience them for herself. No wonder women supposedly dropped at his feet like autumn leaves. Saskia had zero interest in the man yet even she had felt a brief tug of fascinated attraction. The man should come with a warning label.

Nicolas shifted behind her, dragging her attention back to the matter at hand. They still had a couple hundred guests to farewell, and if she wanted to make it home to her bed and her painkillers before lunchtime tomorrow she needed to keep herself focused. Automatically she tilted her head back to offer her

fiancé a reassuring smile, but his expression made
her falter. His green eyes looked cool and distant and
flicked immediately away from her. His hand at her
hip withdrew, and his body canted subtly away as he
murmured something polite and benign to the senior
partner of a well-respected and ancient law firm. She
couldn't quite shake the feeling that she'd been simultaneously rebuked and dismissed.

But for what?

"Great party. Thanks for the invite. Good luck,
and all that."

This time, the voice that snapped her back to
awareness was female, unaccented, and slightly ill at
ease. Instinct and training pressed Saskia to fix that
at once.

"We're so happy you were able to join us," she
said, infusing her smile with extra warmth. She
didn't immediately recognize the woman before her,
but something about the olive-skinned brunette tickled at the edge of Saskia's subconscious. She usually
excelled at remembering names and faces. "Please
tell me you enjoyed yourself at least a little."

The woman grinned in spite of her discomfort.
"Well, the champagne was first rate, and those stuffed
mushroom thingies they passed around before dinner tasted like an orgasm on a plate, so that's something. More than I can usually expect from a work
gig."

Work. Ah, yes. This was the reporter from the
Chronicle. Father had insisted she be invited, even
though she didn't normally write a social column.

Something about a connection with both the Council and the Faerie Summer Court. Saskia eyed her with renewed interest.

"I find that adding in a bit of pleasure tends to make work both more enjoyable and more successful, Ms. D'Alessandro," she said, pulling the name out of her mental database and smiling. "With luck, you'll find that to be equally true."

"'Corinne,' please," the woman said, rolling her eyes. "Don't make me look around this crowd for my mother. I can only take so much trauma."

Saskia laughed, genuinely. She liked people with a sense of humor. "Corinne, then. Can I tell myself you had a good time? Please? It will help me sleep, you know. I'd hate to think anyone found my engagement dinner a chore."

Something flashed behind Corinne's eyes, but it happened so fast, Saskia barely had time to recognize it, let alone decide what it meant.

"It was a great dinner," Corinne said. "Totally yummy. And I should say congratulations. I hope everything works out for you guys."

It wasn't difficult to read the genuine sentiment behind the woman's words, nor the doubt that laced them. It wasn't anything Saskia hadn't encountered before. Very few people anymore understood the reasoning behind arranged marriages, and almost no one in America did. It might be the way the Tiguri had always done things, but Americans had deserted the practice along with horse-drawn plows and whale oil lanterns.

She smiled. "Thank you. I assure you, everything will be perfect." Impulsively she reached out and squeezed the reporter's hand. "Believe me."

Brown eyes locked with her own and studied her for a long minute. When she spoke again, Corinne was frowning and smiling at the same time. Her brows still drew together, but her mouth had curved into a wry expression. "You know, I think you really mean that." She paused, appeared to debate something with herself, then reached into her small evening clutch and pulled out a cream-colored business card. "I have to admit, I'm fascinated by your whole story. If you wouldn't mind, I'd love to pick your brain about it at some point. My office number is on there. Maybe we could have a drink sometime and talk?"

Saskia tucked the card into her own bag. She couldn't explain why, but she liked this reporter right away. Saskia wouldn't mind meeting her for a drink sometime, maybe indulging in some girl talk. After all, Saskia had spent most of the last ten years in Europe and all her close friends were still there. It would be nice to make friends with someone more available.

"If you're hoping alcohol will steal away my inhibitions and loosen my tongue, you'd be absolutely right." Saskia grinned. "I have a pretty low tolerance. But I'm afraid it won't help you discover anything scandalous about my engagement. There's nothing so exciting to it. We're just like any other couple."

Corinne snorted. "Like any *Other* couple, maybe."

Saskia felt her eyes widen and she scanned the

crowd around them reflexively, searching for anyone who might have overheard her but perhaps shouldn't. She knew the Other community in New York still felt very strongly about protecting their secrecy from the humans. In a mixed crowd like this one, the challenge of remaining undiscovered tended to require extra vigilance.

"Oh, don't worry," Corinne said, drawing Saskia's focus back to her. "I'm part of one of those couples myself. My fiancé is . . . special. I wouldn't let the cat out of the bag, even if he did manage to wriggle out of coming with me tonight."

Saskia let herself relax. "Well, then, you shouldn't have any questions about me. It's all perfectly ordinary, I assure you."

The reporter looked from Saskia, to her fiancé, currently schmoozing with her father and the head of a major movie studio, to her future father-in-law, currently glaring at the reporter, and back to Saskia. "Hm. Keep telling yourself that, toots." She stepped back and raised a hand in farewell. "Anyway, call me sometime. Even if I can't pick your brain. You're new in town. I can show you around, introduce you to some of my friends. We all have . . . similar interests, you might say."

Saskia smiled in agreement and Corinne moved away, threading purposefully through the crowd and out toward the hotel lobby. Saskia watched her go for a second, then turned back toward her other guests. Out of the corner of her eye, she could see Stefan still frowning, but now the expression was aimed at her.

What was his problem? she wondered. She'd never

gotten the impression that Stefan Preda liked her very much, despite the fact that he'd pursued the engagement between her and his son with as much assiduousness as her own father. She knew the former head of his streak wanted intensely for the Preda and Arcos clans to be united. As they were two of the oldest and highest-ranking families of tiger shifters left in the world, the move would solidify their power and shove the other four remaining clans firmly onto a lower tier of the rigid Tiguri hierarchy. For it to happen, Nicolas Preda had to marry her. It was that simple.

Pushing the question of her future father-in-law's mood to the back of her mind, Saskia mustered up another social smile and got back to the task at hand. Time to show the crème of New York society exactly how happy she was to have landed herself a man such as Nicolas Preda.

Nic realized early on that the party was going to last until approximately the end of time. The invitations had requested the guests arrive at 7:00 P.M. By 7:45 he had had his fill of glad-handing politicians and schmoozing executives, and by 8:00 he'd had enough of his future father-in-law. Gregor Arcos was a highly intelligent, crafty old sonofabitch, a man who had inherited his place in the world but who hadn't been afraid to fight to keep it, and to fight dirty if he had to. That was a quality Nic could respect. What drove him crazy was the way Arcos seemed to believe that by getting Nic to marry his daughter he'd

somehow acquired the power to control or guide
Nic's actions. Nic would have to find a way to dis-
abuse the man of that notion, and quickly, without
sparking a full-fledged battle of wills. Nic had no
doubt he'd win——eventually——but he wasn't prepared
to risk the collateral damage. Not unless he had no
other choice.

By 8:15, his own father had appeared on Nic's shit
list. Stefan Preda knew better than to let his son see
his attempts at manipulation, but that didn't mean he
wasn't working behind the scenes with all the determination and finesse of a master puppeteer. He might
realize laying a hand on Nic's strings was a bad
move, but he showed no compunction about tugging
Gregor's here and there, or about doing his best to
gather Saskia's strings into his controlling grasp.

Nic couldn't decide how he felt about that. Intel-
lectually, he knew his father's end goal was nearly the
same as his own——to carve out a secure and significant niche for the Preda and Arcos streaks in Manhattan and to ensure the future of the Tiguri in local
Other society, including winning a place on the
Council of Others. The problem was that Nic's social
ambitions ended there. He reserved his other plans
for his business, the family company he'd recently
taken over from his father. Maybe that was part of
the problem. Maybe now Stefan had too much time
on his hands and the elder Preda was out to control
Saskia from a sense of boredom or uselessness.

Maybe that was it, but either way, Nic found himself less than pleased over the way his father had

treated his fiancée over the course of the evening, which was odd. He hadn't expected to particularly care one way or the other. Oh, he would never tolerate anyone treating the woman with disrespect; to do so would be to show disrespect to Nic and his family, as well; that wasn't the sort of thing a *ther*—a dominant male—would countenance. Still, Nic hadn't expected the possessive instincts the small female seemed to call up within him. At least, not at this point in the relationship. Later, after they were mated in truth, he figured thousands of years of species memory would likely make him damned possessive where his woman was concerned. But now? They barely knew each other. It was too early for the beast inside him to be growling every time someone so much as said boo to Saskia Arcos.

Nic had struggled with the feeling all night. First, he noticed it when he and his father had gathered with the Arcoses before the party began. The families had known each other for generations, so the regular meet-and-greet introductions hadn't been necessary. Nic had shaken hands with Gregor and his wife, Victoria, formally slid his ring on Saskia's slender finger, and offered to pour everyone drinks. Fifteen minutes of polite chitchat and the party could get rolling.

Something unexpected had happened, though, the minute Nic slipped the diamond and platinum engagement ring past his fiancée's knuckle. Although he hadn't seen Saskia Arcos in almost twenty years, he hadn't had any trouble recognizing her. With her pale, creamy skin, red-tinged blond hair, and huge blue eyes, she still bore a striking resemblance to the eight-year-old waif who had dogged his footsteps throughout the entire week he and his parents had spent at Shadelea, the Arcos summer home in the English midlands.

While their fathers had taken the first steps in negotiating an alliance between the two streaks, Nic had roamed restlessly around the aristocratic old estate, stretching his legs on long walks, tiring himself out with neck-and-nothing gallops over the hills, and relishing the UK drinking-age laws down at the village pub. Little Saskia had even followed him into that dim, smoky building, settling herself quietly in a corner with a coloring book and a cup of tea, keeping her hands busy even as her attention remained entirely focused on the baffled nineteen-year-old Nic. No one at the pub had commented on her presence, least of all Nic. He'd been deadly frightened that if he acknowledged her presence he would somehow be obliged to take care of her, and he'd had no desire at the time to take care of anyone. He'd still been learning to take care of himself.

Saskia had never asked anything of him, though. Not during that whole vacation. She'd literally become his shadow, following him everywhere, staying a few steps behind him, observing everything but never speaking. It was odd how she'd never said a word to him and yet still managed to drag him through a minefield of unexpected emotions. At first he'd found her dogged attention amusing, maybe a little flattering, but like any nineteen-year-old boy, his amusement had quickly turned to annoyance.

He'd tried a million tricks to get rid of her, but even the few times he'd managed to give her the slip she'd always managed to pop back up within an hour or two, still silent but ever more determined. When he'd run out of ideas for getting rid of her that didn't cross the line into outright cruelty or physical harm, he'd allowed his annoyance to shift into bafflement and then resignation. He still hadn't spoken to the girl, nor she to him, but he'd grown accustomed to her presence just behind him, and when he and his parents had finally left Shadelea he'd felt somehow naked and exposed without her at his back.

Funny, but he'd forgotten all about that strange feeling until tonight, when the grown-up version of that little girl had once again become glued to his side like a shadow. Her presence brought those memories rushing back, but things felt different now. Saskia Arcos wasn't eight years old anymore. She was twenty-eight and very clearly a woman full grown. Her skin and hair and eyes might look just as he'd remembered, but the slight, gangly frame of the girl he had ignored had lengthened, matured, and filled out in some very interesting places, each of them showcased in the strapless gown that floated around her every time she moved. The muted shades of orange and gold made her skin glow and her hair burn and the sweet sprinkling of freckles dusting her shoulders looked like a fine coating of cinnamon sugar. Nic couldn't wait to lean down and taste them.

The only thing about that thought that didn't sit comfortably with him was that he knew for a fact he wasn't the only man in the room imagining the honey-cream flavor of her skin. The head of the Council of Others had made little effort to hide some very similar thoughts of his own.

Nic scowled and scanned the crowd to make sure the good-looking bastard had managed to find the exit. If not, Nic would happily escort him to it. Now that their engagement was official, by Tiguri custom Saskia belonged to Nic, completely. If the Felix De Santos didn't learn to keep his salacious thoughts to himself, Nic would have every right and take every pleasure in pointing out the other man's bad manners. With his fists. And maybe his claws. Possibly fangs. Once the tiger form broke free, no one could predict what it would take to satisfy the beast's need to assert its dominance.

And those were the kinds of thoughts Nic most needed to get ahold of, he reminded himself. He forced a deep breath in and blew it out slowly. He shifted next to his fiancée until he could feel the warmth of her skin soaking through the fabric of his tuxedo jacket. The reminder of her presence beside him soothed his inner tiger and helped him regain control. He knew how little provocation it would take for the Council of Others to disregard the unspoken and fragile truce that currently existed between them and the Tiguri. After centuries of the absence of tiger shifters from most of America, no one knew quite what to make of the Arcos and Preda streaks' decision to relocate both their businesses and their families to New York. It had made most of the Council a bit . . . edgy. If Nic wanted to keep the peace, he needed to keep a tight rein on his more primitive instincts, instincts his fiancée seemed to drag to the surface with unexpected ease.

"Well, I'd certainly call that a success," Gregor Arcos crowed, rubbing his hands together with trenchant glee. "Very nicely done, my boy, if I do say so myself."

Nic skimmed his gaze over the last few stragglers clustered in small groups in the hall outside of the emptied ballroom before turning to his future father-in-law. Behind them, catering staff had already begun dismantling the elaborate decorations. "The staff did an excellent job. I'm very pleased."

"As am I," his father said. Stefan nodded to Nic and Saskia, his patrician features looking almost relaxed after the well-received celebration. "You behaved just as I could have wished, Saskia. You were a credit to our family."

Beside him, Saskia stirred, her shoulders straightening as she nodded at the elder Preda. "Thank you, Mr. Preda. I certainly wouldn't want to disappoint anyone at such a lovely event."

"Your father and I were very proud, Saskia," Victoria Arcos declared. Nic had almost forgotten about Saskia's mother. The woman tended to blend into the shadows behind her charismatic mate. "We only hope you'll continue to demonstrate your value to your new family."

Saskia merely smiled and inclined her head. Nic raised an eyebrow. Her family made it sound like they thought of her as a well-trained spaniel or maybe a schoolgirl who'd just navigated her first formal tea party at the age of seven when Nic knew very well that his fiancée had recently celebrated her twenty-eighth birthday. No one could doubt she was full grown, just as no one who really looked at her would doubt she would always behave with the grace and graciousness of a princess. He knew the practice of arranged matches like theirs was considered old fashioned—by everyone but the Tiguri, who considered the term "old fashioned" to be a badge of honor among their kind—but her family's words made him feel like he'd just been transported into a BBC costume drama.

Slipping his arm around her waist, Nic drew his fiancée against his side and smiled at her parents. "My mate could never do anything less, I'm sure," he said firmly.

"Ah, but she's not your mate yet." Her father chuckled, winking at them. "And I'm sure that's something you'd like to get straight to work on, eh? You kids should go on home now. I had Saskia's things sent over this morning. She should be all settled in by now."

"Thank you, Papa." Saskia leaned forward to brush a kiss against her father's cheek, then settled right back at Nic's side. The surge of satisfaction he felt at the action surprised him. "I'll give you and Mother a call in the morning."

"Not too early, I hope," Gregor boomed, clearly amusing himself and earning a quelling look from his wife. "It takes effort to seal a mating. You wouldn't want anyone to think you weren't dedicated to the task, now would you."

Saskia colored at her father's crude words, and

Nic fought back the urge to snarl. Everyone there knew that by Tiguri custom an engagement merely signaled an intent to form a mate bond and that the union wouldn't be sealed, wouldn't become the equivalent of a marriage, until Saskia became pregnant. Just like the bond wouldn't be considered permanent until she gave birth to a healthy cub. No one had to point that out, especially not so crudely. The unexpected protectiveness Nic felt toward Saskia made him want to strangle her father for embarrassing her in front of both their families.

Fortunately, his father stepped in before Nic could act on his anger.

"Yes, the young couple should be given their privacy," Stefan declared, his voice firm and only slightly tightened in irritation. "I know my son has made every effort to prepare his den for his new mate. He should take her home and show her."

"Gladly." Nic smiled down at Saskia, forcing thoughts of her parents out of his head. She made a much more pleasant thing to focus on. "Shall we?"

She nodded on a deep exhalation, and for the first time Nic noticed the faint shadows of exhaustion under her bright blue eyes. He was feeling pretty tired himself. He should have realized how exhausting the past week since the betrothal had been for his fiancée.

"Yes," she breathed with a tired smile. "That would be wonderful."

"I'll have the car brought around."

Stepping away from her, he beckoned to a staff member and gave instructions to contact the valet desk. Behind him he could hear the stilted conversation between Saskia's family and his father, and Nic felt guilty at his relief that his share of it was nearly over. You would think that in a community as small as the Tiguri, with barely fifty families left, the sense of shared history and shared culture would draw them closer together, but it hadn't. Maybe it was because tigers were solitary animals, but the Tiguri just weren't good at building community, much less maintaining it. For that reason alone, the Council of Others should know that no Tiguri would want to get involved in the intricate business of Others politics. That would be like a hermit running for president—not only wouldn't he get any votes, but also he wouldn't know what to do with them if he did.

It took only a few minutes before a staff member alerted him that his car was waiting, and when he did Nic made short work of extricating himself and his fiancée from their parents' company and whisking her toward the lobby. He collected their coats from the concierge, helped her into hers, and guided her into the back of the black sedan with maximum efficiency and minimum fuss. Within moments, the driver had pulled away from the curb and eased his way into traffic. Nic relaxed back into his seat with a sigh and watched the twinkling lights of the city move past the tinted windows.

The interior of the car was silent for several moments, just the muffled sounds of motor and city and the occupants' quiet breathing. Then Saskia spoke softly. "I'm impressed."

Nic turned his head, his keen night vision having

no trouble making out her delicate features. "Impressed?"

"You decided it was time to leave and had us out of there in under six minutes. If I'd tried to manage that, it would have taken me fifteen. Easily."

He heard the soft echo of amusement in her voice and flashed her a grin. "It's all about planning, timing, and execution."

"And ruthlessness. I admire that."

Both remained quiet for another long minute.

"You're different from how I remember you." Once again, Saskia took the first step to breach the silence. "At the time, I thought you were already all grown up, but now that I can see the man you've become, I realize how silly that idea was."

"You were . . . what? Eight? Last time we saw each other?" He watched her face, tried to read her expression, but all he could see was the tranquil blue of her eyes and the soft cream of her skin. "I'm sure at the time that nineteen seemed ancient."

She smiled. "Not ancient. Just . . . impressive."

He chuckled in spite of himself. "My nineteen-year-old ego thanks you for that."

Nic watched while she turned her gaze forward and stared unseeingly at the front of the car. The driver remained silent and anonymous behind the barrier of smoked glass, but Nic doubted Saskia even thought of him. Her attention all seemed focused inward, as if she barely even realized she wasn't alone. It was quite a kick to the ego. In the past, when Nic had taken the odd moment to envision having a mate he'd somehow never expected that she would be able to dismiss him so easily from her thoughts. It irked him, especially as often as his thoughts had turned to her in the last few hours. Which he also hadn't expected.

He considered and rejected several conversational forays while the limo cruised along the short distance from the hotel to their new home. Nic considered it new himself. He'd only moved in a week ago. His father had been the one to suggest that the new couple should have a place of their own, rather than a section of Stefan's admittedly enormous home. In essence, Nic had chose the new place with Saskia in mind; only he hadn't actually had *her* in mind, just an image of her—an anonymous female figure he'd pictured only as she related to him. His fiancée, his wife, his mate, the mother of his cubs. Now he found himself confronted with an actual person, and he no longer felt sure about what he should do. Should he speak? About what? Or should he keep silent and respect her privacy? Did what he did right now even matter? Presumably, they would have a few decades together to talk, to get to know each other. There was no hurry, was there?

While he debated with himself, Saskia sat silent beside him, her breathing calm and even, her face impassive. The only thing that gave a hint that the thoughts under her serene façade might be half as tumultuous as Nic's was the way her fingers tangled together in her lap, twisting and worrying the large diamond he'd given her just this evening. She made no move to take it off, just spun it around her slender finger as she stared out the tinted windows of the car.

"I should apologize."

Her words cracked the awkward silence, echoing in their automotive cocoon in spite of their soft volume.

"For what?" Nic asked, frowning.

"For my bad manners." She turned to face him then, and he felt her gaze on him almost as if she'd run soft, warm fingers across his cheek. "I never thanked you for my ring. It's beautiful."

His gaze dropped to the four-carat cushion-cut diamond on her hand, seeing the lights from the city outside glint off the brilliant stone. When he'd picked it out at the jeweler's, Nic hadn't thought about how it would look on her pale, delicate hand, but he had to admit, it looked right. As if it belonged. He liked seeing it there.

"There's no need to thank me." His voice came out gruffer than he intended, a low rumble in the dark. "It suits you."

"Still," she murmured, her gaze dropping to the ring. "I do love it. Thank you."

Before he could react, she shifted in the dim space, leaning forward and catching him off guard as she pressed her soft, warm mouth to his.

She might as well have punched him in the gut.

It overwhelmed him. He felt as if he'd slipped into a black hole, drawn by the gravity of this woman. Her soft lips, her warm breath, the rich, sweet scent of her skin, surrounded him, sent his senses whirling. Instinctively he reached out to steady himself and instead caught her upper arms in his hands and groaned. His fingers kneaded the pliant flesh, drawing her against him as he wrestled for control over himself and the unexpected kiss.

He felt her start with surprise when he parted his lips against hers, sensed the instant of hesitation, then the softening of her muscles against him. She had meant the kiss as a gesture, he realized, not an invitation, but she hadn't taken into account his reaction to her. *He* hadn't taken it into account, either. Nic had known his fiancée was a beautiful woman, had seen photos at the beginning of the engagement negotiations, and had felt confident that he would have no trouble when the time came to consummate their relationship. What man wouldn't find appeal in the idea of Saskia Arcos in his bed? He had expected to react to her, to want her once they ended up alone together, but he had never expected to need her.

It gnawed at him like a craving, a mindless, stomach-clenching need that grabbed hold the moment he felt the brush of her lips against his own. Her initial touch brushed against him fleeting, tentative, but he couldn't let her escape. His hands drew her to him even as his lips firmed, pressed, parted over hers. As her hesitation melted, she shivered against him and leaned into the pressure, her mouth softening and yielding to his. He swept forward to claim, to taste, to conquer.

She tasted of champagne, bright and yeasty, of the raspberries that had decorated the dessert plates, sweet and tart, and of herself, warm and rich and intoxicating. Nic felt his own breathing catch, and the beast inside him stirred. Head lifted; nose scented; fangs gleamed. Inside him, hunger stirred and claws flexed as anticipation built. He could already feel the stirrings of excitement that preceded the hunt. He sensed the growing awareness, the narrowing focus. He pressed into the soft figure in his arms and let the adrenaline course into his veins. His tiger had scented a potential mate, and it intended to claim her and mark her as his own. The fact that they still rode in the back of a chauffeur-driven car didn't even factor into it. The beast wanted, and the beast would take.

Two

Saskia's head swam. She had never intended this, and she certainly couldn't figure out how it had happened. She'd just meant to thank him, to show Nicolas that she appreciated the beauty of the ring he'd given her. Okay, maybe she'd wanted to touch him, as well. After all, tonight they would be expected to go to bed together, to seal the betrothal with sex and signal to the entire Tiguri community that they intended to form a mated pair. It was only natural that she'd want to build up to that somehow, to at least learn the shape of her mate's mouth or the dark, woodsy musk of his scent.

She'd learned those things, all right, had gathered those facts up in the half a heartbeat it took to brush a kiss across her fiancé's startled lips. Dozens of hammering heartbeats later, she was still learning things, things she wouldn't have dared speculate on only minutes before. Like the fascination for him she'd felt at the age of eight hadn't dissipated. Or that the press of his body near hers made her dissolve like sugar in warm water. Or that one kiss could make her crave him like a drug, make her tremble and ache, make her mind race and her thoughts cloud. Saskia hadn't expected any of those things, but now she needed to find a way to live with them, with him, in a mating he'd agreed to not because he wanted her but because everyone expected it of him.

The sharp pain in her heart had her gasping for breath.

Nic drew away. He frowned down at her, his green eyes assessing her as if he'd heard the sound and understood where it had come from. Please, no. She couldn't stand it if he guessed so soon. He didn't need to know how she felt; her feelings were irrelevant to their union. She braced herself to be reminded of that, to hear the truth from the lips that had just spurred her into arousal with less effort than it took to strike a match to flame. Her shoulders drew back and her fingers laced together in her lap. She didn't want to hear him say it, but she certainly wouldn't let him see it sting her.

Instead, he laid a hand over one of hers and spoke quietly. "We're here. We should go up."

The car had stopped moving, and Saskia hadn't even noticed. She felt her cheeks heat. "All right."

She felt lucky she'd been able to manage two coherent words, and she knew better than to tempt fate by speaking again as they exited the car and made their way into the lobby of a posh, modern apartment building an entire world removed from either of their family homes.

Old-fashioned in more ways than just their marriage customs, Tiguri homes all tended to look alike. First, they almost always occupied buildings of historic significance, usually ones passed down through their families for multiple generations. If they acquired a new property, it was new only to them and usually had its own listing in the pages of the local historical society. Façades were elaborate, fitting frames for rooms full of antiques and historically significant objets d'art. Her own mother had an obsession with eighteenth-century porcelains, scattered them everywhere in every one of the Arcos family's five homes. Here Saskia could picture nothing that would be more out of place.

The building's lobby, complete with an attentive doorman who greeted Nicolas by name and made polite inquiries about their evening while he called the elevator for them, gleamed with polished marble. Not the predictable and sterile whites and grays she'd seen in so many other Tiguri dwellings, but rich shades of loamy earth and golden brown. The inside of the elevator, too, was paneled in slats of wood that fit together so closely, they resembled vast, solid sheets of mahogany rather than classical wainscoting, the walls above them a shockingly pleasant contrast of dully gleaming steel that reflected light but no images.

Saskia rode up to the seventeenth floor in surprised silence. So far, nothing about this evening had turned out the way she expected. She was beginning to feel like she was on a ship of some kind and the deck beneath her kept rolling and pitching unexpectedly. She wondered how long it would take her to find her sea legs.

When the elevator doors slid open, Nicolas gestured for her to exit before him, then followed closely

on her heels. She felt a tingling go through her at the
warmth of his hand as it settled into the hollow of
her lower back and guided her toward the only door
leading off the small foyer surrounding the elevator
bank. He drew a key from his pocket and slipped it
into the lock, pausing to glance at her with a small
smile.

"I hope you like it," he murmured, pushing the
door open and steering her through.

Saskia paused on the threshold to stare. She
couldn't help it. The apartment opened before her like
a welcoming embrace, less than nothing like she'd
expected. Like the building's lobby, their new home
had sleek sophistication and thoroughly modern
sensibilities, and yet nothing about it seemed cold or
overly slick. Everywhere she looked, she saw clean
lines and warm colors, simplicity and luxury balanced and blended into total harmony.

"It's lovely," she said, and she meant every syllable.

"I'm glad you think so." He set his keys down on
a small entry table. "Let me show you around."

It took several minutes. The apartment was huge,
occupying the entire top floor of the building. Nicolas showed her the enormous, elegant living room, a
dining room large enough to host twenty with ease,
and a gourmet kitchen complete with eating nook and
seating at a center island that probably had its own
zip code. There were rooms for live-in help, he explained, though they were currently unoccupied. On
the other side of the kitchen, he showed her a smaller
sitting room he called the den, a full bath, a library,
and his office.

"I do work from home sometimes, so I tend to spend a bit of time in here."

Saskia stood beside him, taking in the modern, masculine space, the desk already covered with neat stacks of papers, folders, and notepads. "How long have you been living here?"

"Only a week or two. The decorators just finished a couple of days ago." His mouth curved and his eyes twinkled at her. "I told them if they weren't out of here before tonight, I'd dock them five grand for every hour they went over schedule."

"I see that was effective."

"They finished up five days ahead of their estimate."

Looking at her fiancé's powerful form, Saskia didn't doubt the decorators had worked their behinds off to avoid making him angry. She certainly wanted to avoid it.

"Come on. Let's see the rest."

She followed him back into the hall and let him show her three bedrooms, each with its own private bath. The sheer size of the place was beginning to boggle her mind—this was Manhattan, after all!—when he steered her through a set of double doors and waved a hand.

"And this is the last of it. The master, of course. I hope you like it," he repeated his words from earlier, his gaze focused on her face.

"How could I not?"

The room opened in front of her, huge and yet somehow still intimate. Soft earth tones of taupe and ecru provided a backdrop to rich fields of color provided by the rich chocolate of the window treatments, the navy, gold, and burgundy of the rug beneath the bed, and the deep claret of the bedclothes. The mahogany floors gleamed softly. The white-painted woodwork lightened the space and made it seem open and expansive. Saskia could picture him here, reclining in regal splendor against the fluffy pillows.

But could she picture herself with him?

She shivered.

"You have your own closet." He showed her the huge space, larger than her childhood bedroom, her clothes and shoes and luggage already neatly arranged on the racks and shelves. "I had your things put away when they were delivered. I figured it would save you some time."

And keep her from hiding behind the chore while she mustered her courage for what would happen in the rest of the suite.

"Bathroom is through there." He gestured to a door to the right. "There's a whirlpool tub. I know you must be tired, but you look like you could use a soak."

Saskia hadn't expected that. Oh, she hadn't believed he'd throw her down and jump on her the minute she stepped into their bedroom, but she also hadn't thought he would offer her the perfect excuse to delay the inevitable. As much as the kiss in the car earlier had stirred her body into wanting him, now that her brain had seized back control the ability to take a few minutes to center herself—and muster up her courage—held a definite appeal.

"That actually sounds wonderful." Her voice came out hoarse and timid, not exactly the image she wanted to project. Lifting her chin, she cleared her throat and offered him a passable smile. "I am tired, but it's been a hectic day. A bath sounds like the perfect way to relax."

"Take your time." He settled his hands in his pockets and gave her a nod. "I left a couple of things on my desk, but they shouldn't keep me long. Enjoy yourself."

Saskia watched him leave the suite, disappointment and relief warring in her head. She knew all she'd done was delay the inevitable, by an hour at most. She ought to be taking advantage of the extra time to collect her thoughts and prepare herself so that when her new fiancé came to her later he would see only what he needed to see—a calm, willing mate in control of her own emotions.

What those emotions might be Saskia figured he had no need to know.

The first thing Nic did upon reaching the safety and quiet of his office was pour himself a huge glass of whiskey. Three fingers of golden liquid barely had time to splash into the tumbler before he tossed them back with a grunt. God damn it to hell, this was not how this evening was supposed to go.

Like any successful businessman, Nic had mapped out a strategy for his future, one that began with taking a suitable mate. He'd looked through the field of potential candidates, evaluated their strengths and weaknesses, and even weighed the opinions and concerns of his father in his decision. Now that Stefan had decided to step down as head of the Preda clan, it had become Nic's responsibility to lead the family in a manner that respected the centuries of history behind the name. That he would wed a purebred Tiguri was never in question, and with their dwindling population his choices had been limited to brides from the handful of noble families that still maintained their bloodlines and heritage with jealous fanaticism.

Stefan had suggested five names, but his preference for the daughter of Gregor and Victoria Arcos had not been difficult to detect. It had also been easy to understand. While the Preda clan had been content to linger in the eastern parts of Europe, gobbling up wealth and property as the grip of the Soviet system began to dissolve, the Arcoses had migrated west and dug their claws into the meaty flesh of the United Kingdom, France, Spain, Italy, and the other big-name nations. Uniting the two families now would create a business and social power that spanned most of Europe. As Nic was the CEO of Preda Industries, the idea almost made him drool.

As he was a man, the first sight of a grown-up Saskia Arcos had finished the job.

He realized now that the photos he'd looked at hadn't done the woman justice, which just demonstrated how potent a force he now had to deal with. Her classical features and elegant figure showed up just fine on film, but the cameras hadn't been able to capture the creamy glow of her skin, the sweet charm of her shy smiles, or the way her red-gold hair seemed to shift and shimmer like living flame whenever she moved. They also hadn't prepared him for her warmth, the physical heat that radiated off her when he stood close against her, or for the sweet intoxicant of her scent. Just the memory of it, the few molecules that lingered on the lapel of her jacket, made his eyes drift shut as he drew it in on a deep inhalation.

Complexity defined her scent, weaving together layers of sweet and bitter, spicy and delicate. Nic's acute tiger senses detected hints of bergamot and sandalwood, myrrh, lily, and moss. Each note seemed to whisper to him, telling seductive tales of warm nights and deep forests, of passion and feminine power. He wanted to bury his face in the soft curve of her throat and feast on the incredible bounty of her, which was doing very little to aid him in gaining control of himself and his carefully mapped future.

His nose had not been given a vote in his decision-making process, Nic reminded himself. He'd chosen Saskia based on more practical considerations. The alliance with the Arcos clan had topped the list, followed closely by the fact that he knew from her parents and his father that she had been carefully raised to be the kind of wife a man like him required. It might sound like something out of a nineteenth-century melodrama, but the truth was that a man in his position, both financially and socially, needed a mate who knew how to navigate a path through a variety of different social milieus. As the head of an international corporation Nic might have dinner with presidents and kings one night, and as the *ther* of his streak he might spend the next instructing a roomful of adolescent weretigers on the traditions surrounding dominance challenges and territorial marking. His mate would need to charm heads of state and still be able to put cocky young males in their place.

She would also need to form a united front with him against the blatant distrust and hostility of the local Other population. Nic had known when he and his father had made the decision to move the company headquarters to New York that the Council of Others who ruled the city would not welcome their presence. No Tiguri had claimed territory in the American city in longer than even the old families could remember. One reason for that had probably been that with so few Tiguri out there, the tiger shifters had never needed to expand their range to the New World. There was plenty of space in Europe and Asia for the remaining families to support themselves and still keep out of one another's way. They'd been doing so for millennia; no one saw any reason to rock the boat. But the other reason likely had more to do with the deep, instinctive fear and hatred the Lupines harbored for the Tiguri.

Wolves hated tigers; always had, always would. Even in the animal world, their territories never overlapped for long. Tigers drove out the wolves and claimed pack lands for themselves, or wolves abandoned undesirable lands to the tigers and shunned their company. Depending, of course, entirely on who happened to answer the question about the antipathy. As wolf populations had dwindled in Europe and

Asia with the rise of humans, so, too, had the Lupine populations declined. Many Lupines had immigrated to the Americas early on in the development of that nation, and they had staked their claim on New York long before the Tiguri had found any reason to care about that distant country. For centuries, the Tiguri had willingly left America to the Lupines, but in today's world a businessman couldn't afford to ignore Manhattan, and Nic Preda was very definitely a businessman. A savvy and determined one.

The time had come for the Tiguri to take their place in New York, whether the Council of Others liked it or not. Based on the reaction of the Others who had attended the engagement party earlier, Nic thought it was pretty clear that they did not. He didn't care. Despite the history between their races, Nic hadn't come to drive the Lupines away from the city, just to make room in it for himself and his family. He knew it would take time to convince the Council of that, time and a great deal of tact and delicacy. That was where Saskia came in. A woman like her— one who had been raised with the privileged information that conversation was still an art, that diplomacy happened more often at dinners and receptions than in meeting rooms and offices—could win this kind of war in half the time and with none of the bloodshed that would likely accompany a dominant *ther*'s attempt to accomplish the same thing.

That type of skill took years of preparation, education, and training, and Nic had no intention of wasting time with a bride who couldn't keep up with his life. Saskia, he knew, could keep up; he'd seen the proof of it tonight. Theirs would be a union of logical harmony.

At least, it would be if Nic could figure out a way to keep his hands from trembling with the rampant need to throw her down and take her like the beast he was.

He cursed and poured another measure of whiskey.

He needed to get ahold of himself. These emotions that swamped him every time she got too close had to be controlled and concealed. They had no place in the relationship he had planned. He had chosen Saskia Arcos to be his mate and his partner. She would stand at his side in business and in the face of the Council of Others. She would charm his hosts, spoil his guests, support his causes, and bear his children. She would do it all with grace and efficiency, and in fifty or sixty years he would look back on their lives together with the quiet contentment of a man who had benefited from a wisely chosen ally. Nowhere in that equation did it mention burning lust or instant jealous possession. Nowhere had Nic made room for emotions like protectiveness or affection. That wasn't what this was about. As medieval as it might sound, he had agreed to a marriage of convenience; so why was he already having such inconvenient feelings for his new fiancée?

Nic slugged back the whiskey and straightened his shoulders. Time to put things back on solid footing. He just needed to make his position clear, to begin the way he intended to go on. Once he showed his new mate what he expected of her, everything would smooth itself out and he could go back to his comfortable life with a new and comfortable wife.

Simple.

Heading back toward the master bedroom, he stripped off his jacket and tie and left them draped over a chair as he began loosening the studs at his collar and cuffs and slipping them into his pockets. When he stepped into the bathroom, he used the act of rolling up his sleeves to distract himself from the sight that met his eyes. Saskia lounged in the huge tub, her eyes closed and her face relaxed into an expression of innocent bliss. The rumbling whirlpool jets had masked the sound of his approach, and the rich fragrance of the oil she must have added to the water delayed her in detecting his scent. He saw the instant when it finally registered that she no longer occupied the room alone.

Her eyes flew open, and her gaze shot directly to him. Nic leaned against the counter across from the tub and affected a casual pose. He intended to set a tone with this encounter, and he wanted her to see him in a position of power and control. She needed to remember that he was *ther* and he would set the terms of their relationship.

His eyes took in the sight of her creamy, gold-dusted shoulders rising above the gently frothing water. Her skin had flushed from the heat of the bath, lending a rosy glow that made him want to test her temperature with the flat of his tongue. She had left her hair pinned up in the simple knot she'd worn to the party, but the steam had teased strands free and curled them against her temples and brow, plastered others to the nape of her neck. She looked softened and naked and vulnerable, and the way her eyes widened as she took in the sight of him with his shirt untucked and unbuttoned and his trousers stretched over his growing erection made him want to seize her like a conquering invader. Hell, it made him want to invade her, to thrust inside her until she yielded everything to him.

Shit, where the hell was that control he'd vowed he would keep hold of?

"Was there something you needed?" she asked after several minutes of heavy silence had stretched between them. Her voice sounded husky and hesitant, the tone carefully polite, as if she spoke to a dinner companion or a houseguest rather than to her mate.

Nic wanted to change that.

He debated his answer carefully. Part of him wanted to answer with a blunt, blatant, *You,* but he restrained himself. With difficulty. Likewise, his mind vetoed his body's suggestion that he ignore her words and simply yank her from the tub, bend her over the nearest horizontal surface, and claim her in the most elemental way possible. He needed to set a tone here, and losing control would completely undermine his carefully planned strategy.

Leaving the question unanswered, he pushed away from the counter and grabbed a towel from the warming rack. "Time for bed. Before you decide to fall asleep in there."

He stopped at the side of the tub and shook the towel open. Then he waited.

Saskia's eyes widened. He watched her internal struggle play out across her expressive features and saw shock give way to the realization that Nic now had every right to expect the sort of intimacy that came from seeing her rise naked from her bath. He saw embarrassment deepen the color on her cheeks and modesty tighten her shoulders. He could almost see her fingers curling into fists below the surface of the churning, foaming water. She hadn't expected this from him, he knew. She'd probably expected him to stay away long enough for her to finish her bath and prepare herself for bed, to let her have the cover of darkness and enveloping bedsheets when he came to her. Instead, he stood before her now, silently demanding that she come to him wet and bare and vulnerable in the bright, exposing light of the bathroom.

Anticipation drew on already tight muscles as he waited to see what she would do.

She set her jaw first, the sweet curve of it firming as she broke their gaze and looked down at the tub controls. A dripping hand emerged from the water to still the jets. Nic couldn't help the way his eyes dropped to the calming water to search out the sight of her naked flesh. He caught a glimpse of rounded thighs and slim calves before she curled her legs underneath herself and pushed out of the concealing liquid.

The sight of her took his breath away.

All rosy and dewy with moisture, her skin looked

like clotted cream spread thick over strawberry jam. He'd known before that she had a slender, graceful figure, but seeing it now without the concealment of her fancy gown made his tongue thicken and his erection swell until he wondered how his body managed to divide the blood flow between the two heads. Her breasts were not large but heavy and exquisitely formed, the berry-colored nipples tightening at the contrasting chill of the room after the heat of her bath. She had a slim torso that flared deliciously at the hip and a belly that curved just enough to make her look like a woman instead of an emaciated supermodel. The sweet plane dipped down to a small patch of damp curls that looked like an even fierier version of her hair, framed by long, rounded thighs Nic could practically feel wrapped around his hips.

He swallowed hard and beat back an aggressive snarl. Damn, she was gorgeous. His muscles screamed with tension as he fought against the urge to throw her down on the cold tile floor and mate her like an animal. Such a loss of control would be entirely unacceptable to him, not to mention what it might do to his clearly modest mate. He grasped hard at his self-control and spread his arms to open the towel in invitation.

"Come on. Before you get cold."

She stepped from the tub with natural grace and Nic noticed even her feet were small and cute, her toes polished a deep rose color. She curled them into the thick pile of the bath mat as she reached to take the towel from him.

He shook his head and wrapped the cloth around

her, enveloping her in the nubby warmth. "I've got this."

Saskia opened her mouth to protest, but Nic ignored her. He wrapped the towel around her, front to back, trapping her arms at her sides and drawing her tense form against his as he rubbed his hands over the cotton barrier between them and the long, smooth line of her back. He felt her shiver and wondered if it was because of the contrast of cool air against her heated skin or because of the way he held her pressed against him as he dried her. Either way, he savored the small movement, pressing the towel to her shoulders, back, and soft, lush buttocks. He squeezed then and made her jump. With her body pressed against his and her face buried against his chest, Nic could let himself indulge in a grin of satisfaction. His mate might be nervous, but she was also a responsive little thing. It made him look forward even more to the process of sealing their engagement.

Taking a half step back, Nic drew the towel around to dry each of her arms in turn, then dropped into a squat to pat water away from her feet and legs. When he rose back to his feet and cupped his cloth-covered hands beneath her breasts to blot away the moisture trapped beneath them, she shivered. He had to school his features to careful blankness before he could meet her gaze and ask a casual, "Cold?"

She jumped on the offered excuse. "Yes. Getting out of a hot bath is the one downside to taking one."

He smiled and dragged the towel down her belly. "Then we should hurry up and get you dry so you can climb under the covers."

The mention of covers, and by extension the bed they currently stretched across, drew Saskia's muscles freshly taut. Nic ignored it, because he knew he was about to make her twice as tense, if such a thing was even possible. Keeping his gaze locked with hers, he used a foot to nudge her legs apart and slid his towel-covered hand between her legs to cup her damp sex.

Her breath hissed between her teeth like steam from a kettle. Her hands flew up to press into his shoulders and froze there, as if she couldn't decide whether to hold on for dear life or shove him violently away. Nic simply ignored them and continued to rub the towel over her mound, blotting away the moisture from her bath. Any other moisture was something he would address separately. And with relish.

She stopped breathing, trembling against him like a trapped bird, her fingers fluttering against the heavy linen of his shirt. Her wide blue eyes stared up at him as if mesmerized, and Nic found it equally impossible to look away. He could lose himself in those eyes and never even feel the desire to escape.

Slowly and carefully, he dragged his hand out from between her legs, making no effort to conceal his reluctance. He could happily have touched her forever, but the damned towel would have to go. He wanted to feel those soft folds against his skin, wanted to part and explore them, to pinch and nibble and taste, and tonight he had every right to do so.

Thank God for engagement nights.

"All done," he murmured, barely recognizing his own voice. It sounded gruff and rasping in the still quiet of the bathroom. "Soft and dry and ready for bed." He bent down and pressed his lips to the top of her shoulder. "Aren't you, little tigress?"

He felt her tremble and caught the mingled scents of nervousness, uncertainty, and arousal drifting up from her skin. He understood the uncertainty and had every intention of easing his way through the nerves, but the arousal made him purr in satisfaction. Arousal he could work with. Knowing that her body craved his allowed him to focus on her physical reactions and keep both of them so occupied with sensation that emotion would have no chance to intrude. He could still salvage this match if he acted now.

His hands took up the challenge before his mind had finished forming the thought. They released the towel he'd been clenching in tight fists and filled themselves instead with the warm silk of her skin. They settled on her back, fingers spread wide as if trying to touch every inch of her at once, and from there they set about exploring.

She shuddered out a sigh when he touched her bare skin with no barrier left between them. Looking down, he saw her lids drop to half-mast, concealing the expression in the liquid blue depths. That displeased him. He wanted to be able to read her reactions there, but he would have to content himself with what her body told him. Maybe that was better, anyway. Her body wouldn't confuse things with unnecessary emotions. It would be acting purely on instinct.

Nic shifted her closer, pressing her nude form

against his half-clothed body, relishing the feeling of control it gave him. It excited him to feel her bare softness against his hands and his chest where his unfastened shirt had fallen open and tantalized him to realize only the fabric of his trousers separated him from the hot, damp valley between her thighs.

Her nipples tightened where they pressed against his chest, and he shifted her deliberately to allow the curling hair there to abrade the sensitive peaks. Her reaction was a soft, sharp exhalation accompanied by the thrilling sensation of her hands shooting up to grip her arms, as if she felt the need to hang on to something solid. He would be more than happy to do her that service.

He bent his head to hers and shifted forward, throwing her off balance, his hands firming to hold her securely as he forced her body to arch backward until he could set his mouth to hers. Unlike their exchange earlier in the back of the car, this kiss never pretended to innocence. It seized and claimed and devoured, his mouth opening over hers, firm pressure forcing her lips to part and allow him entrance. He took immediate advantage, surging inside to touch and taste. The unique flavor of her acted like a catalyst to his lust, sending pure hunger through his veins with every hammering beat of his heart. His fingers tightened until he thought he must be leaving bruises on her delicate skin, but he couldn't bring himself to ease back. His beast had taken control, and it would not be denied.

Saskia whimpered against his lips, her body arching stiffly for a moment, as if she meant to fight him.

But a second later she melted, her sweet curves easing against his demands for surrender. Her fingers gripped his arms and kneaded, no longer seeking to steady herself but instead taking obvious pleasure in the feel of powerful muscles moving beneath her hands.

This was what he wanted, what he intended to have—his mate heating and yielding and wanting beneath his hands. Nothing else mattered and nothing else was necessary. He would have this relationship, enjoy his mate, get her with cubs, and otherwise live his life exactly the way he wanted. As *ther,* he would accept nothing less than his due.

His beast agreed, roaring its impatience and fighting hard at his already tenuous control. It wanted her now, wanted to come up behind her and cover her, to force the joining of their bodies in the most primitive way. It didn't care about comfort or mutual pleasure; it would take her here on the cold tile floor if Nic didn't get ahold of himself. Even if he did, he knew the beast wouldn't be thwarted for long. About all the man could do now was move them some place where he could ravage her in comfort. He had just enough control left to give her that.

Maybe.

Somewhere in the back of Nic's mind it registered that she wasn't fighting him. In fact, she seemed as involved in the kiss as he was. She sucked on his tongue, tangled and teased it with her own, nipped at his lips, and shifted in his arms to press her breasts tighter against his chest. When he shifted his hands to grip her ass and lift her off her feet, she rubbed her bottom into his palms and spread her thighs until she gripped his hips between her legs. She made tiny little mewling sounds of need and clung to his shoulders as he carried her through the door and into the enormous bedroom. When he moved to drop her on the bed and step back to shed his clothes, she refused to release him and growled low in her throat at any attempt he made to put space between them. Somehow, the press of their bodies together had transformed her from the cool, elegant stranger he'd become engaged to into a fierce, demanding tigress in heat.

Thank God and everything holy.

He sank back into their kiss, reveling in the way her body surrounded him, arms and legs clasping him close. He couldn't wait to feel her sex clasping him, too. He wanted to sink his aching erection deep into the hot cavern at her center and feel them joined together in one sweating, straining body of lust. He wanted to match their stripes until there was no way to tell where he ended and she began.

He wanted her like his next breath.

It didn't appear that she would be all that difficult to convince. Her body writhed and twisted under his, sinking deep into the softly mounded bedding, then rising up with surprising, agile strength. He loved the feel of her female power, loved the knowledge that because she was his Tiguri mate her body had been designed to match his, to take his power in a way few other women could manage. Even other shapeshifters tended to be intimidated by the strength of a dominant Tiguri. The largest of the big cats, tigers possessed an awesome strength comparable to that of any predator on earth, and their shape-shifting cousins, the Tiguri, easily duplicated that power. Even Leos—the Lion shifters—found themselves reluctant to take on the Tiguri in battle. The same could be said for most female shifters of any species; they preferred not to face off against a grown male Tiguri, on the battlefield or in the bedroom.

As for human women, making love to them felt like trying to embrace a soap bubble—it could be done, and the accomplishment offered a certain sense of satisfaction, but it required so much care and patience that it rarely seemed worth the effort. Of course, Nic had had human lovers, but he could never relax around them, never forget to control his strength for fear of seriously injuring them. The freedom he felt in touching Saskia and knowing she could take anything he could dish out nearly drove him over the edge of reason. The urge to take her, to fuck her, had reached flash point. He had to get inside her.

Now.

Tearing his mouth from hers, Nic reared back and ripped at his shirt, his hands bumping into his mate's as they both struggled with frantic fingers to strip him naked. Saskia finally won the battle and yanked his arms free of the sleeves before sending the garment flying into the nearest wall. He heard another purr when her hands settled on the bare skin of his back and shoulders, and the warm, rasping sound shot straight to his groin, drawing his balls even tighter.

He cursed, low and profane, and he forced his

hands between their bodies to deal with the fastening of his trousers. The backs of his knuckles brushed against the wet folds of her labia and he hissed at the sensation of liquid heat coating his skin. Saskia groaned softly and pressed tighter against him, grinding herself against the back of his hand. That was it. He could take no more.

Abandoning the plan to send his trousers in the direction of his shirt, Nic simply shoved the loosened fabric down off his hips and grabbed his mate's trembling thighs, positioning her with rough force until their bodies came into perfect alignment. His lips drew back over teeth he knew had to be growing long and sharp as fangs as he gazed down into her unseeing blue eyes and savored one final moment of burning anticipation.

The sound of the telephone rang like a bullet in the wordless moment.

Saskia jumped, awareness bursting back into her eyes as if some magical spell had been broken. Nic cursed in three languages and dropped his head to his fiancée's sweat-sheened chest. This couldn't be fucking happening.

Brrrrrrrrrinnnnnnnng!

The second ring mocked him, telling him that the fucking was absolutely not happening, thank you very much. Beneath him, he felt the supple quality of arousal leach from Saskia's body until she lay stiffly pinned between him and the mattress. Her hands no longer clung to his shoulders in silent demand but braced against them as if warding him off.

"Whoever that is, I'm going to kill them." He said

the words calmly, his voice quiet and level and utterly rational. And in his head, he was wondering how hard it would be to find medieval torture devices on eBay.

Saskia cleared her throat. The sound of nerves and embarrassment made him long for a rack. Or maybe a nice old-fashioned crucifix.

"It must be important, don't you think?" The third ring nearly drowned out her words, but Nic heard them. It would be hard not to with her mouth practically at his ear. "I mean, I can't imagine many people who know you wouldn't realize tonight might be an . . . awkward time to telephone."

Nic chuffed in wry amusement. " 'Awkward.' I suppose that's one word for it."

With another oath, he levered himself off his fiancée's delectable body to sit on the edge of the bed. Reaching for the phone, he saw the way she snatched at a blanket to cover her nudity and decided crucifixion was too merciful for whoever was on the other line. Maybe he should buy a boat. Keelhauling had definite possibilities.

He snatched up the receiver in the middle of the fourth ring. "What?" he roared, hoping he deafened whoever had the nerve to interrupt what had promised to be the greatest sex of his life. Not to mention the most culturally important.

His father's voice both surprised and worried him.

"You've been summoned before the Council of Others," Stefan announced with no preliminaries. "We both have. They expect us there in fifteen minutes. Or half an hour ago, whichever comes first."

Nic felt Saskia's gaze on him, could see her look of concern out of the corner of his eye, but he ignored her. "What are you talking about?" he demanded. "We're not members of the Council. They can't 'summon' us to the fucking restroom. What the hell is going on?"

Behind him, Saskia pushed herself into a sitting position, the blanket clutched to her chest like a wooden shield. He had to struggle to block her out. He didn't have time for the distraction.

"Apparently there was an attempt a short while ago on the life of the head of the Council," Stefan said, his voice grim and bitter and filled with sarcasm. "In a surprise move, the other members seem to have jumped to the conclusion that the Tiguri must have something to do with it."

Damn it. Nic had known matters between the native Others and the new Tiguri inhabitants of the city would come to a head eventually, but he had hoped it wouldn't be this soon. Hell, he'd been optimistic enough to predict he had at least another month before he had to begin worrying. So much for the best-case scenario.

"Is De Santos dead?"

"No. From what I hear, the jungle beast made his escape without coming to any serious harm." Stefan, like most Tiguri of his generation, viewed all other Feline shifters as inferior species. Nic didn't even bother trying to point out his bigotry. "I think we can assume he'll be present at the inquisition. I'm getting into the car now. I'll have Robert drive by your apartment to pick you up. I think it's best if we present a united front in this matter. I'll be there in five minutes."

Nic was already striding across the room to his closet and yanking out the first things that came to hand. "What about Arcos? Is he on the invitation list, too?"

"I believe he must be, but Gregor is a big boy. He can take care of himself. We'll see him when we get there. Five minutes," he repeated, and Nic heard the click of the line going dead.

His thumb viciously punched the off button on the cordless receiver before he tossed the thing onto the top of his dresser. Before the rattle of plastic on wood had faded, he had fastened a pair of faded jeans and was yanking a dark green sweater in place over his head.

"Nicolas?"

The sound of Saskia's voice startled him. For a second, he'd almost forgotten she was still there. Being accused of attempted murder, even secondhand, could apparently fuck with a guy's mind.

"I'm going out," he said, shoving his feet into a pair of battered loafers and reaching for the wallet he habitually pulled out of his pocket and set on the dresser every evening. "Don't wait up. I have no idea how long this will take."

"How long what will take?" she demanded, squirming to the edge of the mattress and struggling to her feet. "Nicolas, what's going on? Who was that on the phone? Why did you ask if De Santos was dead? Did you mean Rafe De Santos?"

He glared at her and headed for the door. "I don't

have time for you, Saskia," he bit out, his mind already racing toward the interview ahead of him. He had more important things to worry about right now than keeping his new fiancée in the loop, especially since the matter at hand didn't concern her. "Go to bed. I'll see you tomorrow."

With that, he exited the room, leaving his new mate behind him and wondering who the hell had decided to mess with the Tiguri. Whoever it was, they would come to regret it. Nic would make sure of that.

Three

Saskia couldn't decide if she felt more like crying or kicking something.

Scratch that. She knew very well she wanted to kick something, but unfortunately, her fiancé's arrogant, dismissive, chauvinistic ass wasn't available at the moment and taking her aggression out on anything else promised nothing more than bitter disappointment. And the definite possibility of a broken toe.

She couldn't believe the man had left her—just left her!—without a word of explanation. Without so much as a bloody backward glance. One minute he'd been poised to claim her body like an undiscovered country, and the next he'd been marching out the door telling her to go to sleep as if she were a naughty four-year-old up past her bedtime. Just who the hell did he think he was?

With a groan, Saskia slumped back on the bed and stared glumly at the ceiling. She very much feared she knew the answer to that question—Nicolas Preda was a Tiguri male, a *dominant* Tiguri male, and as such he seemed to have been molded very much in the image of all the *theri* before him, men like her father and his, the kind of archaic-minded, pigheaded, mule-stubborn idiots she had vowed as a teenager she would never take as her mate.

So much for the best-laid plans, right?

Saskia's desire not to marry a man like her father had very little to do with her affection for that man. She adored her father and had from the days when he would come home from work in the evenings and indulge her love of dry, doll-filled tea parties every night before bed. She'd loved him when he'd made it clear that she would not be dating like the other girls she went to school with, and she had loved him when he sent her off to boarding school in Switzerland so she could learn to be a proper mate for a man just like him. She still loved her father, and she couldn't deny that her deeply rooted desire to please him hadn't weighed in her decision to accept the proposal offered to her by Nicolas Preda. Of course, her own long-standing infatuation with the man had played a larger role, but now she was beginning to regret her decision.

Not that she had any right to. She had known what she was getting herself into; she'd seen it from the very beginning. The Predas, both young and old, had made it clear from the outset that she—Saskia Eloisa Arcos—had very little to do with the match they were determined to make. Who she was mattered less to them than her bloodlines, her background, and the fact that her family had made very sure to raise her with the traditional values of the Tiguri. As she was growing up, her few friends outside her own kind had teased her often about her family's old-fashioned

ways. She had been the only girl in her middle
school who never wore jeans to class, the last girl to
experiment with makeup, the only one who was
never allowed to attend parties or other events where
boys might be present.

She had known from the beginning that her marriage would be arranged for her, and none of her
friends had understood how she could pretend to accept that. Why hadn't she run away? Or just told her
parents they were crazy if they thought she was going to be traded to another family like a piece of
livestock? Her friends hadn't understood that Saskia
wasn't pretending; she *did* accept that, the same way
she accepted that the sky was blue, the sun rose in
the east, and her parents loved her very much. In her
world, that was just the way things worked. Why argue with inevitability?

That was the million-dollar question, right there.
If she had grown up knowing what sort of marriage
she would eventually have, if she had accepted that
when she was eight or twelve or sixteen years old,
where were these feelings of disappointment coming
from? Was she really going to bother getting upset
because her new fiancé hadn't shared the nature of
what was clearly an emergency with her before he
headed out to deal with it? There was no point to it.
Tiguri men lived by actions, not words. They preferred to tackle problems head-on instead of talking
about them, and they possessed fiercely rigid beliefs
about the role of women in their lives. Tiguri females
were meant to be protected, showered with gifts,
shown off to the world, and set aside when the time

for mating was past. They didn't participate in the family decision-making process, or suggest new ways of doing things, or question their mates' choices. "Seen and not heard" would describe the ideal Tiguri female in the minds of most of the males. Pretty as a picture and half as useful.

Saskia had known what she had agreed to, so why did it sting when that was exactly what she got?

"Maybe my mother was right," she muttered to the ceiling, the sound of her voice all but echoing in the huge, empty bedroom. "What was that Alcott quote she was always spouting? 'She is too fond of books, and it has turned her brain.' Maybe that's my problem."

Whatever she chose to blame it on, Saskia had to face facts—the mating she had agreed to was no longer one she could live with. But what were the alternatives?

Did she tell Nicolas she had changed her mind? Technically, until they actually had sex—the real thing, not just mind-blowing foreplay—their engagement wasn't considered binding under Tiguri law. She could still back out.

She snorted. Yeah, she could really see Nicolas reacting well to that. He might not have any feelings for her in particular, but he had chosen her as his mate and publically declared his intention to keep her. If nothing else, his pride would never allow him to release her from their agreement. Plus, he had seemed to view the whole formal betrothal process the Tiguri still used as a huge pain in the behind. She doubted he'd be very eager to repeat it all with someone new when his current fiancée had no rational reason to back out of their engagement. Disappointment with their first night together would *not* qualify in his mind as a rational reason. Or in the minds of any other of their kind.

So if she couldn't back out, what other choices did she have? She supposed she could try to just live with it, to like it or lump it, as her grandmother would have said. After all, if she'd been prepared before to accept a relationship more akin to the one she had with her banker than the one she'd hoped to have with her mate, she should be able to find that resolve inside herself again. It had to be in there somewhere, right? Maybe tucked behind the frustrated lust, or covered up by the growing piles of self-pity. If she'd felt it before, she could feel it again.

Couldn't she?

Sighing, Saskia twisted onto her side and clutched a pillow to her chest. Honestly, she wasn't sure she could. She couldn't figure out what had changed between the moment she signed the betrothal contract—yes, the Tiguri were the only living beings on earth who still used the antiquated things—and the moment Nicolas had strode out of their bedroom, leaving her alone and frustrated on their engagement night. She thought it had to be more than just the unfulfilled desire that had left her with this restless, hollow feeling. The one in her chest, that is—she knew the one between her legs had everything to do with the desire to feel her mate's body joined with hers in the elemental celebration of their union. But the ache below her breasts felt like more than that. It felt like the insistent drive she felt to put her pencil to paper and draw the images that flitted past her mind's eye, a sort of itching need that could only be assuaged by taking action.

Now she just had to decide what action to take.

She needed to do something. The idea of just sitting back and letting her mate dictate the future of their relationship no longer seemed remotely acceptable, not if it meant she could find herself abandoned at a moment's notice without so much as a word of explanation. It wasn't like she expected her mate to report his every move to her; she had no desire to track his footsteps like some sort of jail warden. But when he stopped in the middle of making love to her and got a phone call about something so important that he climbed out of her bed and into the damned elevators she thought she had every right to ask him what was going on. And she did not want to be told, "I don't have time for you."

Ooh, that statement just chapped her ass. She had the feeling, though, that if she didn't want to hear it again, she needed to start as she meant to go on. She had to set a whole new tone to this relationship, one in which she demonstrated to him clearly the fact that she intended to be a whole lot more than an accessory for him to wear when it suited. Saskia would make herself a partner in this relationship, or die trying.

She just hoped it wouldn't come to that.

Sleep didn't come easily that night, and by the time she finally drifted off Saskia felt as if she'd gone around the world in eighty days. On foot. As a consequence, she woke at her accustomed time shortly after seven feeling about as cheerful as a mortician. When she dragged herself out of bed—still empty except for herself—and stumbled into the bathroom, a quick glance in the mirror told her she looked more like the corpse. Exhaustion had turned her skin even paler than usual, until her freckles stood out in sharp relief, and had painted purple bruises beneath bloodshot eyes.

Oh, yeah, if her mate saw her now, he wouldn't just walk out the door; he'd run straight through it to get away from her.

A scalding shower managed to steam away the worst of her mental fog, but it took twice as long as usual with her makeup to temper the ravages of her restless night. Saskia tried every trick she knew, but in the end she was forced to settle for "not completely pathetic." So much for using her looks to bring her mate in line.

She pulled her hair back into a neat chignon and dressed casually, for her, in tailored gray slacks and a cashmere sweater the color of ripe plums. The cowl-neck drooped just low enough to hint at her cleavage, allowing her to go with the old standby of relying on the power of the breasts to distract a man from the flaws on the face. In defiance of the rules, she ignored the rows of shoes neatly arranged in her new closet and padded out of the bedroom in her stocking feet.

Yup, she'd already turned into such a rebel. The way her hems, cut to allow for the elegant heels she customarily wore, bunched and trailed on the ground would have appalled her mother and every deportment teacher she'd ever had. Take that, rules!

The huge apartment seemed to echo around her, the feeling of emptiness convincing her that her erstwhile fiancé still hadn't returned from his middle-of-the-night mystery task. Still, a niggling touch of hope had her poking her head into each room as she passed until by the time she left his silent office she had to remind herself that anything worth accomplishing took time and dedication. She just didn't like the fact that she couldn't get started convincing her mate how much he needed her until he actually came back to see her.

She found the kitchen easily. After years of training her memory to never forget a name or a face, a simple floor plan offered no challenge at all. Like every other room, this one sat empty and a little cold, the huge expanses of granite counter gleaming in the light that streamed in through the large window.

Saskia might have grown up in a world of privilege, but she prided herself on her ability to take care of herself in any situation. Nicolas had told her he hadn't yet hired any staff for their new home, and she felt glad of it as she located the expensive and complicated coffee machine at one end of the counter. Dealing with her own disappointment at waking up alone the night after her engagement was hard enough; she would have hated to face the pitying looks of strangers if servants had popped out of the woodwork and offered to cater to her every whim. Keeping her hands busy and her mind occupied with

mundane tasks might actually keep her sane until
she could corner her new mate for a serious talk.

It took a few minutes to locate beans and filters in
the massive kitchen, but soon enough Saskia was
cradling an elegant porcelain cup in her hands and
sipping from the heavily creamed brew. She had
contemplated and rejected the idea of a more sub-
stantial breakfast while she rooted through a refrigerator the size of some New York apartments looking
for the half-and-half. Her stomach hadn't settled
enough for her to eat. The coffee would do for now.

Her stocking feet made no sound on the tiled and
hardwood floors as she made her way toward the
front of the apartment. The enormous and deserted
living room felt like a museum gallery or a corporate
function room at the moment, when there was no
one around to fill it. It made Saskia feel even more
uncertain and isolated to perch there on the edge of
a taupe chenille sofa with nothing to do but sip her
coffee and wait. She thought about retreating to the
cozy den at the other end of the hall, but it felt somehow cowardly, and if she sat back there she might
miss the moment when her mate finally returned.
No, she'd tough it out here. It might make her feel
like a little girl at the principal's office, but at least
here she'd be able to hear the click of the front door
opening and to see her mate as soon as he walked in.
For that she would suffer a little awkwardness.

Saskia finished her coffee in silence, then sat there
with the empty cup cradled in her hands for longer
than she cared to think about. She tried to keep her
mind blank and not speculate on where her mate

might have gone and what he might be doing, but she was only mostly human. How could she not wonder about the message that had torn him from her bed—practically from her body—almost six hours ago and still not allowed him to return? Had he been hurt? Had someone else? Was it a business problem, or something more personal? Was he still even dealing with the issue he'd left for, or had he already moved on to something else? Or to some*one* else?

Not for the first time in her life, Saskia felt a twinge of envy for Lupine females. She might be more physically powerful than a she-wolf, but everyone knew that wolves mated for life. Once a Lupine male found his mate, that was it; he was done, no more bachelor ways. Tigers? Not so much. The expression "catting around" hadn't come into being without reason. Tiguri males tended to be infamous womanizers, and judging by the stories she'd heard about her fiancé, she had little reason to hope her mate would turn out to be any different. She'd hoped for the traditional honeymoon period where Nicolas would be so enthralled by her newness and the newness of their mate bond that he would stay close to home and take advantage of having a woman available to him whenever he pleased. She admitted a part of her had even hoped that she could use that time to convince him he didn't need any other women, that she would be more than happy to see to his needs, all of his needs, if he was willing to make an effort to remain faithful. She had known it would be a long shot, but she had wanted to try. Now it looked like she had failed before she'd even gotten a change to make her argument. How was that fair?

Her dark thoughts had drawn her into a good sulk by the time the phone rang. She jumped at the sound, almost as startled as she had been last night when she'd heard the same sound. She hoped this call wouldn't cause the same kind of havoc. Maybe it was even Nicolas. After all, who else would call her on the morning after her engagement? Everyone who knew her would expect her to be spending the day in bed with her new mate. No one else would even think to disturb a newly engaged couple.

Lifting the receiver, Saskia felt a surge of nervous hope. "Hello?"

"Saskia?"

The sound of a woman's voice dashed Saskia's hopes, but the fact that the woman had asked for her rather than Nicolas was some consolation. "Yes, can I help you?"

"You can if you remember me. This is Corinne D'Alessandro. We met at your party last night?"

The picture of the friendly, dark-haired woman popped immediately to Saskia's mind. She never forgot a face. "Of course I remember you, Corinne. I hope you enjoyed the party."

The woman laughed. "More than you, I think. At least no one was staring at me all night. I tell you, being the guest of honor at one of those things is highly overrated."

Saskia agreed, but she couldn't decide how to react. Why was the reporter calling her the morning after her engagement? She made a noncommittal sound and hoped Corinne would continue.

"Anyway. I'm sorry to call so early, but I decided to take a chance that with your man still sitting with the Council, you might be looking for a little company."

Saskia absorbed that information and felt the room tilt around her. "The Council?" she repeated hoarsely.

There was a moment of silence on the other end of the line.

"Uh-oh," Corinne finally said, her voice full of discomfort. "Did I just totally step in it? Am I not supposed to talk about it? I'm sorry. I didn't think. I'm such an idiot. I'm probably the worst person in the world to have an inside line on what the Council gets up to. You'd think Missy and Reggie would know better than to tell me anything. Just forget I said anything. And accept my apology. And forget I called."

"No, wait!" Saskia said, afraid the other woman would hang up and leave her as much in the dark as she'd been since last night. "Don't apologize. You're fine. I just—"

She paused, reluctant to confess over the phone such embarrassing details as the state of her engagement and the closemouthed arrogance of her fiancé. She needed to be able to see the other woman's face if she wanted to be able to tell how her story was perceived. That way, if the reporter gave any indication of being shocked by the truth or of digging for a story in Saskia's and Nicolas's private lives, Saskia would be able to cut things off and repair any potential damage.

She took a deep breath and then took a chance. "You have no reason to apologize," she repeated, infusing her voice with reassurance and a calm she didn't feel. "You surprised me for a second, but not in a bad way. I hadn't realized how nice it would be to have someone I could talk to about this kind of thing. I'm new to the city, and with the engagement and everything, I haven't had a chance to meet very many people yet, especially not other women my age."

"Well, then, I'll just have to introduce you around." Corinne's voice relaxed noticeably. "My friends and I decided early on that we girls need to stick together. Trust me, they'll be more than happy to welcome a new member to our little club."

Saskia blinked. "You have a club?"

"In a manner of speaking. We're all women who found ourselves mixed up with the Others in one way or another, mostly by falling in love with one of the big lugs. You totally qualify for membership."

"Um, thanks. I'll keep that in mind. Listen," she said, taking a deep breath and glancing around the empty apartment. "I've been feeling like an idiot rattling around this place without Nicolas all morning. I don't suppose you'd be interested in meeting me for a cup of coffee? I'd love to get out of here, and the idea of talking to someone I've actually met before would be my idea of heaven right now."

Especially someone who seemed to know more than her about her arrogant mate's current whereabouts. But she didn't say that.

"Actually, that sounds like a great idea," Corinne enthused. "My own worse half is occupied himself at the moment, and the last thing I want to do is find myself with nothing better to do than get some work done. Did you have someplace in mind?"

For a moment, Saskia's mind went blank. She realized she didn't even know what neighborhood her new home was located in, let alone what cafés might be nearby.

Corinne heard her hesitation. "If not, I know a great little place I think you might like." She rattled off an address. "How does that sound?"

"Perfect." Saskia repeated the information to herself, quickly committing it to memory. "I can be there in thirty minutes or less. How does that sound?"

"Better than a pizza." Corinne laughed. "I'll see you there."

Hanging up the phone, Saskia felt her heart pound with excitement. Maybe she'd be able to make a little progress on her fiancé-wrangling project after all. Dashing back toward the bedroom for shoes and her purse, she felt a sense of optimism she hadn't when she woke earlier. This day was finally beginning to look up.

Using the address Corinne had given her and her handy familiarity with cabbies in cities around the world, Saskia made her way to the coffee shop downtown with a minimum of fuss. Stepping into the half-basement space, she spotted the other woman right away, waving at her from a small table tucked up against a low wall that divided the room in two. She smiled and waved back, then wove her way through a maze of tables to take a seat opposite Corinne.

"Thank you so much for this," Saskia began, neatly laying her purse on the empty chair between them. "I know it was short notice, just spur-of-the-moment, really, but—"

Corinne laughed and waved a hand at her. "Don't be silly. I admit, I was hoping to get a chance to talk to you some more after last night. I feel like a jerk admitting it, but I find your whole story fascinating."

"A lot of people do," Saskia acknowledged. "Even most Others find my people's traditions hard to understand at times."

"And that makes us sound like judgmental idiots. Or morally superior assholes. Either way, it doesn't paint me in the most flattering light at the moment."

Saskia smiled as the other woman made a face at her. "No, it doesn't. Trust me, I've certainly met examples of both those types, and you're nothing like either of them. If you had struck me that way, I wouldn't have said more than three words to you on the phone earlier, and I definitely wouldn't be here now."

"Oh, good. Then I can relax and start prying."

Corinne's grin came fast and proved contagious. Saskia found herself smiling in spite of her less than pleasant night, the expression lingering while a waitress stopped by their table and took their orders. When the girl stepped away, Saskia toyed with the spoon at her place setting for a moment while she gathered her courage.

"Actually," she began, hesitating over her words,

"I was hoping to pry something from you, oddly enough. I should confess that my reasons for this invitation were at least three-quarters selfish. Well, maybe more like nine-tenths."

"Oh, thank God." When Saskia blinked, Corinne's grin curved wider. "It makes me feel so much better to hear you say that. I was afraid you would turn out to be just as sweet and kind and polite as you look, and if you were, I wouldn't be able to stop myself from hating you. I can't stand it when people make me feel like the rude, ruthless, self-absorbed person I really am under this charming veneer."

Saskia couldn't help herself. She laughed out loud. "Well! Um . . . give me a minute to try and figure out how to take that!"

"It's a total compliment," Corinne assured her, thanking their server for delivering their coffee and waving away her offer to bring them anything else. "I already have one friend who treads dangerously close to the margin of sainthood. She's a kindergarten teacher, for Christ's sake. So I'm afraid I'm full up on nice people in my life. If you can promise to be at least somewhat selfish and demanding, we'll get along *so-o-o-o* much better in the long run."

"I think I can handle that."

"Good. So, in that case, tell me what horribly selfish reason you had for wanting to talk to me. I warn you, though, I'm tough to impress."

"Actually, it was something you said over the phone." Saskia skimmed the back of her spoon over the foam on her cappuccino as she stalled. "You mentioned that you thought I might be free to talk to you this morning because Nicolas was still dealing with the Council."

Corinne nodded. "And?"

Looking up, Saskia could read nothing but genuine curiosity in the reporter's expression. She looked as if she had nothing more invested in this conversation than her own personal interest. It was enough to give Saskia that last push of courage.

Taking a deep breath, Saskia took the plunge.

"I asked you to meet me so I could ask you what that meant. Nicolas walked out last night just before two thirty in the morning. He didn't tell me where he was going or what he had to do, and I haven't heard so much as a word from him since. So can you tell me what you know about what my fiancé was doing last night? And this morning? Please."

The words tumbled out in a jumbled rush, but Corinne didn't appear to have any trouble following them. No, she didn't look at all confused. Just offended.

Mortally.

"What the fuck?!"

Saskia winced. Not at the harsh language, but at the volume of her new friend's exclamation. It brought the head of every single person in the small café snapping around to see the source of the commotion. Saskia tried to smile at the blatant stares, but there was nothing she could do to prevent the hot color climbing into her cheeks.

"I'm sorry," Corinne said, this time at a more normal volume. She blew out a deep breath. "I just . . . Wow. It never occurred to me that that was why you sounded so tense on the phone earlier. I figured you were worried about what the Council was going to decide, not that you didn't even know Preda had gone to talk to them. That's just—" She shook her head. "And here I thought *my* man could be thoughtless at times. Holy shit."

Saskia shrugged and played with her coffee cup. "I'm sure he just had a lot on his mind after he got the phone call. After all, he's not used to having a mate. It was only our first night together."

Corinne's eyes narrowed, but she made no further comment. Instead, she folded her arms on the table in front of her and leaned forward intently. "Okay, I think we'd better start from the beginning. Tell me exactly what happened last night. Everything. From the top."

"Well, you were at the party, so you know that our engagement officially began last night."

"Sort of. I know last night was a big shindig, but did he propose to you before then? I mean, that's the way things usually work. A couple gets engaged, then they start planning the party, right?"

"Not for the Tiguri."

"Explain."

Saskia sighed. She hated trying to make outsiders understand about Tiguri mating traditions. Outsiders all seemed to think those traditions belonged back in the Middle Ages, but to Saskia they were just the way things were done.

"You know that the marriage between Nicolas and me was arranged, correct?"

Corinne nodded. "Yeah, I had heard. It's kind of a

topic of conversation at the moment. In certain circles."

"For the Tiguri, marriages are always arranged," Saskia said firmly. "For one thing, tradition is very important to us. We pass customs on through families as a way of keeping our culture vibrant and undiluted by other customs. For another, there are very few of us left."

"There are? I mean, I know you're the first Tiguri I've ever met, but I thought that was just because you guys didn't live in the U.S. Don't you usually stay in Europe and Asia?"

"Those of us who are left, yes, they tend to live in their ancestral territories, which do happen to be in Eastern Europe and Asia. But even there, our population isn't what you would call thriving. Only a few families are left, and the ones with any power have dwindled so that I can count them on one hand."

"Wow," Corinne said, frowning. "That's rough. I'm sorry to hear that. But why has that happened? I mean, I don't see the Lupines in any danger of dying off, and I've met plenty of other types of shifters since I found out about you guys."

Saskia made a face. "No, the wolves seem to be in no danger at all, but then, their population has always exceeded ours. I can't point to any scientific cause for our population decline, but I can tell you that our birthrate is low. It's unusual for a Tiguri mated pair to produce more than one offspring, so our numbers continue to drop. That is part of why our mating traditions are the way they are."

"You mean, that has something to do with your engagement to Nicolas Preda?"

"In the way it will progress, yes."

Corinne's dark eyes flashed with interest. "Explain, please."

Saskia could only try. "The arrangement of marriages is important to keep as much variety as possible in our genetic material. Just like in the animal world, a low population of endangered species makes it necessary to consciously work to prevent inbreeding."

"Ew. Okay, makes sense, but . . . ew."

"Exactly. None of us wishes to mate with our first cousin, believe me. Arranging marriages means that our pairings don't inadvertently compromise our gene pool, but the narrowness of that pool has also informed the structure of our matings."

"What exactly does that mean?"

"Human relationships—or really, most non-Tiguri relationships—operate in a series of stages, correct? Couples meet, then date, then become engaged, then marry and hopefully live happily ever after. Am I right?"

"In theory."

"Well, Tiguri relationships have stages, too, but they're geared less toward allowing the mates to get to know each other and more toward ensuring a healthy future population."

Corinne downed a swig of coffee and grimaced. "I have a feeling I'm not going to like this."

"You don't have to like it. I'm just letting you know how this works."

"True." Corinne nodded. "Go on."

"The arrangement of marriages means that those first two stages I mentioned in human relationships are unnecessary for us. Couples don't date. They usually meet at or shortly before the marriage contracts are signed, not before. They get to know each other during the engagement, which becomes official the same night the male presents his mate with an engagement ring, usually just before the reception to announce the union."

"Oh, so that's what last night was for you," Corinne said, her eyes widening. "Wow, then that means that you two barely know each other, right? How weird must that be."

Saskia shifted uncomfortably. "Nicolas and I are a little different," she admitted. "Our families decided early on that an alliance between us made sense, so I've known Nicolas since I was a little girl. I always knew we'd be mates one day."

"But no pressure, right?"

"Right," she agreed wryly. "The pressure starts now. Like I said, the relationship begins with the engagement, which happened last night, but it's not considered official until the couple, er, consummates things."

Corinne stared at her for a second before understanding drew her eyes impossibly wide. Saskia felt her cheeks go crimson.

"Whoa, you mean, even if you're engaged and wearing a ring and telling five hundred guests about your intention to get married and all that, you're still not official until you two have sex?" The reporter's voice strained with incredulity, which wasn't that strange a reaction. Saskia had heard it before.

"Yes, that's correct. The betrothal isn't considered binding beforehand. We have to demonstrate a clear intention to procreate together; otherwise there would be no point in the relationship."

"No point? As in, you can't just be together because you want to be? Because you love each other and you want to spend your lives together?"

Saskia heard the indignation and pointed out the flaw in the human logic. "How would we have become so emotionally attached if we hadn't met before we agreed to marry each other?"

"Well, you— I— You— I mean . . ."

"Exactly. Remember what I just told you—the whole point of a Tiguri mating is to produce children. Which is also why we won't be able to marry unless I get pregnant. Until there's proof that we're fertile together, there's always the chance we'd have to dissolve the agreement and each take another mate. And until I give birth to a healthy baby, we still have that option. We become true mates when I conceive, but it's like a trial run. If I miscarry or produce a stillborn child, the trial period ends and we go our separate ways."

Corinne remained silent for several minutes, long enough for Saskia to drain her cup with a series of nervous sips.

"Okay, wow," the human woman finally managed, sinking back into her seat as if the effort to wrap her mind around Tiguri mating customs had drained her of energy. "I want to say that that's the most disgusting thing I've ever heard, but I can't."

Saskia looked up in surprise. "You can't?"

"Well, I can," Corinne corrected herself, "but it would be stupid of me. I mean, it's horrifying to me, but I'm a total outsider. I'm human. I might be married to a man who's a bit more than that, but I'd be a hypocrite to try and judge another species based on what I've learned about them in two brief conversations and a total of about thirty-seven minutes in your company. In a totally Machiavellian kind of way, it's almost brilliant. It's ruthlessly logical. If what your people need most is more little people and, like all the other shifters I've met so far, you can't make more by biting humans the way the movies want us to believe"—she nodded at Saskia's snort of ridicule—"then what you've described makes a sick sort of sense."

Saskia took a moment of silence for herself. "Thank you," she said after she cleared her throat. "You're the first person I've ever explained to who was even willing to admit that much. Most others are so disgusted by the idea, they can't get away from me fast enough."

"Why the hell is that? Did you design the system? The fact that you're part of it isn't your fault, unless Tiguri have some weird ability to choose their species and parents pre-conception that no one's ever told me about. That would be like someone trying to blame me for the Spanish Inquisition because I'm human and some sick member of my species thought up the idea to persecute heretics back in the Dark Ages. Not my fault, and I'm not about to take responsibility. Neither should you."

It felt almost as if a burden Saskia had been carrying had just been set aside. Impulsively she reached across the table and laid her hand over the back of Corinne's.

"Thank you," Saskia repeated, and squeezed warmly. "I knew there was something I liked about you the minute I met you. I would dearly love to be able to consider you a friend."

Corinne grinned and squeezed back. "Oh, sweetie, with a fiancé who acted like yours did last night, I'm honor bound as a woman to be your friend. We have to stick together against the idiocy of the testosterone-poisoned half of the world. Now let's get back to what your knucklehead did last night. Did he really walk out in the middle of the night without telling you a thing about where he was going?"

Saskia nodded. "When I asked what was going on, he told me he didn't have time for me."

The human woman's expression turned furious. "Oh, no, he didn't," she hissed, her eyes narrowing into angry slits. "You need to tell me everything. Word for word. Right now."

So, Saskia did. Her explanation did little to calm her new friend, though. Corinne's feelings for Nicolas's shabby treatment were stamped all over her face, the anger sending their waitress scampering to deliver their refills with speed never before seen south of midtown. When Saskia got to the part where her fiancé had literally rolled off her naked body at the point of no return, Corinne almost choked on her coffee.

"Wait just a second," the human snapped, setting her mug down with an ominous thunk. "Let me see if I got this straight. Are you telling me that not only did the man leave you in the middle of the night after a phone call where you heard him ask if one of your party guests was dead, but he did it *before* you even managed to have the sex every single member of your family and community expects you to have as a matter of fricking civic duty?"

Saskia squirmed. When she heard it laid out like that, she felt almost as if she should be defending her fiancé, no matter what a louse he'd acted like. "I doubt he thought of it quite like that—"

Corinne cut her off with an impatient gesture. "I doubt he *thought* at all. Clearly, he didn't think about how you would feel to be abandoned on what amounts to your wedding night without so much as a word of explanation. And it doesn't sound to me like he even *thought* about the fact that common courtesy might require him to . . . oh, I don't know . . . make sure you knew he wasn't *lying dead in a ditch somewhere this morning!*"

The woman cut herself off, closed her eyes, and drew in a deep, slow breath. Saskia watched in fascination.

"Sorry about that," Corinne said after a controlled exhalation. "I didn't actually intend to channel the spirit of my mother just then, especially not since she's alive and well and perfectly capable of saying the same thing herself. Which she would, if she heard about this, I can promise you."

"Um, thanks."

"No problem." Corinne fortified herself with a gulp of coffee before continuing. "All right, so setting aside the fact that your man is the hands-down winner of this week's award for Idiot Male–Epic Screwup Category, I suppose that for once, my inside sources on the Council of Others will be used for a higher purpose. It almost makes me feel noble. Usually, I'm just there for the gossip."

"What are your inside sources? Your mate?"

"God, no. Thankfully, the Fae don't sit on the Council, so we get to avoid all that messy political crap. Luc doesn't really have the patience for it, anyway. He's a fighter, not a lover. No, two of my best friends are married to Council members. They always know what's going on, even when their husbands aren't supposed to tell them about it."

Saskia marveled at that. She couldn't imagine a relationship like that, where the male confided everything in his mate, but it sounded like something she wanted. If she was going to try to build a new kind of mating with Nicolas, that was the sort of ideal that would be worth working toward.

"Missy and Reggie," Corinne continued. "Missy is the kindergarten teacher I told you about. Too sweet for her own good, but basically irresistible. You two ought to get along like a house on fire. I think you've got a lot in common. Missy's husband is head of the local werewolf pack."

"Melissa and Graham Winters?" The names clicked into place, opening up Saskia's mental database of people she needed to know. "They're your friends?"

"Yup. Well, Missy is. I think Graham looks at me more as an annoying but amusing accessory in his wife's wardrobe. He's okay, though. He worships Missy, and that's the important part."

"And Reggie?"

"Regina, actually. She's the best source. Graham is on the Council, but Reggie's husband was the head of it for, like, two decades or more. Which is nothing to a vampire, I suppose, but it did give him pretty uncanny instincts for what's going on under the surface there."

Regina. Married to a vampire. A vampire who had led the Council for an unusually long period of time. The facts lined up like symbols on a slot machine.

"Regina and Dmitri Vidâme."

"Hey, you're good." The human looked impressed. "I have trouble remembering the names of all my cousins. How do you do that with people you've never even met?"

Saskia shrugged. "It's my job."

"Huh. I must have missed that section of the want ads."

That earned a smile. "Or you didn't get the Tiguri edition of the newspaper. I mentioned we kinda dig on tradition, right? Part of that includes some pretty intensive protocol training, at least for women in the prominent families. Girls are raised to become . . .

political hostesses, I guess. Remembering names and faces is like a 101 course."

"I'd ask you to teach me your tricks, but then people might start expecting me to remember them, and really that's just more trouble than it's worth." She pushed aside her empty mug. "So anyway, back to the subject at hand. The Council. According to Reggie, the Council called an emergency meeting last night because someone—currently unidentified—attacked Rafe last night after he left your party. Tried to kill him, from what I hear."

Shock pressed Saskia back in her seat. "Rafe? Rafael De Santos? But I spoke with him last night just before he left. Why would someone want to kill him?"

Corinne lifted an eyebrow. "I've wanted to do it a time or two. I'm just not the sort to get the Council into a lather. Rafe's a great guy, don't get me wrong, but he can be an arrogant prick sometimes. And the head of the Council is never the most popular guy in town. Council decisions are always offending one group or another. I don't think anyone was surprised that someone would *want* to kill Rafe, just that they managed to get close enough to him to try."

"Was he hurt?"

"Not from what Reggie told me. She said the only thing he hurt was his pride. The guy jumped him from behind, took him totally off guard."

"The guy? So they know who did it?"

Corinne shook her head. "A figure of speech. I mean, who else would attack Rafe but a man? The only woman who might be big enough to take him would have to be half giant, right? I mean, the dude looks like a useless, elegant cover model, but I've seen him get pissed. It's not pretty. And not something any of the women I know would want to go up against. Including the shifters."

Saskia conceded the point. "Then they don't know the identity of his attacker."

"Not yet, but I think it's pretty clear they have their suspicions."

Another good point, one that Saskia had been trying to avoid. "You mean they suspect my Nicolas."

Corinne shrugged, but her gaze remained glued on her friend's face. "It seems like a pretty logical assumption, given the timing of the phone call you got last night and the mood you said he was in when he left. What I want to know is, why?"

"Why would being accused of attempted murder make Nicolas angry?"

"No, why would anyone think that a newly engaged Tiguri with every reason to look forward to a . . . ahem . . . satisfying night with his new mate would rather be out jumping someone else?"

Saskia groaned. The answer to that question was even more complicated than the traditional Tiguri mating customs. How could she boil it down so the human would understand it without giving her a full-fledged lesson in the history of the Others?

"Has anyone mentioned to you just why the Tiguri and our marriages have become such a hot topic of conversation recently?"

"Not really. I guess I just assumed it was like when a new kid shows up at school one day. People just get curious."

Saskia had heard worse analogies, but . . .

"Think of it less like a new kid just showed up at school and more like you just met your new neighbor and found out he was Genghis Khan."

Corinne blinked. "You plan to sack the city, massacre any resistance, enslave the survivors, and dine atop the bloody corpses?"

"Not me personally, but I think that's what the Council believes is my family's ultimate goal. Mine and Nicolas's."

"That's one heck of an assumption," Corinne mused. "Have you given them any reason to believe that's what you guys are after?"

"I don't think they need a reason." Briefly she outlined the history between the Tiguri and the larger Other population. "So, naturally, the Lupines tend to be the most suspicious, but most other shifters are a little wary of us. The vampires just work around us, and magic users generally could care less. Unless they're trying to get their hands on little bits of us to use in their spells."

"Considering how powerful the Silverbacks are in the city, I'd say you're not going to find yourself making coffee for the Welcome Wagon." Corinne shook her head. "Are your families really sure moving here is worth it?"

Saskia laughed, completely unamused. "Are you suggesting they might have asked me first?"

"You know, I don't understand you at all," Corinne

said, leaning back in her chair and eyeing Saskia curiously. "I like you, but I don't understand you. You're clearly intelligent, you're well educated—I overheard you talking to that NYU professor last night about some Renaissance painter I've never even heard of. You're beautiful and not even remotely airheaded. . . ."

"But?"

"But you don't seem to have any problem letting your father or your fiancé tell you how to run your life. It just baffles me."

"There are days when it baffles me, too."

"No, seriously."

"Seriously," Saskia agreed. "In general, I have no problem with tradition. I like the sense of continuity and safety in knowing what's expected of everyone around me. And no one has ever forced me to do anything I really didn't want to do. My parents love me. Sure, they raised me with certain rules and expectations, but they never tried to take away my sense of self or denied me anything I really wanted."

"But your fiancé sure did."

It took Saskia a minute and a glance at the mischief in the other woman's eyes to catch her meaning. When she did, she flushed predictably. "Well, yes, I suppose so, but I know where he sleeps now. He can't avoid me forever."

Corinne laughed. "True." She glanced at her watch. "Hopefully, he can stop avoiding you any minute now. Missy and Reggie told me that come hell or high water, the Council would be adjourning by ten.

Even Others need to sleep eventually. With any luck, your man is already on his way home."

"Really? Just like that?" Saskia sat up and reached for her purse. "They won't try to hold him, or anything, will they? Has he been officially accused of the attack?"

"I seriously doubt it. If they had any proof he was involved, I doubt they'd have issued a polite summons to ask him to come to them. They would have shown up on your doorstep and dragged him away in chains."

"The summons wasn't all that polite, remember?"

Corinne stood and left cash on the table to pay for their coffee, waving away Saskia's attempt to take care of it. "This is on me. Trust me, though, for the Council, that summons was as polite as it gets. Those folks don't mess around."

Saskia feared she was right.

Four

Saskia hurried home from the café, tapping her foot impatiently until the cabbie turned up his radio to drown her out. Thankfully, the music also covered up the sounds of her growling every time they got stuck at a red light. By the time they pulled to a stop outside Nicolas's building, she was so anxious to get upstairs that she threw enough money at the man to pay for a dozen trips just so she wouldn't have to wait while he counted. She positively ran past the doorman, not even pausing to acknowledge his greeting as she pushed impatiently at the elevator button and all but danced in place while she waited for it to arrive.

She darted into the car the minute the doors opened and got a look at the way the doorman frowned at her with the phone to his ear while she stabbed at the "doors close" button. Less than thirty seconds later, the doors opened again, disgorging her into the lobby of Nicolas's private floor. The door to the apartment swung open even as she fumbled in her purse for the key she'd snagged from the hook in the kitchen.

"Just where in hell have you been, woman?" Nicolas roared at her, the force of the demand literally backing her up a step.

Saskia froze, her eyes widening. "What do you mean?"

"I mean, where the *hell* have you *been*?" he repeated, reaching out to grasp her arm and pull her into the apartment. The door snapped shut behind him with a tone of finality, and suddenly Saskia found herself standing in the barely familiar living room wringing her purse in her hands while the fiancé she'd spent the morning worrying and obsessing over glared at her like an accused criminal.

Wasn't that an ironic about-face?

"Well?" he prompted, crossing his arms over his chest and staring down at her from his intimidating height.

The female inside her urged her to open her mouth and confess, apologize, mollify her mate, but Saskia bit back the urge. She hadn't done anything wrong. If Nicolas hadn't wanted her to leave the apartment, then he should have told her that last night before he left. Even better, he should have stayed put himself. Then she would have had no reason to try to pry information about her own fiancé out of a near stranger.

"Saskia . . ." The low growl was a warning.

She drew back her shoulders and mustered a glare of her own. "I went out for coffee, if you must know."

"If I must know?" he repeated and prowled a step closer. "Oh, believe me, little tigress, I definitely *must know*. But why did you need to go out for coffee? I searched the entire apartment for you when I got back. I saw the pot of coffee you brewed, and your used cup in the sink. Was there something wrong with the coffee you made here?"

He had dropped his arms and stepped forward until he loomed over her, clearly trying to bully her into feeling guilty. Well, Saskia wouldn't have it. Deliberately, she turned her back on him and stepped away, heading toward the bedroom as if she hadn't a care in the world. She heard him curse as he followed her, and laid a hand against her stomach to try to calm the butterflies that cavorted inside.

"There was nothing wrong with the coffee in the kitchen," she said, setting her purse down on the low table in the sitting area of the huge suite. After taking a fortifying breath, she turned to face him and lifted her chin defiantly. "But I like company when I drink it, and since I didn't know when you might be back, I went out to get some."

The muscle in the side of Nicolas's jaw clenched so tight, Saskia thought it might burst right through the skin. His eyes darkened to a shade of green that reminded her of dense, dimly lit forests, and when he spoke she didn't think he managed to separate his teeth by so much as a millimeter.

"We announced our engagement last night and you went out this morning to have coffee with another man?" he asked, his voice so deep and low, Saskia had to strain to hear it. That, more than anything, sent a chill of apprehension shivering through her.

When the words finally registered, she gasped with indignation. "What? No! Of course I didn't meet another man. What sort of person do you think I am?"

Her mate's nostrils flared and she saw his hands clench into fists at his sides.

"I don't know, Saskia. Why don't you explain it to me."

It wasn't a suggestion.

"I had coffee with a friend. A female friend," she clarified hastily when she saw his lips draw back to reveal the beginnings of fangs where his canines would normally be. "Like I said, I didn't know when you'd be home."

She hated that she sounded defensive, but that was how she felt. Actually, she felt so many things at that moment, she couldn't begin to separate them all. Anger over his disappearing act, indignation at his accusations, relief that he had returned home safely. Frustration with his typical *ther* attitude.

A stirring of unwilling arousal.

Saskia swallowed a curse and hoped he was too distracted by his own emotions to detect that last bit in her scent. For him to know she still wanted him after the way he'd treated her last night and this morning would be the final blow to her self-respect.

"And it never occurred to you to wait for me?" he rumbled. "That it might concern me to come home and find you gone? That I might fear something had happened to you?"

"Apparently not," she snapped, fisting her hands on her hips and stifling the urge to scream in frustration. "Just like it apparently never occurred to you that I might worry when *you* left. In the middle of the night. Without a single word about where you were going or why you had to leave or when you might be back. Looks like we're both thoughtless rudesbys."

Nicolas stilled in mid-prowl, his breath coming out in a hiss. "What? Is that what this was about? About getting even? Were you trying to punish me for not stopping to answer all your questions last night? I told you, I didn't have time to explain. I needed to hurry. But somehow you decided that gave you the right to disappear like a spoiled brat playing hooky instead of waiting for me to come home?" He stalked toward her again, herding her backward until she had to dart sideways to keep from being trapped against the wall. "Because if that's what this was, I need to tell you, it's completely unacceptable."

Saskia felt her jaw drop and her eyes widen until she felt sure she resembled nothing so much as a goldfish in an oxygen-poor fishbowl. "Unacceptable?!" she sputtered.

"Unacceptable," he repeated, following her around the side of an armchair and toward the other end of the room. The end occupied most noticeably by the enormous carved walnut bed. "When I tell my mate to wait for me, I expect to return to find her where I left her. I do *not* expect to find her missing with no explanation about where she's gone or when she'll be back. Not that a note would have saved your ass in this case," he mused, his eyes glinting dangerously, "but it might have kept me from spending quite so much time planning your punishment."

Punishment???

That was it. Saskia reached the end of her rope and snapped free with a howl of indignation. She launched herself at her fiancé with the ferocity of a raging fury, all fiery eyes and snapping teeth. How dare he tell her she needed to be punished when he wouldn't even acknowledge his own rude, arrogant, inconsiderate, and downright *mean* behavior from the night before? Oh, he was going to regret that, from the balls up, if Saskia had anything to say about it.

He caught her attacking form in his huge, powerful hands, but he clearly hadn't expected her to be quite so strong. That's what blind outrage could do for a girl. He had to struggle to keep her at arm's length, and even then avoiding her kicking feet and striking knees presented an altogether different challenge. Saskia heard him curse and hoped she was hitting something vital. She knew she hadn't gotten at his groin yet, but just give her a chance; she was determined.

"God*dammit*, Sass! What the hell is wrong with you?" he bellowed, finally giving up on holding her away from him and twisting to tumble them both to the bed, where he could pin her more effectively with the weight of his body. "Would you calm down?"

"Calm down? I'll show you calm, you arrogant son of a bitch!" she screeched, and bucked beneath him like a wild animal. Which was very nearly what she'd become.

Saskia was holding back her change by the skin of her teeth. Her already elongating and sharpening teeth. Her tigress stretched and clawed beneath her skin, demanding release. The beast had no compunction about showing an arrogant mate what Saskia thought of his ideas about crime and punishment. With four-inch claws and three-inch fangs she felt more than capable of taking on the angry male. Even if she didn't win, she'd certainly inflict enough damage to make him pay for the way he had treated her.

She felt her skin begin to ripple and tried to remember why shifting just now would be a bad move. She couldn't focus. Her anger burned too hot. The tigress yowled too insistently.

"Sass! Saskia!" Nicolas shouted above her, his green eyes burning intensely down at her. She felt his hands tighten around her wrists, shaking her, trying to snap her out of the change. She wanted to tell him he was probably too late.

She felt him shake her again, hard, then felt him wedge his legs between hers, spreading them wide and preventing her from striking him the incapacitating blow she had so looked forward to. He cursed, the sound a distant echo behind the fierce impulsion to let go, to let her beast shape slip through the human covering that imprisoned it. Her body began to twist, the hair on her arms standing erect, beginning to thicken and lengthen. She could feel it coming and threw back her head, her mouth opening to welcome her savage self—

Then Nicolas bent down and seized her lips, surging inside and transforming her fury into lust with the hard, dominant stroke of his tongue.

Saskia froze for the space of several heartbeats; her tigress offered only a token protest, growling in surprised indignation, then melting into a purring mass of heated desire. She stopped fighting to hit her mate and instead fought to get closer, arching her body into his and wrapping her legs around his hips to pull him tight against her. In that breathless instant, she forgot why she wanted to fight him or to hurt him. Her tigress made the split-second switch from killing frenzy to mating frenzy without a whimper of protest. To the beast, passion was passion and the flavor of it mattered less than drinking it down.

The animal sank back beneath her skin as Saskia gave in to the impulse to join with her mate. She writhed beneath him, no longer trying to get free but wanting to rub every inch of herself against every inch of him. She mewled into his mouth, torn between wanting the intimate kiss never to end and needing to lay her tongue against his skin to take in the rich, spicy taste of him.

She felt the instant when he realized that she no longer struggled to escape him. His body stiffened, then relaxed into the intense focus of a predatory male. His fingers loosened cautiously from her wrists, hands sliding down her extended arms, ready to snap back into place should she attempt to strike him. Saskia had no such plans. As soon as she could, she lowered her arms and insinuated them between their bodies to grasp the hem of her sweater and yank the offending garment off over her head. The touch of cloth between them had become unbearable. Saskia needed to feel his skin against hers. When he drew back to give her more room, she expressed her impatience with an angry hiss.

Nicolas growled in return, a low rumble that orig-
inated deep in his chest and that Saskia could feel
vibrating against her sternum. The sensation made
her shiver and reach impatiently for his sweater next.
Too much cloth still lay between them. He took matters out of her hands, stripping bare to the waist, then
pressing down over her, letting her feel the rough
heat of his lightly haired chest pinning her to the
mattress. Saskia purred her pleasure and twisted to
rub her breasts against him, the sound turning to an
expression of displeasure when she realized her bra
still separated them. Almost before the thought had
registered, Nicolas lifted a hand and swiped at the
lacy fabric, slicing the garment down the center with
one precisely controlled claw.

Her breath hissed out in relief when her nipples
made contact with his chest, the buds tightening into
painful little points of arousal. She saw her mate's
eyes narrow, their green depth all but glowing as he
stared at the hard points for a heated instant before
swooping down to capture one between his lips.
Saskia moaned in reaction, her arms curling around
his head to cradle him against her even as she lifted
to press herself into his mouth. Nothing in her life
had ever felt as good as the hot furnace of his mouth
drawing on her with ferocious strength. Sharp little
stings of pain only seemed to make the pleasure that
much greater, until she found herself whimpering
with every expert tug.

God, how she wanted him.

Intent on urging him faster, she squeezed her legs
around his hips, the heels of her gray flannel pumps

digging into the small of his back as she ground her
pelvis against the arousal she could feel straining
between them. Again, the feel of layers of fabric
separating them made her furious and she released
his head to grab at the waistband of his jeans and tug
angrily. She didn't even notice the sound of denim
ripping, just allowed her hands to skate appreciatively over the bare skin she exposed.

Nicolas released her nipple with a pop and reared
over her, ignoring her furious roar as he efficiently
rid himself of the last of his clothing. Saskia's eyes
greedily drank in his nude form, roaming happily
over the heavy width of his shoulders, the long plane
of his torso, and the thick muscling of his thighs.
When her gaze skated to his erection, she felt her
eyes widen with a mixture of hunger and apprehension. As impressive as the rest of him, his penis
stretched long and thick over the taut muscles of his
belly, the head gleaming with proof of his arousal.
As if the size of him had left any doubts.

While she stared, her mate moved swiftly to deal
with her own unnecessary garments. He flung her
shoes in the general direction of her closet, flicked
open the fastening of her trousers, and yanked the
cloth down and away, taking her lacy panties with
them. Clearly uncaring, he tossed everything aside
and took a moment to stare at her pale, creamy na-
kedness before dropping his knees to the foot of the
bed and crawling toward her like the hungry predator he was.

Her muscles tensed involuntarily. Instinct screamed
at her to run, flee, escape, before she found herself

devoured whole. But Saskia didn't want to escape; she wanted to be devoured, and she wanted this man to do it. Under her skin, her tigress recognized its mate and stretched in luxurious welcome.

Nicolas's eyes glowed a bright, intense emerald as he flowed toward her, muscles rippling and flexing in a breathtaking display of masculine power and beauty. Instinctively Saskia gathered herself into a crouch, pulling her legs up under her and shifting her weight forward until she balanced gracefully on her palms and the soles of her feet, her eyes fixed on her approaching mate. With her knees drawn up to her shoulders and her hands pressed to the mattress between her legs, she presented a tantalizing picture to the hungry male. The position stretched her open, placing her sex on vivid display, but her arms partially shielded her, leaving her mate to catch fleeting glimpses of his ultimate goal.

He prowled closer, lowering his head and inhaling deeply to draw her scent inside him. She saw the way his eyelids drooped and his nostrils flared, as if he found her intoxicating, and she felt a surge of feminine satisfaction. He pressed his face to her chest and nuzzled, then trailed a path up to her shoulder with broad swipes of his tongue. When he reached the graceful curve he bared his teeth and nipped sharply. Rather than causing pain, the sharp bite made her purr, and she tilted her head to rub her cheek against his. The crisp rasp of stubble told her he hadn't bothered to shave when he returned to the apartment, and she savored the tactile pleasure of emerging whiskers.

Her mate growled softly, more a promise than a threat, and crowded closer to her. If she'd had a tail, it would have twitched in response. As it was, her tigress made do, sending her body twisting and turning until she dropped to her knees and faced the head of the bed, insinuating herself between Nicolas's arms and backing into him. With her bottom nestled against his groin, she arched her back like the cat she was and rubbed skin to skin in blatant invitation.

Nicolas didn't need to be asked twice.

With a dark rumble of satisfaction, he shifted his weight forward, covering her like a blanket. His chin hooked over her shoulder and nuzzled briefly before his teeth closed around the tender lobe of her ear in a primitive warning. He was done playing. Now he intended to claim his mate.

Saskia shivered at the feel of his big body surrounding hers. Warm skin pressed against her everywhere, his muscled thighs to the backs of hers, hard stomach and chest pinned against her back. His arms braced just under hers to bracket her in place. With his size and strength, he had her trapped. She couldn't have gotten away if she'd wanted to, but escaping was the furthest thought from her mind. She reveled in his overwhelming presence. Her body heated at the mere smell of him, the sensation of bare skin against bare skin making her soften and flood with moisture at her core. She wanted him, woman to man, mate to mate.

Needed him.

Desperately.

Her breath caught in her throat as he moved behind her with elegant power. A twist of his hips, a curve of his spine, and she felt his erection slide between her swollen lips, searching for her entrance. She tilted her pelvis eagerly, choking on a gasp when he found his mark and began to sink into her. The broad head of his cock spread her open, stretched her to receive him. She felt a sharp sting, then a steady, itching burn as her body struggled against his invasion. The rough texture of the spines that encircled his glans rasped against her inner walls and made her whine, high and desperate. Instinctively she shifted as if to escape, and her mate snarled a warning. Saskia panted, pleasure and discomfort blending in a tangled mess of overwhelming sensation. She needed more, needed to get away, needed something so badly she could taste it, dark and bitter at the back of her throat.

Her fingers scrabbled at the bedclothes and she shifted her weight forward, trying to slide out from under her aroused mate. Nicolas roared and thrust his hips forward, even as his head dropped, teeth closing hard over her shoulder to pin her in place. She felt him enter deeper, working his way into her with shallow digs of his hips until, with a lunge, he broke through her internal barrier and slid home on a single, powerful thrust.

Saskia screamed. It started out as a sound of shock, of outrage at the physical insult to her body, but within the space of a heartbeat it became a primitive expression of exultation. Nicolas echoed it with a yowl of his own. She heard the savage satisfaction in his tone, the possessive note that told her he knew no other man had ever claimed her, and she shivered in reaction. Her virginity had never mattered to Saskia; she had kept it merely from a lack of motivation to be rid of it, and because in the back of her mind she had always felt as if she already belonged to Nicolas. The fact that he noticed and gloried in being the first to touch her thrilled her to her core.

Impatient to experience more, she pressed her shoulders down into the mattress and wriggled her hips with obvious demand. Her mate purred and laved the skin where he had bitten her moments before. Then he set his teeth to her again and held her still as he began a hard, steady rhythm of claiming.

She choked back ragged cries of pleasure as his body moved deep and strong inside her. His spines, designed to stimulate her to ovulation, rasped against her inner walls with every withdrawal. The sensation was like fingernails on her clit, one part pain and three parts ecstasy. She thrust back against him, trying to match his demanding tempo, struggling to wring every drop of sensation from the fierce mating.

The sound of high-pitched whines and sobs almost distracted her until she realized they came from her own mouth, broken and ragged because of the way she had to struggle for breath. She might as well have been running a marathon, because every ounce of oxygen became a rare and precious resource. Under the sounds she made she could also hear the rough slap of flesh against flesh as his hips thudded against her backside on every powerful thrust. She heard the raw, wet sounds of her sex clasping around him, and the animal grunts he made as he worked furiously over and within her trembling body.

She lost all track of time. They could have strained together for hours, or days, or seconds; Saskia had no idea. All she knew was that *this*, this was what her tigress had been craving, hungering for, since the moment she set her eyes on her childhood crush all grown up and glorious. The beast within her had needed to be taken, claimed, possessed, and the disappointment of the night before had driven her to the brink of her self-control. Now that control had snapped, and Saskia had become a creature of pure lustful instinct, a needy, greedy female at the mercy of her ferocious mate.

Oh, how she gloried in it.

The firm grip on her shoulder didn't hurt in the least; instead it acted like a live wire from her mate's mouth straight to her quivering pussy. Every swipe of his tongue, every sting of his teeth, every draw of his mouth as he swallowed and purred and pinned her in place made her muscles clamp around him like a fist. In fact, she clasped around him so hard, it amazed her he could still manage to pull out far enough to power his mind-numbing thrusts.

Her breath worked in and out like a bellows, making her head spin and her throat go raw. She strained for air, strained for pleasure, strained for *more* until she thought her heart would burst, and she didn't even care. All she cared about was this moment and this man. This mating.

The climax snuck up on her. It stalked her like another tiger, crouching low in the camouflage of the forest, waiting and watching for its moment to strike. The moment came, unexpectedly, when strong white fangs released their grip on her shoulder and grazed a careful line up the curve of her neck to the sensitive hollow behind her ear. Hot breath stirred the tendrils of hair that curled there, caressed the tender skin into trembling softness. Then, a tongue came out, swiping at the tiny trickle of blood at her shoulder, following the path of the tendon back to that magic patch of flesh, and lapping away a salty film of sweat. A cry tore from her throat, rough and aching, and her body clenched, quivering endlessly on the edge of the precipice. Until her mate shifted, pressed himself high and hard inside her, parted his lips, and let his teeth graze the delicate shell of her ear. In a soft, toneless, airless whisper, he purred one word directly into her head and heart, and Saskia leapt blindly into climax.

He whispered, *"Mine."*

She woke feeling as if either she'd just been in a car crash and trauma had wiped away all memory of the incident or someone had snuck into her room while she slept and beat her soundly with a baseball bat, for some reason concentrating rather obscenely on the sensitive area between her thighs.

Wincing, Saskia rolled and stretched and discovered her muscles would scream in protest. She groaned, the sound oddly hoarse, and memory came rushing back. With about the same force as the previously mentioned baseball bat, this time aimed right at the back of her head.

She was mated.

Quite thoroughly, from the feel of it.

Flipping onto her back, Saskia pulled the rumpled blankets to her chin and scowled at the empty bed beside her. Judging by the light spilling in through the windows, she had dozed until mid-afternoon—hardly surprising given the vigorous bout of pre-nap exercise—but the scene before her bore a disturbing similarity to that morning. Once again, she had been deserted in her own bedroom, her mate nowhere to be found.

Clearly, the two of them still needed to discuss a thing or two.

Saskia pushed herself into a sitting position and winced at the tenderness between her legs. When she slid her feet to the floor and took a tentative step toward the bathroom, she actually groaned. She'd known that the use of a bunch of unfamiliar muscles in an unfamiliar activity might leave her a little sore, but this seemed excessive. She could barely walk.

Hobbling carried her into the master bath, where she used the toilet, hissing in a breath when the tissue came away stained pink with blood. Knowing that a ruptured hymen led to virginal bleeding was one thing, but seeing proof of it in her hand felt like something very different. She felt a little contemplative as she stood at the sink washing her hands, then removed the few remaining pins from the tangled mass of her hair. It had fallen halfway down her back sometime during the wrestling match with Nicolas, and sleeping on the resulting birds' nest hadn't done her any favors. She brushed it out quickly and secured it in a no-nonsense ponytail before returning to the bedroom to dress.

She couldn't quite decide how she felt as she tugged on comfortable, stretchy yoga pants—about all her body would tolerate at the moment—over a plain set of cotton bra and panties. She had always thought that joining with her mate for the first time would leave her feeling content, at peace, secure in her mating and her place in the world. Instead, she felt as if she'd opened a door with excitement brimming over, only to find herself stumbling into a dark room without having any idea where to find a light switch. Sure, the sex had been better than anything she'd ever read about or heard spoken of or even contemplated in the furthest reaches of her subconscious, but that didn't mean she had any idea how she ought to feel about it.

She tugged a soft jersey pullover on over her head and stared into the full-length mirror that decorated the inside of her closet door. Her face looked pale, and with her makeup from the morning a distant memory, the dark circles had returned to the skin under her eyes. She looked tired and vulnerable and a little uncertain. Was that really the way she wanted to appear when she went to beard her tiger in his den?

Was there really anything she could do about it?

Making a face at herself, Saskia closed the closet

door and once again padded barefoot out of the master suite, searching for her mate. This time, at least, she managed to find him.

He'd left the door to his office slightly ajar, lamplight spilling out into the hallway. The interior room lacked windows, so when she poked her head inside she saw Nicolas's face lit by the glow of the banker's light atop his desk and the tall floor lamp beside it. He didn't look up when she stepped closer, but she saw his fingers tighten around the pen he held and she knew he had sensed her presence.

She pushed the door fully open and hesitated on the threshold. She felt like she should say something, but she couldn't think what. Did she apologize for screaming at him earlier? It didn't seem appropriate, considering she'd meant every word she'd said; and thanking him would feel ridiculous, not to mention pathetic. She supposed she could ask him what he was doing, but she wasn't sure she cared. What she really wanted to know was what he was thinking, but she couldn't ask him that for fear he might tell her.

Was it supposed to be this hard to talk to the man she'd be spending the rest of her life with?

Her weight shifted from one foot to the other, and Nicolas finally raised his head. For a minute, they stared at each other, neither speaking. It felt like the longest minute of Saskia's life. Then Nicolas carefully laid down his pen.

"How are you feeling?" he asked, his voice even and very controlled.

It made Saskia shiver. "Fine."

Another awkward silence.

"Did you sleep well?"

She nodded stiffly. "Very well."

"Good."

He stared at her, his eyes dark green and impenetrable as virgin jungle. She could almost see the vines and bushes blocking her path.

Saskia cleared her throat. "I, uh . . . I thought that . . . since we both missed lunch . . . I thought you might be hungry. I could make something to eat."

She held her breath, hoping he would recognize the offer as her tentative overture of friendship. Not that "friendship" seemed even remotely to describe their complex relationship, but it was the best Saskia could do while she still nursed both anger at the night before and the soreness from their earlier encounter.

He waited a long time to answer, so long that she wondered what she would do when he rejected her, but his words, when they came, almost reassured her.

"That sounds good. I just need a few minutes to finish up here."

As reassurances went, it wasn't much, but Saskia would take it. At this point, any positive sign made the engagement between them feel less like a chain around her neck.

"Great." She tried a tentative smile, had no idea if it succeeded. "I'll just go get started."

Nicolas watched his mate walk away from him with an impassive expression on his face and the feel of his own claws digging into the flesh of his thigh behind the concealment of his large, heavy desk. The expression was meant to keep her from seeing how quickly and deeply her presence disturbed him, and the self-inflicted pain was to keep him from leaping over the polished furniture and dragging her to the floor for another round of primitive mating sex.

Christ, she got to him like a drug. No man would ever need heroin if he could just spend five minutes in Nicolas's mate's addictive company. Not that he intended to let another man within fifty feet of her anytime this century. Even her father would need to be evaluated on an individual basis. Never in this life had Nicolas felt possessive of a woman before, but when it came to Saskia he felt himself turning into a jealous monster. What the hell was going on?

Tossing aside his pen, Nicolas ran a hand roughly over his face and scrubbed restlessly at his short-cut hair. Less than twenty-four hours since their engagement, and the woman had him tied up in knots so tight, he didn't think anything but a chain saw could hack them loose. This did not fall in line with his plans.

He snorted. Every time he saw her, his plans skittered further and further out of his grasp. He reminded himself of a clumsy puppy chasing an ice cube across a kitchen floor, only he wasn't having nearly so much fun. Instead, he felt himself running in circles, somehow ending up further and further away from his goal of a peaceful, orderly, traditional life with the peaceful, orderly, traditional mate he had selected. About the only traditional thing he'd discovered about Saskia was that she'd somehow managed to come to him a virgin, a fact that had blown his mind a few hours earlier and that still had the power to make his dick hard just thinking about it.

He hadn't been expecting that, he admitted, and the sharp, sudden scent of blood, the abrupt tensing of her muscles, the unexpected resistance he'd encountered inside her, had nearly given him a stroke. He'd known his mate had been raised strictly by parents who still valued the old Tiguri ways; it had been one of the reasons he'd agreed Saskia might suit him. But he'd never expected innocence. What woman these days made it to her late twenties without ever having sex? Tiguri or no, his mate was beautiful and tempting and so stunningly sensual, he wanted to hide her away from all the men who must have noticed it just watching her walk down the street. How was it that none of them had managed to seduce her before this afternoon? Nic knew that if he had met her some other way, just run into her at a party or a club, he would have chased after her like a hound on a rabbit and he wouldn't have stopped until he'd had her under him, until he'd tasted all that hot, wild passion he now knew bubbled beneath her elegant surface.

The memory of it made him grateful to be sitting down. It weakened his knees even as it hardened his dick. He recalled the way she had fought him so fiercely in the beginning and the moment when his last, desperate attempt to subdue her had flipped that internal switch and transformed her anger into lust. He'd been able to taste the change on her tongue, a spill of heavy sweetness washing away the metallic tang of her rage. He'd felt the way her body softened and yielded to him, the way she began to struggle not to get away but to get closer, to feel and experience more of the electricity their two bodies generated.

Nicolas groaned and sank back in his chair. He could almost feel her sweet flesh wrapped around him again, so tight and hot he'd almost lost his mind. Hell, he *had* lost his mind. Otherwise, there was no excuse for the rough way he'd taken her. Even when he'd registered her broken barrier, he'd been unable to pull back, unable to slow down, unable to do anything but rut hard against her. He'd staked a primitive claim on her, marking her with his scent and his teeth. He remembered the feel of her soft flesh under his jaw, recalled the taste of her blood in his mouth, the way she'd uttered the tigress's version of a purr, a deep, rumbling *reowwwr* escaping her with every exhaled breath. He shuddered, the sensory memory literally washing over him like an ocean wave, dragging him under and flipping him ass over elbow until he barely knew which way was up. That was how his mate made him feel, and to Nicolas that was utterly unacceptable.

He shoved away from his desk, unable to sit still any longer. Obviously, the time had come to set down some rules for his new mate. She needed to understand the way he intended for this relationship to work. He had every intention of caring for her, providing for her, and treating her with respect, but if she thought he would allow himself to be led around by his dick, she was sorely mistaken. He would make it clear now that he had taken charge of their union and he would steer it in the direction he deemed most appropriate. If she had a problem with that, she'd better start learning to cope, because Nicolas Preda had a plan, and he intended to see it through.

Five

Nic had himself back under control a few minutes later when he made his way into the kitchen. The sight of his wife—politically incorrect and clichéd as it might be—standing barefoot at the expansive counter contributed nicely to his newly acquired calm.

She looked at ease in the space, her classical features and feminine delicacy somehow striking a pleasing balance with the slick, dark modernity of the utilitarian room. She held a large, sharp knife comfortably in one hand, the other guiding a pile of cleaned and stemmed mushrooms into the path of the flashing blade. She barely hesitated when he approached, offering a tentative smile across the granite peninsula.

"I thought a stir-fry would be quick and easy," she said, and he noticed the small prep bowls of neatly chopped vegetables spread around her.

He tried to look pleased. "The vegetables look . . . pretty."

She laughed. "Don't be scared. The beef is marinating in the fridge."

Nic relaxed in relief. "Ah." He lifted his head,

sniffing at the fragrant air. "Something already smells pretty good."

"I put the rice on first. It should be ready by the time I have everything else cooked up."

"How long?" He didn't really care. As hungry as he was, he just wanted to keep her talking, and the subject of food seemed like a safe territory to explore.

She glanced over her shoulder at a digital timer. "About ten more minutes."

He nodded and slid his hands into his pockets, scanning the room for something else to say. When in doubt, he told himself, offer assistance. "Is there anything I can help with?"

"No, I've got it under control." She kept working for a couple of minutes, then glanced up with a tentative smile. "You could get us something to drink, though. I wouldn't mind if you wanted to keep me company."

Right. Drinks. Nic could handle that. He glanced at the clock on the double oven. Just after four. That meant the sun was over the yardarm, right?

"How about a glass of wine?"

"That sounds nice."

Crossing to the well-stocked cabinet against the wall, he scanned labels thoughtfully before reaching for a heavy green bottle. "Red okay?"

"Mm-hm."

He busied himself with the production of opening the wine, letting it sit on the counter to breathe while he pulled down a pair of balloon goblets. The cozy domesticity of the scene, each of them working at their chore, companionably sharing the family space, eased a bit more of his tension, and Nic found himself almost relaxed and he took a seat on the stool at the other side of her work surface.

"Where did you learn to cook?" he asked, pouring them each a glass of wine.

She thanked him for hers but left it on the counter as she moved on from mushrooms to carrots. "I'd love to say Paris, mostly because I wish I'd gotten the chance to spend that much time there, but oddly enough, it was in Bern."

"Switzerland?"

She gave a small grin. "Yeah, not exactly famous for the cuisine, is it? But it's true. My school was just a couple of miles outside of the city, so I got to go there a lot. I spent so much time in this one little bistro that the owner finally got exasperated at my taking up space and decided to put me to work. She dragged me back into the kitchen so she could show me how to make my own crêpes, and after that she had trouble getting rid of me."

"You enjoyed it?"

"Very much. I like to use my hands, and I like to make things. The fact that cooking means I can make things that also taste good is like a big bonus."

He asked her more questions about her years in Switzerland and about her childhood and found himself actually listening to her answers. Her words painted a picture of a pleasant but somewhat isolated existence. Her parents had constantly reminded her of the importance of her heritage, and while they had encouraged her to pursue the things that interested

her, like cooking and art and—to Nic's surprise—
needlepoint, they had always made her aware of
how her choices and her hobbies would have to fit in
with the life for which they believed her destined.
He wondered whether it was some sort of miracle
that Saskia's interests all seemed to suit her role as
Tiguri mate so well or she had subconsciously only
chosen to pursue things she knew wouldn't upset her
family. The idea made him somehow uncomfortable, and he had to make an effort to push it away.

"University was sort of overwhelming at first,"
she confessed, sliding her prepared ingredients to
the side of the huge cooktop. She set a wok on the
top of a burner and lit it, leaning down to expertly
check the level of the flame. "I mean, I'd spent eight
years at the same school tucked away in the moun-
tains of Switzerland and suddenly I was trying to
navigate my way around Edinburgh without a single
familiar face around me."

Her mouth curved into a wry smile as she pulled
a covered bowl from the refrigerator and set it beside
the vegetables. "I probably spent the first month
looking like a deer in headlights."

She reached for her wine finally, took a sip, and
gave an appreciative little hum. Nic shifted on his
stool and tried to ignore the way that sound altered
the fit of his trousers.

"What made you decide to go to school in Scot-
land?" he asked, mostly to distract himself.

"Because my parents wanted me to go to Oxford."
Her smile widened into a grin and her eyes sparkled

as she added oil to the hot wok and then tossed in garlic and shallots. "That was my rebellious phase. My parents were living mostly at Shadelea at the time, and they liked the idea of me being so close to home. I didn't."

She moved with graceful efficiency, adding carrot, celery, and broccoli flowers to the wok, using a rounded metal spatula to keep it all moving. "Big rebellion, I know. A whopping three hundred and fifty extra miles. But at the time, that seemed like a grand gesture."

"Not every gesture needs to be a grand one. It looks like yours worked out fairly well."

"It did." Beef went into the wok, got tossed around, then coated with a splash of the marinade. "I had a wonderful time in Edinburgh, and I got the taste of independence I wanted. I was still able to visit often enough to keep my parents happy, but I wasn't so close that they felt compelled to check in on me constantly. I enjoyed it." She turned to look at him. "This is just about ready. Should we take it into the dining room?"

The table there sat at least twelve, even without the extending leaves. Nic shook his head. "Let's eat in here. Would you mind?"

"Not at all. Can you grab place mats or something?"

He dug out a pair of colorful mats, folded linen napkins, and chopsticks. Somehow after seeing her expertise with the wok, he doubted the wooden implements would present her with any sort of challenge. Setting two places side by side at the counter, he moved around to pick up her wine as she dished rice, meat, and vegetables onto two plates.

"That smells wonderful," he commented. He watched while she reached across the counter to set out the food, then circled around to take the stool beside his.

Because he was watching her closely, he saw the slight grimace of discomfort when she sat, even with the stool's padded seat. Damn, he'd been too rough with her.

She didn't betray herself with so much as a grumble, just smiled and spread her napkin daintily across her lap. "I hope it tastes good."

It did, so good he gave an involuntary grunt of pleasure the moment the first strip of tender, flavorful beef crossed his tongue. Saskia said nothing, but he saw her smile over the rim of her wineglass.

They ate in silence for several minutes, Nic working his way steadily through a healthy pile of meat, rice, and vegetables while his mate lifted each bite-sized morsel to her lips with the delicate grace of a house cat. The contrast made him feel like an even bigger brute for the way he'd handled her earlier. He wracked his brain for a delicate way to broach the subject but came up empty. Did a polite way even exist to ask a woman if you'd fucked her hard enough for her to require medical attention?

Finishing his meal, Nic pushed his plate away and angled his body toward his mate. She glanced up at him, caution and curiosity mingling in her expression. He decided the only way to get answers was to ask the damned question and worry later about who blushed harder. He felt pretty safe in assuming it would wind up being her, anyway.

"Did I hurt you earlier?" He tried to keep his voice soft and undemanding but surprised himself when it came out low and intimate. As he'd predicted, her cheeks turned the color of ripe apples.

She also nearly choked on a mouthful of rice.

"N-no!" she coughed, reaching for her wineglass and taking an indelicate swig. After clearing her throat again, she shook her head, her eyes watery and unable to look straight at his. "No, you didn't hurt me. I'm fine."

"Are you sure?" he persisted. "You looked like you were feeling a little . . . tender."

Her cheeks burned even brighter, if such a thing was possible. "It's nothing. Really."

He wanted to press further but feared his little mate might actually burst into flames if she felt any more embarrassed, so he dropped the subject and raised his hand to tweak the end of her ponytail. "Good, because I have to admit, I'm glad you're officially mine now."

My *mate*. Officially my *mate*. That's what he had meant to say. Really.

Either way, the confession did nothing to reduce the color in her cheeks, but Saskia nibbled on her lower lip and nodded shyly. "Me, too."

Good, they had agreed on something. Nic let the small triumph buoy him and turned his attention back to his master plan. Now that they were both fed and rested and feeling relaxed, it might be a good time to begin clarifying what he expected of their relationship. Being careful to keep any hint of scolding or accusation from his voice, he ventured, "I think maybe we need to talk about this morning. Don't you?"

To his surprise, his mate nodded eagerly. He'd been expecting her to try to avoid the subject; no woman liked being lectured on what she'd done wrong, even if it was for her own good. Still, Nic wasn't about to look a gift horse in the mouth. Especially not when it had teeth like a tigress.

"I thought about what you said, and I realize that it was partly my fault for not saying anything," he began, trying to begin with a gesture of goodwill. "I regret that, but you still need to know that leaving here without saying a word or even leaving a note behind was very inconsiderate. I was worried when I got back and found you gone. Really worried. Just think how you would have felt if you were in my place. Now can you understand why I'm going to ask you not to leave the apartment again without first telling me where you're going and when you'll be coming back?"

His mate's eyes widened as he spoke until, by the time he fell silent, the vivid blue had been drowned out by the ever-expanding ring of white visible around the edges. She looked like a lemur with those wide, blinking eyes. Her mouth opened, then shut, then opened again, like a fish, and when she slapped her palms lightly against her temples she made the journey through the animal kingdom complete with the startlingly chimplike action.

Nic frowned. He hoped she wasn't having some sort of breakdown brought on by the stress of her guilty conscience.

"Inconsiderate?"

She nearly gargled the word, and he had to wonder if some more rice had gotten lodged somewhere in her throat. That definitely wasn't a natural sort of sound.

"*I* was inconsiderate?!"

And neither was that. He tried not to wince, but the high-pitched shrieking noise felt like an ice pick on his sensitive eardrums.

"I. Cannot. Believe. You!"

Jerking back, Nic stared at his mate, his eyebrows drawing together as he realized she might not be in complete agreement with him after all. In fact, judging by the look on her face, it occurred to him she might be about to take his gesture of goodwill and shove it up a part of his anatomy he really preferred to keep to himself.

"You arrogant, selfish, egotistical, medieval, despotic, swollen-headed, *dumb, idiot penis owner!*" Leaping off her stool, Saskia clenched her hands into fists and drew them up in front of her torso as if she had already half-decided to take a swing at him. "I can't believe that after the way you treated me last night, you have the *nerve,* the unmitigated *indecency,* to talk about what *I* did wrong! You've got to be *kidding* me!"

She opened her mouth for another attack, changed her mind, spun on her heel, and left, stalking out of the kitchen and down the rear hall toward the

bedroom, her footsteps surprisingly loud given her
lack of even the most basic footwear. His acute Tiguri hearing allowed him to detect her muttered
words, uttered under her breath all the way to the
other side of the apartment; and he would have had
to be deaf not to hear the echoing slam of the bedroom door when she reached her destination.

Hm. He glanced around the kitchen, grabbed
both nearly empty glasses of wine, downed the contents of each, then reached for the rest of the bottle.
That certainly hadn't gone according to plan.

Saskia started the night on the sofa in the sitting area
of the master bedroom, absolutely unwilling to share
the bed of so clueless, heartless, and hopeless an excuse for masculinity as her erstwhile mate. It had
taken her hours to calm down enough to settle into
the plump cushions, but considering her mate stayed
away until almost the wee hours of the morning, she
was well asleep by the time he entered the room and
spied her lying on her makeshift bed for the night.
His quiet curses woke her, along with the feeling of
his hands lifting her and carrying her gently to the
large bed where they had tangled together just hours
before. She thought about admitting her wakefulness, slapping his hands away, and stalking back to
the sofa, but he made no attempt to touch her after he
settled her on the mattress, just pulled the covers up
over her still-clad form, climbed in beside her, and
settled down to sleep.

Damn his considerate hide.

By the next morning—when she woke for the third

time to a cold and empty bed—she'd had plenty of time to calm down, and also enough time to reach some tough conclusions. Her mate was not going to spontaneously reach an understanding about what he had done to make her angry, let alone apologize of his own volition. It just wasn't in the cards. She needed to accept that and move on. What she was not prepared to do was allow their small war to continue. He had made her angry; she had made him angry. They each needed to accept the past failings of the other and go forward from there. Since Saskia was the woman in the relationship, and therefore the one with the larger capacity for both logical thought and forgiveness, it would be up to her to broker the peace deal.

But if she was going to do that, first she needed coffee.

This time, she managed to get out of bed without so much as a twinge of discomfort. One of the blessings of a shifter metabolism—ultraquick healing—apparently extended to, ah, more intimate injuries as well. She felt as good as new, if a little grungy from sleeping in her clothes.

A quick shower put everything to rights, and Saskia found herself minutes later standing nude in her cavernous closet wondering just what a woman with a plan wore to talk some serious sense into a pigheaded male. Silk? Cotton? Denim?

Plate armor?

She settled on one of her favorite stay-at-home outfits, comfortable enough to lounge around in but attractive enough to give her the boost of confidence she felt pretty sure she would need. The dark jeans had just enough stretch to combine comfort with curve-hugging visual appeal, and the vivid blue of the V-neck pullover accentuated the color of her eyes while simultaneously drawing attention to the shadow of her cleavage. A shadow she ensured looked its best with the strategic application of a push-up bra in lace-covered satin.

This time, she coached herself silently as she padded down the hall to her fiancé's office—what she was already coming to think of as his lair—she wouldn't wait for an apology or a lecture. She would state her grievances straight out, outline the compromise she had in mind to guide each of them in their future behavior, and reach an amicable settlement with a minimum of fuss.

Or bloodshed.

Unlike the previous afternoon, Saskia found the door to the office firmly shut, but the thin strip of illumination shining just above the floor told her she would find her mate inside. She could hear the low rumble of his voice through the thick wood and guessed he must be on the phone. All the better; she could slip in and make herself comfortable while he finished the call. Then she would be able to begin the conversation from a position of power.

She knocked lightly, but she already had one hand on the knob, and she twisted without waiting for a reply, swinging the door open and stepping inside before her fiancé could invite or rebuff her. He glanced toward her, a frown marring his features. Apparently, Nicolas didn't like to be interrupted.

She had an idea why when she saw that he hadn't been alone.

Rather than speaking on the phone, Nicolas had been carrying on a conversation with a tall, lean figure currently sprawled in one of the armchairs facing the large mahogany desk.

"Excuse the interruption," her mate grumbled, fixing her with an impatient scowl. "Saskia, is there a problem?"

"Only that I didn't realize you were entertaining, Nicolas," she answered smoothly, refusing to be intimidated, especially not in front of a guest. "I had no idea you had made an appointment for this early in the morning. It's barely past seven." She stepped toward the desk and offered her hand to the man she suspected her fiancé hadn't wanted her to meet. "I'm so sorry I wasn't there to greet you. I'm Saskia Arcos. Can I get you anything? Coffee?"

The visitor had turned at her entrance and now rose to take her hand, demonstrating the good manners Nicolas hadn't bothered with.

"No, thanks, I'm fine," he said, his mouth quirking in a charming smile. "It's a pleasure to meet you, Ms. Arcos. I'm McIntyre Callahan, but please, call me Mac."

"Mac," she repeated, smiling warmly. The touch of his hand confirmed what her nose had already told her. Callahan wasn't human. Not entirely. "And you should call me Saskia. I apologize for the interruption, but as I said, Nicolas didn't warn me he'd be entertaining this early."

"I'm not entertaining," her mate snapped, sounding as if he'd like to shove her out the door and turn the key in the lock. She hoped he'd think twice about that while there was a witness present. "This is a business meeting."

"Oh? What sort of business are you in, Mac?"

She heard Nicolas growl low in his throat, but she ignored him. He needed to learn that being old fashioned didn't make her a doormat.

"I'm a private investigator," Mac answered, clearly aware of the fierce undercurrents flowing between his hosts and just as clearly amused by it.

Saskia felt her eyebrows lift and took another, closer, look at her husband's visitor. She thought the man looked more like a carpenter or an artist than a PI. He had blond hair, worn long and pulled back into a queue at the back of his neck, and blue-gray eyes that sparkled with humor. At six feet and change, he was a tall man, though not as tall as Nicolas, and while his lean build spoke more of a runner than a weight lifter, Saskia didn't doubt he was stronger than he looked. He wore a pair of battered jeans, scuffed boots, and a long-sleeved thermal, topped by a button-down shirt he wore both unbuttoned and untucked. Instead of looking sloppy, it looked comfortable and casual, as if he was a man who dressed not to impress but to take care of business.

Since she didn't much believe in coincidence, Saskia was willing to bet she knew just what sort of business Nicolas had called him to deal with.

Ignoring her mate, she offered Mac a look of wide-eyed innocence. "An investigator? Oh, then you must be here to look into the accusations the Council has made against my fiancé. Have you discovered anything yet?"

"Saskia!" Nicolas snapped, slapping his hands down on the desk and shoving to his feet. "This is not your concern."

Saskia dug in her heels, clenched her teeth, and did her best to appear both baffled and guileless. "But of course it is," she protested, counting on the chance that her fiancé wouldn't want to make a scene in front of a man who was essentially an employee. "Anything that affects my mate affects me. Tell me, Mac, have you been able to find any information about who might really have attacked Mr. De Santos?"

She heard Nicolas swear, but her stomach settled a bit when she saw him sink back into his seat behind the desk and scowl at her.

"This is actually only our first meeting." Mac kept his tone professional, but she could see that he understood she was using him to manipulate her mate. Thankfully, it seemed to amuse more than offend him. "I haven't yet started my investigation. Your fiancé was just filling me in on the meeting he had yesterday with the Council."

"Oh, I'm sorry. Please go on, Nicolas. I promise not to interrupt again." With that, she planted herself firmly in the seat opposite Mac's, tucking her crossed fingers under her thighs and hoping frantically that Nicolas wouldn't give in to his temper and throw her bodily out of the room. Judging by his expression, he thought about it, long and hard.

Finally, though, he clenched his jaw and turned back to Mac. "As I was saying, after I got the call from my father letting me know about the attack and that the Council wanted to see us immediately, he drove over to pick me up and we met with the Council in their chambers at the Vircolac club."

Mac nodded, picking up a pen and small notebook Saskia had overlooked earlier. "Was the full Council is session?"

"No. From what I understand, it was only the Inner Council."

"And was anyone else called before them? Other than you and your father."

"Just Gregor Arcos. Saskia's father." Nicolas glanced toward her, his expression tight but unreadable. She fought to keep her own from betraying any emotion. "He'd brought his wife along, but her presence wasn't a requirement."

"Why just you three?"

"We're the only three Tiguri males currently living in the city."

Mac looked up from his notes. "So, they were absolutely convinced that a Tiguri was behind the attack on Rafe?"

Nicolas nodded, and his eyes narrowed. "Are you acquainted with the head of the Council?"

Saskia saw the way the investigator's expression hardened and the subtle tension that invaded his frame.

"I know him," Mac admitted. "My wife knows him better. She's close with the wives of his close friends. I can assure you, though, that I have no conflict of interest in finding out who's responsible for the attack. The Fae have never been interested in getting involved in the Other politics of this city, and while I might be only half Fae, that's the half I agree with in this case." He paused and cast the Tiguri a level look. "Are you okay with that?"

Saskia watched her fiancé evaluate the other man's statement and nod briefly. "Fine."

She blew out a breath she hadn't realized she'd been holding. She had a feeling that Mac was going to be the key to keeping abreast of this business, since her fiancé clearly refused to talk to her about it directly. So far, she liked the investigator, though. And she was glad to learn her instincts had been right. Half Fae made him a changeling, definitely more than human.

"So the Council came right out and said they believe the culprit was Tiguri?" Mac asked again.

Nicolas shrugged. "Some of them. De Santos himself said he couldn't be positive. He knew it was a shifter, and he knew it was Feline, but beyond that he couldn't swear to it. Most of them seemed to make the assumption based on how he described the size of the thing."

"Big?"

"According to him."

"I suppose it would have to be to take down De Santos." The changeling grinned. "At least, according to him, it would."

Nicolas snorted, the sound almost passing for

amusement. Maybe he was beginning to lighten up
and forgive her for forcing him to include her in his
business.

"Okay." Mac flipped to a fresh page in his notebook and settled back down to work. "Now tell me
everything De Santos reported. As much as you can
remember."

Saskia curled her feet up under her as she listened
to her mate describe the meeting before the Council,
complete with Rafe De Santos's testimony. It sounded
like a nightmare, which on the one hand made Saskia
almost glad she hadn't been invited to attend but on
the other made her even more furious that she hadn't
been allowed to stand beside her mate and support
him through the indignity of the inquisition he'd en-
dured. It made her want to hug him and smack him,
probably in that order.

She struggled to remain silent while he described
the insulting questions of the Council members,
most of whom had clearly decided on the identity of
the guilty party well before the summons that had
brought the Tiguri before them. According to Nicolas, it had actually been De Santos who had prevented
the others from issuing a formal accusation, backed,
surprisingly enough, by the Alpha of the Silverback
Clan. Though Lupines were usually the first to jump
on the bandwagon to run the Tiguri out of town on a
rail, Graham Winters had proven surprisingly level-
headed. From what Nicolas had seen, Winters seemed
to be fairly close with De Santos, which might have
influenced his decision. Either way, the Council had
reluctantly declined to issue a formal charge, but they

had made it clear that they were going to keep a very close eye on Nicolas.

"Just you? Not your father or Arcos?"

Mac's question drew a sneer.

"Just me. After all, Saskia's father and mine are both old men," Nicolas pointed out. "How could one of them possibly take down the head of the Council, a Felix in his prime?"

"Ah. Understood." Mac glanced over his notes and nodded. "Well, it's not a lot to go on, but I've started cases with less. Rafe might be able to fill in some holes, too, when I talk to him."

Saskia frowned. "You're going to interview De Santos? Do you think that's wise? Won't that tip him off to the fact that Nicolas is trying to find the real attacker?"

"I don't see that being a problem," the investigator said. "First, it will make it clear that your fiancé is prepared to back up his innocence. A guilty man doesn't hire someone to do digging in his own backyard. Rafe knows I'm honest, so he'll know that by hiring me, Nic is doing more than making an empty show of trying to clear himself. Second, Rafe's already met Nic. Believe me when I tell you, there isn't a man or beast alive who could look at that man and not just assume that he'd move hell and high water to defend his reputation. That means none of this will come as a surprise, and it may even make the Council curious enough to look past their prejudices to find out who really made a try for their leader."

She supposed that made sense. Uncurling her legs, she rose from her chair and held her hand out to the investigator. "In that case, I'll let you get to work, Mac, and wish you luck. I want you to find out who was really behind the attack on the head of the Council, so that my mate can clear his name and we can get on with our lives together."

Mac shook her hand. "I'll do my best."

"Then I'm sure this will all be cleared up in no time." She smiled and turned to leave. "It was lovely meeting you, Mac. I hope you'll stop by again, under more pleasant circumstances."

Her graceful exit stopped halfway to the door when her fiancé spoke her name, his tone cool and hard as steel. "Saskia."

She froze. Schooling her features into a mask of bland inquiry, she glanced at him over her shoulder. "Yes, Nicolas?"

"I'm going to be another minute with Mac, and then I have a couple of phone calls to make," he said. "I trust you don't have any plans to go out this morning?"

Translation: You'd better not set foot outside this apartment, or I'll blister your hide so badly, you won't sit straight for a week.

"Not at all," she said calmly. "I thought I'd take the opportunity provided by a quiet morning and get a start on the thank-you notes for our party."

"Then I'll see you later."

"Of course, Nicolas."

When she closed the door behind her, she nearly sagged against it with relief. That hadn't gone exactly as she had planned, but it had worked out even better. She'd learned everything she wanted to know about the issue with the Council, and she'd been able to hide behind Mac Callahan while she pried loose the information. Not bad for an hour's work. In fact, Saskia realized she'd managed to work up quite an appetite.

Smiling in satisfaction, she straightened and headed for the kitchen with a definite bounce in her step. Maybe this relationship would work out after all.

Her optimism lasted until shortly before noon, which was when her fiancé finally cornered her in the small spare bedroom she had decided to commandeer for her own purposes. It didn't have quite the right light for a studio, but it had a pretty, streamlined desk perfect for writing thank-you notes, and she found herself quite comfortable there as she began making her way down her list of the party guests who required notes of thanks for their gifts or their attendance. This was the sort of task Saskia could perform with her eyes closed, so she allowed her mind to drift as she inscribed, folded, stuffed, and sealed.

She would need to explore the apartment a little more thoroughly soon if she wanted to find a space that might suit her as a real work space. Or maybe she should call it a pleasure space. Her parents always referred to her drawing as her "little hobby." It had taken her a while to overcome the instinctive surge of anger the dismissal aroused. She knew they had their own ideas about her future, about what she should focus her attentions on—namely, her mate— but Saskia had realized while still a teenager that she would need more than that to make her happy, so she had quietly forged her way ahead, taking art classes and perfecting her techniques and keeping quiet about the goals her family didn't care to know about.

By the time she finished university, she had begun to earn commissions as an illustrator, her drawings adorning the pages of books from children's stories to academic texts. She never took projects so large or so numerous that she had to work the equivalent of a full-time job, but the work fulfilled her, brought her joy and satisfaction, and made her feel as if she were leaving her own mark on the world, separate from her family and her species.

Saskia had left the door open while she worked, so she knew when he approached, not because she heard him—he moved as silently as a tiger, after all—but because she smelled him, the spicy musk of his scent already indelibly printed on her senses.

He stepped into the room and paused to watch her. She saw him in her peripheral vision, but her pen never paused in her task. This time, he could make the first move.

Finally, he moved closer, prowling across the carpet toward her with the focus of a predator. She couldn't quite get a read on his mood; they still hadn't spent enough time together for that. His tone of voice didn't help, either. The man could make a fortune as a professional poker player.

"Saskia."

Deliberately, she finished the note she was work-

ing on, signing it on both their behalves before fold-
ing it carefully and slipping it into the envelope she
had already addressed. Setting it aside calmly, she
turned in her chair and raised her chin to meet his
gaze. "Nicolas. Is there a problem?"

If he noticed her using his own words against
him, he didn't acknowledge it. "I think there is. Actually, I think there might be several."

"That sounds serious. Maybe you'd better sit
down." She waved him to an armchair in the corner
near the desk, then rose to angle her own chair to
face it. Resuming her seat, she crossed her ankles,
folded her hands neatly in her lap, and looked directly into his eyes. "Please, tell me what's bothering
you."

Her mate stared at her for a long moment and
then did something that surprised her. He laughed.

"I'm sorry, did I say something to amuse you?"

"Sass, in the last twenty-four hours you've infuri-
ated me, taunted me, aroused me, defied me, and in-
trigued me, but I can't honestly say you've done
anything as innocuous as amuse me." Nicolas lounged
in the comfortable chair, his arms extended to curl
along the sides, the picture of the relaxed, powerful
male; but Saskia knew that if he'd had a tail, it would
be twitching.

"Don't call me that," she said, ignoring his pro-
vocative words. If he wanted a reaction from her, he
needed to get to the point.

"Don't call you what? Sass?" His mouth curved
into a smile that spoke of a bitter kind of humor. "I

don't see why not. As far as I can tell, it suits you. Rather perfectly. You've spent most of our time together sassing me, wouldn't you say?"

"No," she snapped, her fingers curling tightly together. "I wouldn't. I think it would be quite inaccurate to class any of my behavior as 'sassy.' First of all because that's a ridiculous word that makes me sound like a misbehaving five-year-old, and second because I don't consider it 'sass' to ask my mate reasonable questions about his whereabouts, intentions, or welfare, nor to defend myself against his unreasonable attempts both to control my every move and to exclude me from areas that clearly concern me."

Nicolas's eyes narrowed and his fingers began to drum lightly against the arm of his chair. "Just which of those erroneous statements would you like me to address first, Sass?"

"My name is Saskia, and not one of my statements was anything but accurate, not to mention admirably restrained."

"I beg to differ."

Saskia snorted at the idea of this arrogant beast begging for anything. Ever.

"To begin with, I'm having trouble remembering the point at which I ever gave you the right to demand answers about where I go or what I intend to do," he continued, his eyes glinting. "Perhaps you'd care to enlighten me?"

"I'd love to. I think it was around the same time you agreed to make a commitment to me as my mate and the sire of my cubs. You recall that, don't you? It was about twelve hours before you decided it was acceptable to treat me like a child breaking curfew in what I'd like to point out constitutes a rather stunning display of hypocrisy."

He snarled his displeasure, green fire sparking in his eyes, but Saskia refused to back down. She would not be intimidated.

"Maybe that's the problem here," he rumbled, rising from the chair and stalking toward her with predatory menace. "Maybe this all boils down to your lack of understanding over what our mating actually means. So let me spell it out for you."

He leaned down and braced his hands on the arms of her chair, trapping her in place. The position let him lean in close so his face loomed only inches from hers, full of arrogance and irritation. She wanted to back away, but not only did he have her cornered, but also she refused to give him the satisfaction, so she just pressed her lips together and glared straight into his annoying face.

"I might be a man of my times," he said, his voice low and gravelly and full of dangerous power, "but I'm Tiguri first. I have no tolerance for modern human notions of 'marriage.' This is not a relationship of equals. I am *ther*. My word is law. As my mate, your role is to obey my commands, support my decisions, and bear my cubs. *I* decide what areas do or do not concern you, just as I decide what you need or do not need to know. If I think you need to know where I'm going, rest assured I will share that information. If I don't share it, it's because you do not need to concern yourself.

"On the other hand." He leaned in closer, his

breath stirring against her cheek and lips, making her clench her jaw to keep from the instinctive urge to touch him that their completed mating had caused. "Everything you do and everywhere you go is of concern to me. As my mate, your actions reflect on me, but more than that, your safety and welfare are now my responsibility, and I can't protect you properly if you disobey my commands and disappear. Which means that from now on, you will never leave this apartment unless I know where you're going, who you'll be seeing, and when you'll be back. Am I making myself clear?"

He waited for an answer. Did he really want to hear what she thought of all of that?

"Saskia," he repeated, his voice low and menacing, "did I make myself clear?"

"Perfectly," she spat out, glaring at him. She shook with anger so intense she wasn't sure she could manage anything more coherent than the single word.

"Good; then we shouldn't need to talk about this again." He pushed himself away from her and strolled casually toward the door. "I have one or two loose ends to tie up before I'll be ready for lunch. Give me half an hour before we eat."

Half an hour? That would give her plenty of time to prep the poison. Did this arrogant bastard actually think she intended to cook for him like an obedient little mate after what he had just said to her? Could be possibly be *that* misguided?

Seizing her temper with both hands, she fought for enough self-control to speak. There was one very important message she needed to get across to her mate before he disappeared back into his office, thinking he had solved all of their relationship issues with one ignorant decree.

"Nicolas," she ground out, stopping him just as he stepped across the threshold.

He paused and turned his head back to her, one eyebrow arching in supercilious response. "Yes, Saskia?"

She kept her tone very even and polite, an effort that had her trembling with the strain. "I'd just like you to know, Nicolas, that as far as I'm concerned, you can take your relationship rules and choke on them. I agreed to be your mate, not your Stepford wife broodmare. If that's what you're looking for, then as far as I'm concerned, this engagement is null and void."

He turned on her, fury rising on every line of his face. "That's not the way this works, Saskia," he bit out. "The engagement is sealed. We *are* mates. This isn't like a human relationship where you just tell me you've changed your mind, you give back the ring, and we each go our own merry way. We were bound together the minute you took me into your body. There is no going back."

"Trust me, I know what having sex with you means," she hissed, her own fury rising. After all, she was the one who would suffer as a consequence of their mating, not him. "Do you think I'm an idiot? I'm fully aware of the way my own body works. When you mated me, you induced my ovulation. Sometime in the next two or three days, I'll be as fertile as a bloody earth goddess and as horny as a rabid mink.

But you know what? I'll get through it, because I will kill you before I will let myself be impregnated by and permanently bound to a mate who has so little respect for me, he can't even treat me like a person in my own right."

The force of her words finally gave her the strength to move, and she rose to her feet as she spoke until she stood before him, spine straight, shoulders back, chin up, her whole body vibrating with pride and defiance. She waited for the explosion, the ultimatum, the lecture. Every muscle tensed to spit and claw and do whatever it took to convince her mate of her sincerity. She had drawn her line in the sand, and now she would hold back the tide, if that was what it took.

"I have never treated you as less than a person."

"You've treated me as less than you. Isn't that enough?"

She expected the explosion; what she got was ossification at lightning speed.

In the space between one heartbeat and the next, the man in front of her visibly turned to stone. His jaw set, his body hardened, and his expression solidified into something about as warm and welcoming as a slab of rough-hewn marble. When he spoke, she expected something to crack, like the earth's crust above a fault line.

"We'll see," he said tightly, and exited.

Saskia watched the door long after it had closed behind her mate, and blew out a deep breath. The strength went out of her in a rush of cascading adrenaline, leaving her groping for support as she lowered herself back into her chair.

"Okay," she breathed. "That went well."

Then she lowered her head between her knees and stared blankly at the floor.

What the hell had she done?

Six

What in God's name had he done?

Nic left the apartment in self-defense, like the proverbial rat, only what he'd fled wasn't a ship; it was his engagement, and it wasn't sinking. It had just gone up in flames.

"Holy hell."

Just what had he thought he was doing, issuing his mate those sorts of ultimatums? Was he out of his mind?

Completely, he acknowledged, pacing down the sidewalk with long, angry strides. He had no idea where he was going at the moment; he just needed to get away from the mess he'd created of his own life. He knew he'd just screwed up on an epic scale, and he even had a pretty good idea about why—it was all Sass's fault.

The minute he got within ten feet of his fiancée, he lost his ever-loving mind. He didn't know how it happened; he just knew that one minute he was a sane, logical, amiable fellow and then his mate appeared and in an instant he became a jealous, irrational, possessive, controlling Neanderthal nightmare not sufficiently evolved to beat his own chest or pick his own ass. All he could do was bellow at the cause of his insanity, as if raising the volume on his inane ranting would make it sound any less ridiculous. How had this happened?

Just at the moment, he would have been perfectly content to blame the whole thing on Rafael De Santos, the absolute bane of his existence. Nicolas had never had a nemesis before, but the head of the Council had just won the title in a single round of unanimous voting.

It had started at the engagement party.

Nicolas had been on guard before that, of course. He'd known before Preda Industries ever made the decision to relocate its headquarters to New York—a purely practical decision based on the city's position as de facto center of the business universe—that the Council of Others would not likely roll out the welcome mat for an influx of Tiguri. He had planned to remain civil, though, to prove to the Council and its head through his actions that he had no interest in and no intention of wresting control of the paranormal community from the hands of those currently in charge. Nic had enough on his hands, between running the company and starting a new phase of his life, complete with a mate and the new family they would start together. Why would he want to get mixed up in politics? As far as he was concerned, they were a thankless endeavor. He'd much rather concentrate on making money and cubs. He knew he was good at one and had no doubt he would thoroughly enjoy the other.

At the party, though, De Santos had set Nic's

downfall in motion by the simple and seemingly innocent fact of his conversation with Saskia. While Nic had been occupied by another guest, the slick werejaguar had moved in and engaged his mate in a seemingly idle conversation, all about how pleasant the party had been and how pleased she and Nic were that De Santos could attend. Nic had heard the words, but more important, he'd heard the tone within them and his attention had immediately snapped from an important business acquaintance to the woman at his side and the way the eyes of Rafael De Santos had raked over every inch of her lovely form.

The fierce rush of jealousy had startled Nic. He'd wondered at himself, not previously having experienced such an intense feeling of possessiveness over any woman, and although Saskia had agreed to become his mate, they had yet to form any real bond between them. That was supposed to come later that night, after they were alone. And naked. He had tried to tell himself not to act like an idiot, that he had nothing to worry about, but then the Felix had smiled at her, and Nic had seen the predatory heat behind the charming gesture, and he had known he had every reason for his jealousy. De Santos had all but devoured Saskia with those damned yellow eyes of his, and Nic had seen the moment when she became aware of it. He'd drawn her closer and attempted to diffuse the situation by deflecting the other man's attention to himself, but he suspected now the plan had backfired.

Very few people had paid attention to De Santos

flirting with Saskia. She was a guest of honor, after all, and the head of the Council had a reputation as a notorious Romeo. People almost expected a little bit of charged banter; but when Nic stepped in, the dynamic changed, all of a sudden becoming a lot more interesting for the nonhuman guests still present. More than one person had taken note of the ruthlessly restrained confrontation between the two men, neither Nic's jealousy nor De Santos's appreciation of Saskia's charms going unnoticed. Nic more than suspected that the exchange had only fed the fire of suspicion against him once word got around of the attack on the head of the Council. Who had a stronger motive for attempted murder than a jealous mate publically challenged?

Nic supposed he should be grateful that no one thought to suggest that he'd been anywhere other than at his apartment during the time of the attack. Everyone knew that to say a newly engaged Tiguri would be out roaming the streets looking for revenge when he had a new mate waiting for him at home, ready and willing to seal their relationship in the most intimate manner possible, would do nothing other than make the one suggesting such a thing look like a fool. Especially when the mate in question looked like Nic's Saskia.

And there Nic's mind brought him full circle back to his current dilemma. What was he going to do about Sass?

He contemplated turning right around, crawling back into the apartment, and begging her forgiveness, but he saw one major flaw in that plan. Other than the possibility that she would take one look at him and slam the door on any and every protuberant part of his anatomy. Right now he might be thinking rationally, but all he had to do was get in the same room with Sass and he'd bet his entire business that his capacity for logical thought would once again fly right out the window. In other words, while he might go in intending to apologize, he had a sick, over-whelming feeling that once he caught sight of her he would once again transform into an ignorant jackass and only manage to further alienate the one woman he most wanted to keep happy.

How was that for a kick in the balls?

Nic grumbled to himself as he turned yet another corner and found himself in a familiar neighbor-hood. He recognized it instantly, even though he had last approached it in the wee hours of the morning. There, on the next block of the upscale, tree-shaded street, lay the classical stone edifice of the Vircolac club.

His lip curled in a snarl. From what he had heard, every other Other in New York City considered the private club to be a home away from home. Every respectable Other, that is. Membership only required that a being prove to be Other or to be mated to one. Inside the walls, vampires and shifters, changelings and magic users all congregated and enjoyed what was rumored to be truly outstanding service, includ-ing a highly regarded restaurant, private and public meeting spaces, select guest accommodations, and one of the finest bars in the city. In the basements, however, a whole other level of socialization took place—all run by the Council of Others.

The Council chambers took up at least half of the sprawling building's underground space. Nic had gotten an impression of the size of them during his rather unwilling visit the other night. Decorated more like a medieval dungeon than a state building, the room had possessed an atmosphere that suggested one would be well served to remember that civilization was merely a construct of human history and not something to which the Council of Others felt itself bound. Needless to say, Nic had not enjoyed his visit.

The memory sparked a surge of resentment. At any other time and in any other city, a private club for Others would be falling all over itself to open its doors to Nicolas Preda, member of a noble supernatural race, *ther* of his streak, business owner. If the owners were looking for bloodlines, power, and conspicuous wealth, Nic possessed all those in abundance. There was no logical reason why he shouldn't be welcomed into such a club, but the fact remained that he felt barred from the place as surely as if the owners had erected a fence around the building, something with heavy iron bars and about a hundred and twenty volts.

He felt about that level of shock when he saw the doors to the club open and a familiar figure step out into the afternoon sunshine. Nic blinked, but the sight didn't change. He'd crossed half the distance between them on pure instinct before he even realized he was moving.

"What's going on? What happened?" he demanded.

Stefan Preda fixed his son with an icy stare and jerked his head slightly toward the club. "The Council 'politely requested' that I return this morning to answer a few more questions," he sneered. "They detained me for almost three hours demanding explanations for the most errant nonsense I have ever been forced to endure hearing. I had to cancel two very important meetings, and now I'm about to be late for a third because my driver couldn't obey a simple instruction to *wait. Here.*"

"Why wasn't I informed of this?"

"There was no time." Stefan glanced at his watch, then down the street where a sleek black town car had just turned the corner several blocks away. "One of their little functionaries came to my home to escort me this time. I wasn't even permitted to call my secretary. I had to have Robert call about rearranging my schedule after he dropped me off."

Oh, the indignity. Nic heard the subtext; he just didn't care at the moment. "Then she should have called me."

"Didn't she? Then how did you know I would be here?"

He returned his father's frown. "I didn't," he admitted. "It was purely a coincidence that I happened to be walking by when I saw you come out of the building."

"You were out walking?" Stefan's voice rang with incredulity.

"I needed some air."

"Don't be ridiculous. You *need* to be making use of the time you cleared in your schedule for your new mate and ensuring that she becomes pregnant as quickly as possible." The town car pulled up to the curb and Robert climbed out to open the door for his employer. "You agreed to this arrangement, Nicolas, and now you need to follow through on your commitment. You have a responsibility to the future of our streak."

As if he didn't realize that, he thought, biting back a stinging retort. Sometimes he wondered if his father had paid any attention to the man Nic had become, except, of course, when he needed Nic to do something, like take over the company so he could retire or take the daughter of his old rival as a mate to further the purity of Stefan's bloodlines.

"I'm more than aware of my responsibilities, sir," he said, keeping his voice even with effort. "I've yet to fail at any of them."

"Good."

Stefan slid into the backseat of the car, clearly finished with the discussion, but there were a few things Nic still wanted to know.

"What exactly did the Council have to say to you that they neglected to say on Friday night?" he asked, holding up a hand to delay Robert from closing the car door and driving away.

Stefan snorted impatiently. "Just as before, they *said* very little. They asked intrusive questions about our people, questioned our motives for moving to the city, and generally made themselves look ridiculous. It was a waste of time, and mine is still of some value."

"That sounds just like the other night. They didn't mention anything new? Any new theories about who might be behind the attack?"

"Nicolas, who they think is behind the attack was never in doubt. They are convinced it was one of us, either you, or me, or Gregor. I can't imagine there's anything that could change their minds outside of the real culprit stepping forward and confessing. On the other hand, they have no proof to back up their suppositions, obviously. We all know we're innocent. Eventually, the Council will realize that there's no proof to be had, they'll throw up their ineffectual hands, and they'll move on. You should put them out of your mind and concentrate on your new mate."

"You might be able to ignore it when someone accuses you of an attack on a head of state, Father, but I'm not quite so laissez-faire about the matter." He leaned down into the car, his face set in grim lines. "I resent the hell out of the fact that the Council is trying to blame me for a crime I didn't commit. I intend to prove that I wasn't behind it, and then I intend to tell them exactly how little I care about the political power they think they wield. When I'm done, there will be no doubt in the mind of anyone on the Council that I wouldn't take one of their jobs if they paid me for it."

"Oh, relax, Nicolas. You sound ridiculous," Stefan dismissed him. "You invest too much importance in the whole matter. As I said, the whole thing will blow over soon enough, and if it doesn't . . . well, since none of us are guilty, the only alternative left to the Council will be to turn on themselves and tear each other to pieces. It would be no great loss, as far as I can tell. I've seen better organization at some of the properties we've pulled out of bankruptcy."

Nicolas stepped back and shook his head. Clearly, his father really didn't care about the accusations, beyond the annoyance he felt at having his schedule disrupted. Maybe that was what came of sixty years of playing the arrogant despot. Was that what Nic had to look forward to in another thirty? He grimaced.

"Now, go home, and put this entire matter out of your mind." When Robert shut the car door and walked around to climb back behind the wheel, Stefan lowered the window halfway and leaned forward to get in one last jab. "I expect to hear I'm to be a grandfather within the next two weeks, Nicolas. Get to work."

Nic watched the sedan disappear down the street and shoved his hands into his pockets. He'd love nothing better than to work on making those grandbabies his father seemed to want so badly, but in order to do that Nic would have to get close enough to touch his mate. Without her cutting off any important parts of his anatomy. Judging by the mood she'd been in when he'd left her, he thought his chances of that happening were what might politely be called slim-to-none.

He turned away from the Vircolac club and continued his way down the block, walking in the same direction he'd taken before he'd spotted his father.

Until Nic figured out the way to make amends with his furious mate, he thought it might just be safer to keep walking. With any luck, he'd formulate a strategy before he reached Delaware.

"Oh, no, he didn't."

"He did. I can't believe I'm saying this, but he so did."

Saskia and her guest sat curled up on opposite ends of the sofa in the cozy den of her new apartment, sipping cups of coffee and marveling over the idiocy and unmitigated gall of her darling mate. It had taken her a good thirty minutes and half a plate of the cookies she'd dug out of the cavernous pantry to bring Corinne up to date on the saga of her war with Nicolas, but she'd finally gotten through the fight they'd had in the spare room. Now Corinne stared at her with eyes so wide she looked like a cartoon character.

"Oh. My. Lord." The reporter shook her head slowly. "I mean, I got he was dumb from when we talked yesterday, but I had no idea he was *this* dumb. How did you keep from just killing him?"

"I think it had a lot to do with the fact that I was unarmed at the time. And since there's no fireplace in that guest room, there weren't any useful weapons near to hand."

"No weapons? Excuse me, but aren't I talking to the girl who can turn into a five-hundred-pound Siberian tiger anytime she darn well feels like it? Sweetie, you *are* a weapon."

Saskia made a face. "Maybe, but you're forgetting

that if I do that, Nicolas can turn himself into a *seven*-hundred-pound Siberian tiger. It's not like I have some sort of unfair advantage. If anything, it's the other way around."

"Oh, right. There go my fantasies about what it would be like to have the upper hand over a man once in a while."

"If you're looking for stories on that subject, don't come crying to me."

Corinne reached forward to pat her hand. "Don't look so gloomy, sweetie. You're not alone in the man trouble arena, you know. Far from it. Every woman I know, including the stupid-happy ones—hell, especially the stupid-happy ones—had to whack some sense into her man before he was any use at all."

"Think they could give me some pointers? Because I just told you about the last time I tried that. We gave each other a set of ridiculous ultimatums, remember?"

"Yeah, that strategy probably wasn't destined for success, but that doesn't mean you can give up. I mean, not unless you've decided he's not worth it. . . ." Corinne trailed off and looked at Saskia curiously.

"I don't know," Saskia said, feeling hope and doubt and anger and confusion all bounding around inside her like puppies on speed. "I thought he was worth it. I mean, I've always thought he'd be worth it, but—"

"Uhhhh-ohhhhh."

"Uh-oh?" Saskia repeated. "What-oh?"

"You've been holding out on me," the reporter accused, her lips curving into a teasing smile. "Nicolas Preda isn't just your fiancé; he's your girl crush!"

Saskia felt her cheeks burst into flame, which made her immediate denial lack a certain something.

Like credibility.

"Girl crush?" She tried to make the words sound as implausible and distasteful as fat-free chocolate. "I don't even know what that is."

"Sure you do. Everyone's got a girl crush, the boy you just fell madly and passionately in love with somewhere before the age of twelve. Mine was Jimmy Devellano. He lived next door to my aunt Renata. I was ten; he was fourteen. In his mind, I didn't exist, but in mine, we were going to get married, move to Long Island, and have, like, five kids. And die of old age before thirty-five, of course. Most girl crushes never go beyond writing your first name with his last name over and over and over in your notebook while you're supposed to be working on math problems, but some of us get luckier than that."

Saskia shoved aside a mental flash of her childhood diary, the pink leather and little gold lock concealing line after line of "Saskia Preda" written in a loopy childish hand. "That's just ridiculous. I never had a girl crush on Nicolas."

Which was the truth . . . sort of. Saskia had never had a crush on her fiancé. She'd just had the infinite bad luck to fall in love with him at the age of eight and had never managed to find her way back out again.

"Don't lie to a new friend, Saskia. It will set our relationship off on the wrong foot."

Saskia gave an inarticulate cry and dropped her head to the sofa cushions.

"What is wrong with me?" she groaned, banging her head a few times for good measure. Too bad the cushion wasn't a brick wall. Maybe that would knock some sense into her.

"A man," Corinne shot back. "I thought we'd already established that."

"That, and the fact that I must be an idiot to still be here angsting about it. The way he behaved was inexcusable. I should just cut my losses and leave, right?" She raised her head and looked to her friend for agreement. "Right?"

"If it was that easy, why did you call me and ask me to come over here to talk you out of it?"

"That's not why I—" Saskia gave up and set aside her empty cup to rub her hands over her eyes. She laughed helplessly, mostly at herself. "I had to ask you to come here because he told me I wasn't allowed to leave the apartment without his permission."

Corinne sucked in a deep breath, held it for a moment, then exhaled, her lips pursed in consideration. "Okay, setting aside for the moment the complete assholery of that whole 'without his permission' bullshit, I'd say it just proves the point that after he left the apartment you called me to come keep you company instead of grabbing whatever wasn't nailed down and running as fast as you could go in the opposite direction of wherever he went. Am I right?"

"You're right."

"So, what does that tell you?"

Saskia made a disgusted sound, this time directed

entirely at herself. "That I'm a spineless idiot with pathetic taste in men?"

"Stop that." Corinne frowned at her. "No one is allowed to call you spineless, Saskia Arcos, least of all yourself. A spineless woman would never have stood up to her big, bad fiancé in the first place, let alone handled him as neatly as you did this morning in his office. You're a long way from spineless. What you are is, well, kind of submissive."

"Submissive?" Saskia couldn't have felt more shock if the other woman had reached out and punched her. "I'm submissive? Since when?"

Corinne shrugged. "Can't say. I haven't known you that long. But judging by your personality and what you've told me about your family, I'm going to guess since you were a twinkle in your daddy's eye. There's nothing wrong with it. Some people are just born that way."

"I am not submissive. Whips and chains? So not my thing!"

"Good; that will leave more for Reggie." Corinne chuckled. "I'm pretty sure she and Misha wear out the ones they've got pretty regularly. Oh, stop blushing. Reggie isn't ashamed of who she is, and you shouldn't be, either. Not that I'm saying you're exactly the same. There's more than one kind of submissive in the world, and I'm pretty sure you and Reggie are completely different kinds. Reggie's a sexual submissive. She likes her man to dominate her in the bedroom; it turns her on. You're more of a . . . well, I don't know what the technical term is, but you've just got a submissive personality."

"You're contradicting yourself," Saskia grumped. "You're the one who just told me I wasn't spineless."

"That's because you're not. Look, stop getting hung up on the terminology and just follow along with me, okay? When I say you're submissive, I'm not saying you'll just let anyone who wants to walk all over you. That's not submission, it's pathologically low self-esteem, and it's the sort of thing that requires years of intensive therapy. You just have the sort of personality that means you're perfectly happy not to run the show, you know what I mean?"

Saskia just stared at her.

Corinne sighed. Setting her mug on the coffee table, she leaned forward as she tried a different explanation. "So far, we've only known each other a couple of days, right? But let me tell you all the different ways you've demonstrated to me, in that short period of time, that you prefer not to take the dominant role. Ready?"

No, she wasn't, but she nodded anyway, because that's what Corinne seemed to expect.

"Okay, first, when we met at the party, you were perfectly sweet and polite. In fact, you're like a small-talk guru, but that was as far as you took it. I was the one who put us on a first-name basis, not you. If it were up to you, we would have exchanged a couple of words of chitchat and gone our separate ways. You might have thought later that I was nice and wondered if we would have had anything in common, but you would have left it where it was. Am I right?"

Saskia frowned. "It was my engagement party. I

had responsibilities. I couldn't just think about who I felt like talking to most."

"Mm-hm. Who threw that party, by the way?"

"What do you mean, who threw it? My parents did. It's tradition. The bride's parents always throw the couple's engagement party."

"Right. But who did the planning? Drew up the guest list? Chose the location? Picked the food?"

"My parents. They wanted to be certain we included everyone who might expect an invitation, and it only made sense to have it at the Predas' new hotel. But I certainly did my share," she hurried to add, starting to feel uncomfortable. "I consulted over all the major decisions."

"Of course you did. It was a lovely party. And I meant it about those mushroom things." The woman smiled, but her gaze remained serious and focused. "Second, after we talked a little bit and developed a rapport, I was the one who gave you my card. I passed you my digits, thereby offering the possibility of us making contact in the future and potentially exploring the possibilities in friendship. If we'd been in a bar and at all inclined toward lesbianism, the correct terminology would be that I picked you up."

That startled a laugh from Saskia, and Corinne grinned back.

"Not that you're not gorgeous," the reporter continued, "but I'm unfortunately straight and madly in love and lust with my sexy fiancé. But this brings us to point number three—even after I gave you my card with all of my contact information on it, I am still the one who made the next move by calling you the next day and suggesting that we get together and you let me introduce you to my friends."

Saskia did not like the direction where this was heading and she struggled to find some way to refute Corinne's points. Which, unfortunately, were all true.

It took Saskia a second, but she did manage one point in her favor. "You did call me, but I was the one who suggested coffee!"

See! See! she wanted to shout. *I'm not just a passive follower! I can do stuff, too!*

"You did," Corinne acknowledged with a nod, "and I was very proud of you. But I will just point out that there are points deducted for only doing it after I already had you on the phone and for letting me suggest the coffee shop."

"Hey! I told you I hadn't been in the city for very long. I couldn't think of anyplace."

Corinne hummed noncommittally. "Then there's the matter of our conversation over coffee. I'm the one who got it rolling and set it on a personal level, allowing you to treat me like a friend and confide in me the way you were dying to do. And I'm the one who came right out and declared us to be friends. I'm afraid the evidence is stacked against you."

"Sheesh. What are you, a lawyer?" Saskia grumbled.

"Nope, but my good friend Danice is. She's a total shark. If you ever need representation, give her a call. But in this case, even she would tell you the jury's a lock. You, my friend, are the opposite of a dominant personality. Which, according to the rules of antonyms in the English language—and I can say this because I'm a writer, so I use words—makes you submissive."

Defensiveness made Saskia hunch her shoulders in a resentful shrug. "So what does that mean? That secretly I want Nicolas to treat me like an inanimate possession, so I should just stop complaining about it?"

"Lord, no!" Corinne scooted closer and gave her friend a one-armed hug. "That's not what I intended to say at all. Not even close. As far as I'm concerned, that man deserves a bloody lip at the very least, but that's my personality talking, not yours. And that's my point. You're the only one who can decide how you're going to deal with your fiancé, but I think you need to understand yourself and what you really want before you do or say anything irrevocable.

"You're not a dominant person, so you're never going to want Nicolas to defer to you all the time any more than you want him to let you make all the decisions. There's nothing wrong with that. The important point in all my psychobabble was that you have to realize that not everything is going to be worth fighting over, not to you. You're the type of person who can be happy living within a certain power structure and a certain framework of rules, so recognize that and then decide which ones you really *can't* live with and make those the ones you fight over. If you try to battle over every single thing, all you'll do is exhaust yourself and make both of you even angrier."

It made total sense.

Saskia quirked the corner of her mouth and looked at her friend. "So, basically, this was all your long-winded way of saying I should pick my battles?"

"Hey, even Dickens got paid by the word."

Impulsively she reached out and hugged Corinne. "Thank you. I appreciate you coming over and talking through this with me. Between this and trying to find the real attacker, I feel like it's been seven years since the party sometimes."

"Don't worry," Corinne reassured her. "I know Mac. He's Danice the lawyer's husband, actually, and he's good. If anyone can find the real culprit, Mac will."

"That's good to hear. I think Nicolas is fairly convinced that the only way to clear his name is to find the real attacker and bring him to justice."

She hesitated, something Corinne picked up on.

"You don't agree?"

"No, I think it makes sense," Saskia allowed. "I'm just not sure there's not something everybody is missing . . ."

"Like what?"

"Well, the timing really bothers me. I mean, maybe I'm just being paranoid, but it seems strange to me that the attack would happen on the night of our engagement party, after it had broken up and everyone went their separate ways, but while the Tiguri were still on everyone's mind. But I don't know." She shrugged. "Maybe I'm just still sensitive about Rafael De Santos and Nicolas having their little squabble in front of everyone. Like I said, the timing just makes me uncomfortable."

Corinne looked thoughtful. "I did see Rafe and Nicolas have a discussion before Rafe left. I think that was right before I talked to you, wasn't it?"

"Yes."

"Yeah, they didn't exactly look like the best of friends, did they? In fact, your fiancé actually looked a little bit mean."

"You're not the only one who noticed. I just worry that someone might have remembered that and taken it the wrong way."

"And done what? Used it to try to frame Nicolas?" The reporter shook her head. "That seems like a bit of a stretch."

"I know it does, and I'm not even really suggesting that. I just think it might be worth looking into who already had a grudge against De Santos who might want to use the general sentiment against the Tiguri as a kind of smoke screen for an action they already planned to take."

Corinne whistled between her teeth. "Sweetheart, I hate to break it to you, but Rafe is a public figure. He's rich, he's gorgeous, and he's the head of a powerful organization. The list of people who haven't wanted to kill him at one point or another is probably smaller than the one of people who have."

"I don't suppose it really matters, anyway." Saskia forced a smile. "My major in art history didn't exactly give me a lot of training in digging up dirt on nasty grudges. Unless they involve painters and notorious ballet dancers."

"Maybe not, but I happen to be an expert on digging up dirt. If it will make you feel better, I'll do a

little poking around. I can't promise I'll find anything, but I've always believed it never hurts to take
a look."

"You would do that?" Saskia felt truly touched. "I
think that's the sweetest thing you could possibly do
for me."

"No," Corinne corrected. "The sweetest thing I
could do for you would be to kidnap your husband
and have him taken in for a lobotomy and forced
asshole deprogramming. This is the most practical
thing I could do for you."

Saskia laughed. "Well, it works for me. Thank
you."

"No problem. What are friends for?"

Corinne left a few minutes later, leaving Saskia sitting in the den and trying to figure out the best way
to follow her friend's advice. Saskia knew she had
made a mistake earlier by issuing Nicolas an ultimatum to change his behavior or consider their engagement over. As he had pointed out, a Tiguri engagement
wasn't that easy to break. In fact, the agreement
could only be dissolved if the mated couple failed to
conceive after a minimum of one full year of living
together. Unless Saskia wanted to condemn them
both to another eleven months, three weeks, and four
days of living hell, they would have to come to some
sort of compromise.

Besides, in her heart, Saskia knew that she didn't
want to end the engagement. She wanted Nicolas for
her mate; she just wanted him to talk to her a little,
the way he had in the kitchen last night while she

made dinner. Then, he'd spoken to her like a person, asking questions about her life and her hobbies and really listening to her answers. He hadn't ordered her around or accused her of doing something wrong; he'd just talked to her. When he did that, Saskia found herself even more attracted to him than she had been for the last two decades. Those were the moments when being his mate felt like the most natural thing in the world. Surely they must be able to work out some way to have that kind of relationship for more than thirty minutes at a stretch.

It must be possible.

First, Saskia reminded herself, she would have to pick her battles. Which were the ones she really wanted to win?

It didn't take long to decide that she didn't care what he thought or said about her leaving the apartment while he was out yesterday morning. She had left because she was worried about him and angry that she didn't know where he'd gone or when he'd be back. Leaving him in the same predicament had been a petty form of revenge she had enacted without even realizing her own subconscious intention. It had been wrong, not because she should be required to clear her every move with her mate before she made it but because common courtesy dictated that if she wasn't going to be where someone expected to find her, she should at least leave a note to explain where she was. She would have done it for a room-mate; she could certainly do it for a fiancé. So as far as past mistakes went, she decided the wisest course would be to set them aside and move on.

She also didn't think they should waste time arguing about her interruption of the meeting with Mac. She could explain that she had only barged into the office unannounced as a last resort after Nicolas refused to explain about the trouble with the Council that had dragged him out of her bed on their first night together. She still felt he should have opened up to her when she asked, so she didn't regret her actions. In fact, she would do the same thing again if presented with the same choices. But she would also explain that to her mate—calmly and rationally— and put the responsibility for that back on him. If he didn't want her to manipulate him into sharing things with her, he could either share of his own accord or give her a good—read: not "because I said so"— reason why he couldn't share.

That was where the real trouble lay, and that was the battle she would pick to fight. Saskia wanted to be a good mate to her fiancé. She wanted to do all the things he needed her to do, from running his social calendar to bearing his children. She wanted to be his companion and support him in his decisions. She wanted to *love* him, damn it, but he had to let her. He had to accept that she wasn't an accessory but a mate, that in order for her to share his life, he had to actually share his life *with* her. She didn't need to know what he was thinking every minute of every day, but when something happened to threaten him or her or their life together, then she expected to hear about it. From him. That was her one and only requirement, the one battle she could not afford to lose.

She just hoped he would be able to respect her stance on that.

She sat alone in the den for a long time, lost in thought, until the sound of a key in the lock of the front door caught her attention. Her Tiguri hearing picked up the noise easily, and her sense of smell told her immediately that Nicolas was home. She detected none of the sharp, bitter smells of fury that had clung to him when he left, and she felt hope surge in her chest. His footfalls were naturally quiet, but if she strained, she could just barely pick them out. They sounded even but not precisely measured. He sounded as if he was walking, not marching, toward her. She found herself holding her breath.

Her eyes fixed on the doorway even before he appeared in it. She thought he looked tired, too tired for barely five in the afternoon on a Sunday, but otherwise his expression remained neutral. Not frighteningly blank and hard, the way it had looked the last time she had seen him, just even. And cautious.

They stared at each other for a minute; then Nicolas sighed and crossed to the sofa, lowering himself wearily to the cushion beside her. He didn't touch her and he left several inches of space between them, but he chose the seat beside her instead of the chair to the side or the far cushion where Corinne had curled up earlier. Saskia's heart rose.

When she spoke, the words ran right over Nic's, uttered in the same moment.

"I think we sh-h-hou—"

"I've been hoping we m-m-migh—"

Each stuttered to a halt. Nic's mouth quirked. Saskia smiled shyly.

"You first."

Saskia took a deep breath. This was it. She had to take the risk. "I think we should start over." She had to force the words out, but once they were there, hanging in the air between them, it felt like a vise releasing her chest. "I never should have said what I did this afternoon. I didn't really mean it. I don't consider our engagement null and void. I was just upset, but I handled it badly. I apologize. I won't say you haven't done anything to make me angry, but I think I've done a pretty good job angering you, as well. So I think we should set that aside and let it go. I think we should start over, from here, and agree to treat each other with respect and consideration."

Nicolas watched her in silence. His green eyes looked like slivers of jade, opaque and mysterious, but his expression remained relaxed and open while he listened to her words. When she finished, he nodded slowly.

"You did make me angry, but I responded by being cruel, and that's something I'm not proud of. I regret that I made you feel like less of a person, because that isn't what I want. I don't want a mindless slave, a Stepford wife, or a broodmare. Any one of those things would bore me to tears and have me pulling my hair out within a week. I want a mate, and I want you to be that mate. I think starting over is a wonderful idea. I just wish I'd suggested it first."

Saskia's eyes widened and her heart sped up. She

felt like she'd just woken up and realized it was Christmas morning. "Really?"

Nicolas nodded. "Really."

"Wow," she breathed. "That was a whole lot easier than I thought it would be."

Nicolas gave her a strange look and burst out laughing. He laughed so hard, it made the sofa shake. Saskia held on to the cushions and waited for it to run its course. It took several minutes.

"What?" she finally demanded, once her mate had settled down into the occasional guffaw.

"I just love that you thought this was easy." He chuckled, flopping his head back on the sofa and turning to look at her. A wide grin softened his harsh features, making him look years younger and shockingly handsome.

"Well, not all of it." She rolled her eyes and harrumphed. "You know what I mean. I was just talking about this." She waved a hand between them. "This last bit. I wasn't sure you'd agree with my suggestion. I thought I'd have to spend a lot more time convincing you."

Still grinning, Nicolas reached out a hand and took one of hers. He played with her fingers while he watched her face. "Well, I hate to spoil your plans," he teased, his gaze turning hot. "If you feel the need to convince me of something, I'd be more than happy to let you."

Saskia felt a low hum of arousal begin in her belly. She'd spent all day in her head, trying to come up with a solution to her problems with her mate, which was almost a relief, because it had kept her from frantically monitoring the state of her body. Tiguri, like their fully feline cousins the tigers, were induced ovulators, which meant that they only released fertile eggs after being stimulated by a male during intercourse. Unlike tigers, though, who entered heat on a regular cycle regardless of whether a male was present for mating, Tiguri females, like human females, were always receptive to mating. Consequently, while a tigress would go into heat, seek out a mate, and then ovulate, a Tiguri would mate first, *then* go into heat, and then ovulate. Which meant that Saskia hadn't been lying earlier when she'd said that within the next couple of days she was going to become about as horny as a rabid mink.

Thankfully, she didn't think she'd entered heat quite yet, but it didn't seem to matter. Nicolas did a fine job raising her temperature without any help from her hormones.

He tugged her toward him, and she went willingly, shifting across the sofa cushions with shy enthusiasm. Nicolas guided her into his lap, encouraging her to straddle his thighs until he could nestle his groin against the apex of her legs. Saskia was so much shorter than her mate that even in this position, she didn't have to look down at him. Instead, it brought their eyes level, and Nicolas stared into hers while his hands drifted teasingly over her back, hips, and bottom.

"Go ahead, Sassy," he encouraged, lips curving, fingers slipping beneath the hem of her top to drift in feather-light strokes over the sensitive skin at the small of her back. "Start convincing me."

At that moment, Saskia couldn't have convinced herself to keep breathing. She just shook her head and leaned closer, shivering at the feel of his breath caressing her cheek.

"Hm, then maybe I should convince you," he rumbled, and when his mouth settled on hers Saskia melted.

She was convinced.

Nicolas wasn't Catholic, but he still wanted to light a candle and say a prayer of thanks that he held his mate once more in his arms. He had feared, really feared, that he had made irrevocable mistakes. All afternoon as he'd wandered the city on foot, he'd mentally kicked his own ass. If he'd been able to reach, he would have kicked it literally, too. He'd thought long and hard about ways to make things right with Saskia, and the only thing he'd come up with was that he needed to apologize. He needed to admit he'd been wrong in the way he'd behaved and say he was sorry.

For a Tiguri *ther,* this amounted to cutting off his own testicle with a rusty spoon. Nothing could have been more difficult.

Still, he had believed Saskia was worth it. He still believed it, now more than ever as he cradled her in his arms and savored the sweet, rich spice of her mouth. He would pay a higher price than his pride to keep this woman as his mate, but he couldn't deny that a part of him roared in relief that she hadn't demanded he pay a single sacrifice.

Her apology had floored him. Of all the things he

had expected when he returned to their apartment, of all the scenarios he had braced himself to face, a calm, sweet-faced Saskia offering an apology of her own and a face-saving compromise for their future hadn't even featured on the list of possibilities. Nicolas had prepared himself for weeping, screaming, claws, fangs, stony silence, flying projectiles, and even the absence of Saskia and all her worldly possessions, but not for this miracle.

And, Lord, but it felt like a miracle.

She returned his kiss with sweet, eager passion, welcoming him inside her mouth and exploring his own in turn. Every caress he pressed on her she returned twofold, until the feel of her soft hands threatened to snap his control and end the moment far sooner than he intended. Struggling for control, he drew his lips from hers and pressed them to her temple.

He meant for the moment to allow him to catch his breath, to regroup, refocus, and regain the patience he would need in order to love this woman the way he wanted to, but the skin at her hairline was so soft, so smooth, so richly scented with the sweet perfume of her hair, that he just had to reach out and taste. That led to him running a trail of kisses down to her ear, where he teased the delicate whorl with the tip of his tongue, then closed his teeth around the plump lobe and tugged. The slight pressure made her breath hitch in her throat, which made him want to explore a little farther.

She shivered when his teeth scraped down the long, slim column of her neck, his tongue following to lave away the tiniest sting. He discovered that the hollow of her throat tasted like salted caramel and he paused there for several minutes, licking and sucking the fair skin while her breathing became faster and more ragged. When need finally spurred him onward, he tugged aside the neckline of her top with an impatient hand and growled in satisfaction at the sight of the mark he'd left there the day before. Her rapid Tiguri metabolism would have healed any other slight injury she might have sustained during their mating, including the soreness of a torn hymen, but the mating bite was special. It would remain visible for days, and even after it faded, other males would continue to sense its presence and know that this woman belonged to him.

The thought filled him with savage satisfaction.

A moan escaped her lips when he placed his teeth over the mark and squeezed gently. He wouldn't pierce her skin again, but echoing the moment when he'd claimed her excited him desperately. He remembered how he had done it while he'd pressed inside her, and the memory of her tight sex clenching around him would have brought him to his knees if he'd been standing. As it was, it made his head spin and his fingers clench, flexing in the warm flesh of her hips.

Saskia whimpered at his touch and shifted against him, rubbing her denim-covered core against his groin with hungry little rocking motions. He could feel the heat of her, smell the growing arousal rising off her skin, and suddenly he needed to taste it there as well.

Swiftly he stripped away her shirt, yanking it up over her head and dropping it to the floor. He dealt with his own, as well, then reached around her for the clasp of her bra and froze. Her rapid breathing made her breasts rise and fall, making the pale mounds strain at the edges of their lacy prison. Nic had seen breasts before, plenty of them, and some had been decorated in truly artful scraps of fabric, but somehow he'd never seen anything quite like this. The bra his mate wore looked deceptively innocent, a concoction of pale pink satin overlaid with lace in a slightly darker shade of rose. The concealing cups offered him not so much as a flash of nipple or a shadow of areola; they simply cuddled the full globes like a pair of gentle hands, lifting them high against her chest as if offering them to him to savor and treasure. His mouth actually watered at the sight.

Shaking his head at his own fanciful thoughts, Nicolas unfastened the garment and tugged it down her arms, peeling the cups away like wrapping paper off a much-anticipated gift. Immediately his hands took over the job of support, cupping each breast and lifting it in turn to his lips. He pressed a kiss on each peak, then settled one broad palm over the first while he opened his mouth over the second and drew the nipple deep into his mouth.

Saskia hissed in pleasure, the sound turning into a moan that trembled and broke when his tongue pressed the nub against the roof of his mouth and he began to suckle strongly. The hands that had gripped his torso during his explorations rose, her arms twining about his head and cradling her to him. She leaned into his worship, and her knees tightened around his hips.

"Oh, God," she whimpered, and dropped her cheek to his hair, as if she could no longer support the weight of her head.

Nicolas hummed in pleasure and turned his attention to the other breast. Within minutes, he had turned each nipple into a deep pink splash of color against her pale, creamy skin. The sight made him smile, but his work was far from done.

He slid one hand over her shoulder, fingers dancing over his mark, before skimming down between her breasts, detouring to draw a circle around each peak, and sliding over the quivering flesh of her abdomen. A quick twist of the wrist dealt with the fastening of her jeans, allowing him to spread them open and insinuate his hand into the hot delta of her thighs.

She cried out, the sound sharp and breathless, echoing in the quiet room. Her hands clutched his shoulders and her head fell back even as she lifted herself slightly away from him to offer him better access. He thanked her by stroking deeper, parting her soft folds to find the tight bundle of nerves at the top of her crease. He pressed his thumb against the little nubbin, flicking gently even as he sent two fingers delving into her sweet liquid core.

Her body clenched around him helplessly, her hips rocking to try to compel him deeper. He teased her with slow, shallow strokes that circled her opening, then barely slipped inside, keeping her constantly craving more. Her breath came in ragged pants now, and she whimpered like a hungry kitten. The sound drew his arousal even tighter until he could no longer bear the constriction of his clothing.

When he pulled his hand from between her thighs she gave a muted roar of protest, then purred her approval as he swiftly divested them of their remaining clothes. With no barrier between them, she crawled eagerly back into his lap, gasping at the sensation of bare skin against bare skin. He returned his hand to her sex, reveling in the freedom of movement her nudity offered him, and he petted her for long moments, savoring the slick feel of her plump folds. Her hips pressed against him in demand, trying to capture his fingers inside her. When he gave in and filled her with two long digits, she chuffed happily and rode his hand with abandon.

A creature of sensation, she lived for nothing but pleasure in those moments, and Nicolas watched her with rapt desire. She moved as gracefully as water, burned as hot as fire, and became as necessary to him as air. He ached to be a part of her, needed to be inside her, and when she lowered a hand between them to wrap her fingers around his shaft his control deserted him.

With implacable movements, he brushed her hand away, gripped her buttock in a punishing hold, and lifted her over him. He took a second to position himself, but when he slammed her hips down over his, his gaze was locked on her beautiful blue eyes. They went blind as his and Saskia's bodies merged, the beautiful mountain lake color losing focus as all her attention turned inward to the feel of his body invading hers, stretching, filling, claiming. Her breath escaped on a long, thready moan, the sound like broken music in his ears.

He took a moment to savor the connection, the feel of her clamped warm and tight around his aching arousal. Nothing on earth could ever feel as perfect as this, he acknowledged, surging helplessly inside her. No place could ever feel more like home than the sweet, warm depths of her body. She was his home, his haven. His mate.

The thought sliced through the ropes holding back his beast, unleashing the full force of his voracious hunger on his unsuspecting mate. In an instant, he went from holding still to better savor the moment of their joining to imprisoning her in a punishing grip while he pounded her depths with primitive fury. A part of him was appalled by his own actions and railed at him to be slow, be gentle, treat her like the treasure she was, but that softer voice was drowned out by the roar of his hunger. If she represented a treasure, then he would mark every inch of her to be sure no one else would ever mistake that she belonged to him.

To slow down was impossible, to be gentle a battle he could never win. All he could do was push and push and push her along with him, to pour on sensation until it overwhelmed her and swept her along in the frantic rush to fulfillment.

Saskia arched her back as she rode him or, rather, as he moved her over him with insistent clenching hands. Her head fell back between her shoulders, her throat a quivering arch as she choked on a never-ending litany of cries and incoherent pleas. She braced her hands on his chest, using him to anchor herself in the storm of passion. The sane corner of her mind knew he must be hurting her and roared in self-directed fury, but the expression on her face appeared nearly beatific, as if she gloried in every hard, ruthless thrust, every place where his fingers bit into her flesh hard enough to mark the pale surface of her skin with deep purple bruises. She uttered not a word of complaint, just flexed and gripped and shuddered and moaned while he pushed her harder and higher toward release.

Nic could feel it coming. It built low in his spine and snaked around to his groin in an involuntary clenching of muscle and tingling of nerves. It drew his balls up tight to his body, hardened the erection he already felt had been carved of stone, and tore the breath from his lungs in raw, painful exhalations. Determined to make her come, to give her at least that much in apology for her brutal treatment at his hands, he shifted her hips, changing the angle of their connection so that the base of his shaft dragged hard across her clit with every forceful thrust.

Her moans turned into helpless, high-pitched whines, and he gritted his teeth against the need to explode before her. He would take her over the edge if it was the last thing he ever did. Since he thought this experience might just kill him, that represented more than an empty promise.

"Nicolas!"

Her voice broke on his name and he knew he had her. Pinning her hips in place, he held her with desperate intent and gave three short, hard thrusts, each one a slow, pointed assault on the knotted bundle of nerves at the top of her slit. On the third thrust, she shattered like spun glass.

He came giving thanks, emptying himself into his mate in endless, aching streams of pleasure, knowing he'd just done something irrevocable and hoping like hell that whatever it was, it made this woman his forever.

Seven

Their truce lasted not only through the remaining hours of the weekend but well into the next week. With their promises to each other kept constantly in mind, they began to establish a routine of time spent together and apart, of conversations that began stiltedly but quickly warmed into the easy, comfortable exchanges of a committed couple. Nicolas never went to his offices at the headquarters of Preda Industries, but he did spend time working in his office while Saskia staked a claim to a nook off the kitchen that Nic referred to as the sunroom. The light made the space perfect for her work, and her customized work surface—a sort of cross between an easel and a drafting table—took up residence among the lush plants beneath the enormous skylight. Her current project kept her just busy enough to occupy herself in the few moments when Nic failed to express the desire to occupy her in an entirely different manner. It didn't hurt, of course, that by Tuesday Saskia's heat had struck with a vengeance and she could barely go three hours without waving her proverbial tail under his nose and begging him to touch her. Devoted mate that he was becoming, he never uttered a word of complaint.

She would have said that Tuesday and Wednesday were spent mostly in bed, but the truth was that that particular piece of furniture entered into the picture only on occasion. Most of the time, she couldn't wait for him to drag her to that room and instead teased, and taunted, and enticed until he took her right where they stood. Or sat, or knelt, or lay. They christened every room in the apartment, some more than once. He took her several times bent over the kitchen counters and on one memorable occasional standing pressed up against the front of the refrigerator. She remembered it because it had taken her ten minutes to polish her ass prints off of the stainless-steel doors.

By Thursday morning, she knew if she wasn't already pregnant, she would be soon. Maybe as soon as Nicolas walked back in the door from his errand. He'd left the apartment almost an hour ago to deliver some important paper to his office. While he'd worked mostly from home the last few days—and even then, only when she left him alone long enough to catch his breath for a few minutes—the move to New York meant that the company couldn't let him go completely. While he delegated as much as he could, some things only the boss could handle.

He had told her he wouldn't be long, so she was expecting him, not a visitor, when the doorbell rang a little after 10:00 A.M. The sound surprised her and it took a moment to register what it meant before she hurried to the door and checked the peephole. Her father shifted impatiently on the other side of the door.

"Papa," she said, yanking the barrier aside and waving him in. "What on earth are you doing here? Is something wrong?"

Gregor Arcos stepped over the threshold and swept his daughter up in a forceful embrace. "What? A father can't come to check up on his little girl without her getting suspicious? I've missed you, poppet. I wanted to make sure this Preda character is treating you right."

"Of course he is. Don't be silly." She returned the hug, then stepped back and led Gregor into the living room. "Come in and sit down. Can I get you something? Coffee or tea?"

Gregor started to wave away the offer, then stopped. "Actually, tea sounds lovely, poppet, if you'll brew it for me. It's impossible to get a good cup in this city, I swear."

"Make yourself comfortable, Papa, and I'll be right back."

Gregor nodded and hitched up the legs of his trousers before sinking to a seat on the elegant chenille sofa.

Saskia hurried into the kitchen to put on a kettle and assemble the makings of tea. A quick glance at the clock confirmed her suspicion that Nicolas could return at any moment. She had gone from wishing he'd hurry up already to hoping his errand might take longer than he expected. She'd rather he didn't get back while her father was in the apartment. She had no desire to conceal the visit from her mate; she just feared that with the hormones of her heat still surging, she might not be able to keep her hands off him once he returned. There were just some things a father shouldn't see his daughter doing, and crawling all over a man was one of them.

Stacking a serving tray with cups and saucers, sugar, cream, lemon, strainers, and, of course, the teapot made for a heavy load once she added the boiling water to the leaves, she walked very carefully back into the living room. As she approached the sofa her father rose and relieved her of her burden, setting the tray down on the coffee table before resuming his seat.

"I hope English is all right," she said, setting out the cups while the leaves steeped. "I haven't had time to lay in a selection yet. This is all I could find."

"It's fine. Fine. I'm sure you've had other things on your mind just lately."

Saskia blushed and murmured, "It's been a busy few days."

"Of course, of course." Gregor reached for his cup, remembered it was empty, and drew his hand back, cupping his knee and rubbing in tight circles, a nervous habit Saskia remembered well.

She frowned. "Papa, what's wrong?" she asked. "Something's bothering you, which is clearly the reason you've come for this visit. Why don't you tell me what's bothering you?"

"Don't be silly." He laughed too heartily. "There's nothing bothering me. Nothing at all."

She paused with the teapot poised over his cup. "Papa," she scolded.

"All right, all right." He sighed. "I suppose by now you've heard about this business with the Council?"

"Yes." She nodded, her expression tightening as she added two lumps of sugar to her father's cup and a tiny splash of cream to her own. "The whole thing is ridiculous, if you ask me. As if any of us would have any reason to harm Rafael De Santos. Besides which, you and Mr. Preda were at home at the time of the attack and have Mother and your staffs to vouch for you. And Nicolas was here with me. None of you could have committed the attack, even if you'd wanted to."

Gregor appeared surprised that she knew quite so many of the details of the event in question, but he didn't ask about it. He probably assumed that Nicolas had shielded her from most of the worry, as he had likely done with her mother; but he hadn't counted on his daughter's determination to share her mate's worries, nor would he have understood if she had tried to explain.

"Yes, well. Clearly none of us was involved in the dreadful business, but that hasn't kept the rumor mill from working overtime. Our reputations are being ground down like soft summer wheat."

"What are you talking about?"

"I'm talking about the fact that this damned attack is all anyone can talk about lately," Gregor snapped, his fingers clamping around the handle of his cup until his knuckles turned white.

Saskia gave a little prayer of thanks for the deceptive strength of porcelain.

"Everywhere I go, every Other in a five-mile

radius can't manage to discuss a single, solitary subject without the conversation circling back to the
Tiguri, and the way the Council of Others is treating
us like serial killers who just haven't yet been linked
back to the crime scenes yet."

Saskia winced. "It's that bad?"

"It's worse!" Gregor slammed down his cup and
surged to his feet to pace restlessly around the room.
As he spoke, he gestured wildly, his hands slicing
through the air in testimony to his agitation. "I received a call last night from Milan Voros."

"Voros?" Saskia couldn't keep the shock from her
voice. Voros was *ther* of one of the powerful old Tiguri streaks still hanging on to territory near Rostov
in the northern Caucasus. Of course, he and Gregor
knew each other, but she would never have called the
men friends. "What on earth did he want?"

"To express the concern of several of the old families that perhaps our families had not been the wisest choice to test the idea of our people moving into
the new world."

Okay, Saskia wouldn't touch that "new world"
stuff with a stick. It just showed how wrapped up in
tradition the Voros *ther* still was. But that stuff about
there being a deliberate choice to expand the presence of their kind to America . . . that gave her pause.

"What could he have meant by that?"

"I think his meaning was obvious, Saskia." Her
father glared at her. "He wanted me to know that if
Preda and I continue to have problems with the
Council, the old families will not hesitate to remove

us from this city, undoing all of our hard work and installing themselves in our place."

"Whoa, wait a minute, Papa. What's this about hard work and installing someone in New York? I though this move was about business. You said Preda Industries and Arcos Enterprises need to move here in order to stay competitive in the global market. You said that New York represented the hub of the business world and it would benefit the companies to relocate their headquarters here. You didn't say anything about this being a coordinated effort among our people to establish some kind of toehold on new territories."

Gregor froze and turned to look at her. He wore an odd expression, a combination of guilt and calculation. She didn't like it one bit.

He smiled at her, and the paternalistic gesture made the hair stand up on the back of her neck.

"What aren't you telling me, Papa?"

"It's nothing. Nothing you need to concern yourself with."

"I beg to differ," she gritted out, clenching her teeth. "If it involves my race and my family and now my mate, then it involves me. Therefore I have a right to know. Are you telling me that the old streaks came together to make the decision to move into America? Is that actually something that happened without my knowledge?"

Gregor scowled. "And why would you need knowledge of something like that, eh, little girl? That is a matter for *theri*, not females or cubs."

She drew a deep breath, searching for calm. "I can't believe I'm hearing this. I can't believe you did that. Did someone forget that keeping our paws off of North America is a large part of how we've kept the peace with the Lupines all these centuries? Did that slip someone's mind?"

The old refrain of "not for women and cubs" was a familiar one, but that never seemed to make it sound any better to Saskia's ears. She wanted to shout about how she and her mother probably had a better grasp on the nuances of the Tiguri political atmosphere than Gregor did, but she knew the information would fall on deaf ears. Bound up in tradition, her father really believed that women didn't get involved in politics. Never mind that her mother and grandmother had steered their clan into the alliance with both the Voros and the Berec clans, or that Saskia herself had given him the outline of the solution he and another *ther* had used to rein in a young male without a streak who had been attempting to siphon members and power off an old and weakened clan.

Her father might know that Saskia had as deft a political hand as he did, but she knew she would never hear him admit it. She tried not to let that knowledge upset her.

"Of course it didn't," Gregor said, "But times have changed, and some among the *theri* believe that we need to change with them. The expansion of territory was only a by-product of our discussions. The important part . . ."

He trailed off, and Saskia shook her head emphatically. "Oh, no, Papa. You've come this far. Now I need to hear the rest."

"Yes, I suppose you do, since your role in the whole situation has become so crucial."

He paused to draw a deep breath, clasping his hands together behind his back and rocking back on his heels the way he always did before he made a big announcement. The last time she'd seen him do it, he'd been about to tell her that Preda had approached him about a mating between her and Nicolas.

She waited, nervous tension tightening her belly. She felt as if the sword of Damocles hung above her head.

"Over the last few years, there has been . . . rumbling among the streaks. Some of the newer groups have begun to question whether the old families should really have so much influence over our laws and customs."

Saskia nodded, not finding that particularly surprising. While she'd been raised in an old family, she realized that many of the Tiguri who grew up in the newer, less entrenched clans often saw her kind and their traditions as antiquated. Almost obsolete.

"The things we heard told us nothing new," Gregor continued, "but the volume of some of those dissenting voices has increased in the last year or two. It prompted five of the old families to get together last year and discuss our options."

"Your options for what?" she wanted to know. Or actually, she didn't, but she felt she needed to in order to understand.

Her father looked grim. "For consolidating our power and enhancing our authority over the rest of the Tiguri. The *theri* who attended the meeting took a vote to determine which of us would step forward as representatives of the old guard."

The knot in her stomach drew painfully tight. "So who won the vote? You, or Stefan Preda?"

"Neither of us. Both of us."

"I don't understand."

Gregor sighed. "During the discussions, the subject of the betrothal agreement between you and Nicolas came up. A couple of the *theri* were swayed by the thought that the mating, especially if it were fruitful, would make for a powerful leading force by tying two old families together for a single purpose, behind a single leader."

"A single leader? Who was that supposed to be? You, or Mr. Preda?"

"Nicolas."

Saskia felt as if she'd been slapped. "Nicolas?"

"That was the main reason why Stefan stepped down as *ther* last year. With Nicolas as head of their streak, and the two of you engaged, it would seem perfectly natural if he became the official head of both our families, and therefore of all the old guard. Of course, his position would only be strengthened if you were known to be carrying his cub." Gregor's blue eyes, so like her own, bored into her. "Tell me, Saskia. Are you pregnant yet?"

If she had managed to conceive, she hoped an iron-rich diet would be good for her baby, because Saskia felt angry enough to chew nails. Fury had struck her so hard, she'd barely managed to keep from throwing her father bodily out of the apartment. As it was, her demand that he get out had left him looking wounded and her feeling like a horrible child.

Just not horrible enough to look at his face at the moment.

She felt betrayed, as if she'd just discovered that her father wasn't really her father or her mother not her mother. Saskia felt like an orphan, abandoned by parents who cared more about their own position in society than about her happiness or well-being. How could they do that to her?

Saskia knew she was painting her mother with a fairly broad brush, since Gregor hadn't mentioned Victoria taking any active role in the big plan, but it didn't matter. She always followed her husband's lead. Victoria was the perfect mate, obedient, loyal, and content to let Gregor steer the course of their lives while she rode around in his wake, content with luxurious houses and pretty jewels and the occasional fond glance.

At the moment, Saskia didn't feel that kind of fondness for anybody, including her own mate.

Had he known about this? Had that been the reason for their sudden engagement, after years of knowing that they would be mated as soon as he got around to setting a date? Had Nicolas, like their fathers, cared more about the political implications of their match than about actually building a life with her?

God help him if he did, because that would be one

injury to their relationship that no compromise could heal.

He returned about fifteen minutes after her father left to find her still sitting on the sofa, the remains of the tea cooling in front of her. She heard Nicolas's greeting as he stepped into the living room from the foyer, but she didn't turn. She sat staring into space like a trauma victim. She supposed she was.

"Sass?" His voice rumbled as he walked up behind her, her face concealed by the position of the sofa, which faced away from the entrance to the room.

When she didn't answer, his voice became concerned. "Saskia?"

He circled the sofa in a rush of movement and dropped to his knees in front of her. He peered into her face, then took stock of the scene around her, the two half-full cups of cooling tea, the fancy English service. Looking back at her, he raised a hand to her cheek.

"Saskia, what's wrong?" His deep voice held a world of concern. "What happened? Who was here? What did they do to upset you? Sassy, talk to me, sweetheart."

Her eyes shifted to his face, but she didn't move. She had to clench her teeth against the jolt that coursed through her when his fingers touched her skin. Her hormones didn't care that she'd been betrayed, probably by him. But her heart did.

"Did you take me to mate because you wanted me, or because you wanted to lead the old families against the upstart Tiguri?"

She watched his face, searching carefully for his reaction, and saw only confusion. But was that all there was or all her lovesick heart wanted to see?

"Sweetheart, what the hell are you talking about? What kind of nonsense is this?"

She repeated the question, her voice flat and unemotional. "Just answer me."

He sat back on his heels, his hand dropping to her knee. His expression shifted from concern to annoyance. "I'll answer, but then I expect you to tell me what this is all about. When I left here this morning, I thought we'd moved beyond making stupid assumptions about each other. I would hate to think I was wrong. Agreed?"

Saskia nodded. She'd hate to think that, too.

"Okay, then." He nodded and fixed her gaze with his, the green depths serious and intense. "We've been over this before, but I'll say it this one last time, because obviously, you need to hear it. Saskia Eloisa Arcos, you are my mate, and I took you for my mate because no other female would do. You suit me as if you'd been made for me, from your beautiful red-gold hair to the tips of your delectable little toes. Even when you're driving me crazy and making me behave like a mindless fool, I know that you're the only woman on earth with that power. And when you take me into your delicious body, I know no other woman has ever fit me so perfectly. For the last four days, I've gone to sleep tasting you on my tongue and woken up with the feel of you in my arms, and I know that I'll never be able to get a night's rest again if you're not there beside me. You challenge me and you comfort me, and I will never want another woman as my mate. Does that answer your question?"

Tears welled in Saskia's eyes and she nodded. She fought to keep her lips from quivering, but she doubted she succeeded. She certainly didn't manage to bite back that sob that tore from her throat in a choking wail.

With an expression of mingled horror and tenderness Nicolas watched her break down. Gathering her against his chest, he pressed her cheek to his shoulder and stroked her hair gently.

"Oh, sweetheart," he murmured, and the rumbling of the sound in his chest made Saskia feel somehow safer. "Baby, don't cry. You need to tell me what happened so I can go out and beat whoever did this to you into a bloody pulp."

Saskia just sobbed harder.

Murmuring soothing nonsense, Nicolas scooped her up into his arms and took his seat on the sofa, arranging her carefully across his lap. "Hush now, Sassy girl. It can't be that bad. I promise, I'll make it better, but you have to tell me what happened."

It took her several more minutes to stop crying hard enough to prevent speech. Even then, the words tumbled out in fits and starts as she explained to Nicolas about her visit from her father. She felt Nic's muscles tighten steadily under hers, but his hands remained gentle as they rubbed soothingly along her spine.

She told him about the meeting among the *theri* and about the unrest moving through the Tiguri families. She also told him about her father's summary of the agreement with Stefan and his concern for the possibility of her pregnancy. Her mate remained silent through the whole telling, but the glances she cast up at his face revealed an expression of intense anger. Luckily, she didn't think it was directed at her.

"The worst part," she said, after she'd reached the point in the story where she threw her father out of the apartment, "is that I've been just sitting here thinking this whole time, and I'm not sure it matters anymore whether you were in on our fathers' plan."

His arms tightened around her. "Saskia, I swear to you that—"

"No, I know," she cut him off. "I'm not saying I don't believe you when you tell me you had no idea what they were doing. I just mean that if there really is such serious trouble brewing among the streaks, you might have no choice but to take charge. I mean, would you rather have my father do it? Or yours? They've already proven they can't be trusted to put anyone's welfare above their own agendas. Not even their own children's."

"Oh, no." Nicolas tightened his mouth into a grim line. "I will not be manipulated into going along with their little scheme just because they've created a de facto role for me. My father and I have been over this ground again and again, but apparently he's not getting the message any more than the Council of Others is. I. Am. Not. Interested. In. Politics. End of story. Not the politics of the Others, and not the politics of the Tiguri. Any man who wants to try to control the destinies of others is out of his ever-loving mind. I'd rather spend my days mining for diamonds in a pile of horse shit. It would be a hell of a lot more pleasant, not to mention about equally as productive."

Saskia could see his sincerity; it radiated from him like music from a concert hall. He meant every single word. "So what could our fathers have hoped to accomplish?"

"I have no idea, but trust me when I tell you, I mean to find out." He eased her off his lap and set her on the sofa beside him. "I don't care if my father is in a meeting with the Queen of England at the moment, he's going to want to get rid of her so he can answer to me. And when I'm done with him, I'm going after yours."

Saskia grabbed hold of his hand and prevented him from rising. "Don't. Not now." She lifted his hand and guided it around her shoulders until she could snuggle back into his embrace. "Nothing is going to change in a few hours, and I'd rather have you here right now. I've had a very upsetting morning."

Nicolas glanced down at her, some of his tension melting at the way she rubbed her cheek against him, like a kitten begging to be stroked. "You have, hm-m?"

She nodded, feeling the pressure of arousal growing inside her again, her heat returning in the wake of the release of her tears. They had already made love once on this sofa, but she didn't necessarily mind if they repeated themselves. As she recalled, the experience had been worth repeating.

"I have. And as my mate, it's your job to stay here and comfort me."

He used his arm to snug her closer and slid the other hand along her side, drifting over her sweater-clad breast and stomach to press gently at the tops of her inner thighs.

"I guess you might be right," he purred, and leaned down to nuzzle her ear. His tongue flicked over the sensitive tip, making her shiver. "I wonder what you might find comforting after such a difficult morning."

His fingers pressed gently, slipping a bare inch between her thighs to tease along the seam covering her crotch. Her legs parted helplessly and her hips lifted into his hand. She adored his touch. It made her head spin like raw whiskey, and somehow after all the times they had come together over the last few days it still managed to show her new things about herself and her own capacity for pleasure.

"That's my girl," he murmured, sliding his fingers down, cupping his palm over her heated core. "Did you miss me while I was gone?"

He ran his thumb along the ridge of material above her clit, pressing the cloth against her sensitive nerves until she moaned and shook against him. "Did my girl get hungry while I was away?"

God, he had no idea. His deep voice teased her as surely as his hand, the low vibrations moving through her like an inner caress, as if he touched more than just her body. He touched the heart of her with his quiet words and the emerald heat of his changeable green eyes.

"Do you need me, Sassy girl?" His fingers shifted, hovered over the fastening of her trousers. "Do you need me inside you? Do you need to be mated, my sweet little tigress? Need to be filled?"

She hissed her response, growing tired of being teased. With the heat on her, she could be readied just by thinking about him. She required no preparation to drip with welcome and ache with need. She just wanted her mate. Now.

Her mouth opened on a muffled roar of demand, and she could feel fangs drop from her jaw as passion brought her beast to the surface. The last time she'd come so close to changing had been the first time she and Nicolas had mated. The glint in his eye told her he remembered the event well.

Abruptly the teasing stopped. Efficiently his fingers dealt with the fastening of her trousers and the buttons of her sweater, stripping her of both garments in economical movements. His own clothing followed, though unlike his habitually barefoot mate, he got his jeans caught on his shoes for a second and cursed roundly as he paused to deal with the obstacle. Finally nude, he reached for her, shifting her to lie back on the sofa and coming down over her like the warm darkness of a summer night.

His weight pressed her into the cushions, and she stretched luxuriously against the velvety nap of the soft chenille upholstery. Arms and legs opened in welcome, wrapping him in her embrace. She gloried in the feel of him, the scent of him, the raw masculine power of him as he dispensed with any show of preliminaries and joined their bodies in a single smooth thrust.

She arched into him, purring her pleasure as his

barbed shaft rubbed along her sensitive inner walls, urging her to pleasure and fertility. Grunting, he gave her more of his weight, pressing their bodies together from chest to groin. The intimate connection allowed him to stroke her with his whole body, undulating against her as he thrust and retreated.

With her eyes open, she watched his gaze locked on her, watched his face tighten with his own intense arousal. She could read his rhythm in his eyes, the way they sparked with each withdrawal and darkened with pleasure each time she closed fully around him, taking his entire length. His parted lips allowed his breath to caress her face with short, sharp puffs of air. He breathed heavily as the pleasure peaked, but so did she, gasping for air to keep her moving, keep her open and accepting for her chosen mate.

Their loving didn't last long. It couldn't, not with the whip of her heat driving them forward and the intensity of the pleasure they knew they could achieve in each other's arms. Neither had any interest in delaying that ecstasy. Each reached for it with greedy fingers, and when they grasped it each dissolved crying the other's name.

Nic dozed for a few minutes, enjoying the softness of his mate beneath him and the warmth of her body clasped around his softening flesh. He savored their connection as he drifted back toward awareness, but when he looked down into Sass's pretty blue eyes he found them shuttered in sleep. Whether he had worn her out or the demands of her emotional outburst had accomplished the task he couldn't tell. Either way, she slept soundly enough that she barely moved when he separated their bodies, and he took that as a sign that she needed the rest.

Lord knew nether of them had gotten much of that over the last few days.

The thought made him smile as he scooped her into his arms and carried her carefully into their bedroom. Pulling back the covers, he tucked her beneath the blankets and brushed the hair away from her face with gentle fingers. She didn't stir.

He had definitely worn her out.

His sense of satisfaction barely followed him to the bathroom door. As he cleaned up, his thoughts drifted back to the story his mate had told him and renewed anger flooded through him.

What the hell had their fathers been thinking?

He snorted and reached for a towel. He had a pretty good idea what *his* father had thought. It qualified as a familiar refrain in the story of their relationship. Nic had refused to do as his father expected, so rather than fighting about it, Stefan had simply gone ahead and arranged matters in such a way that his son would have no choice but to fall in with his plans. Only Nic did have options. He'd learned early in his life always to keep some open and to be able to locate new ones where none appeared available.

In this case, his choice was clear: he would straighten out the mess with the Council, tell his father and Arcos to go to hell, and remove himself and his mate from the arena of Tiguri politics through any means necessary. If that meant he would have to abandon his position at Preda Industries and move the two of them to Antarctica to start a new life together, then that was what he'd do. He would regret that his cub would never know its grandparents, but that was a price he would pay if it meant that he and his mate could live together in peace.

And woe betide any man, woman, or Other who threatened that peace.

Striding naked into the bedroom, Nic paused by the bed to check on his mate before getting dressed. He had just pulled the covers up over her shoulders when the shrill noise of the telephone shattered the quiet. He snatched up the cordless receiver halfway through the first ring.

"What?" he growled softly, keeping one eye on Saskia to see if the sound had disturbed her. She slept on in peace.

"Oh, wow. You must be Nicolas," a woman's voice declared, sounding both amused and concerned. "You sound grumpy. You and Saskia aren't fighting again, are you? Last time I talked to her, she said you had worked things out. What happened?"

Nic scowled and carried the phone with him into the hall. He didn't want to risk waking his mate. "Who is this?"

"Sorry. This is Corinne D'Alessandro. I'm a friend of your fiancée. You didn't upset her again, did you? She was starting to sound really happy."

Nic thought about being offended at the woman's prying, but he liked the way she defended his mate so fiercely. "No," he informed her, softening his tone. "I'm sorry if I sounded 'grumpy.' Sass is asleep right now and I didn't want the phone to disturb her."

"Ah, taking a nap, is she?" Amusement crept back into Corinne's voice. "She mentioned yesterday that she hasn't been getting as much sleep as she's used to. She probably needs the rest."

"As you say." He couldn't quite manage to keep the purr of satisfaction out of his voice.

Corinne laughed. "Ri-i-ight. Okay, if she's sleeping, I'll try back another time. But let her know I called, okay? We've been trying to find a time to get together again, but she's . . . ah . . . had other things on her mind lately."

"I will. No, wait," he said abruptly as a thought occurred to him.

He really didn't want to wait to confront his father. It always benefited him to have the element of surprise when he had to upset his father's plans. But he didn't want to leave Saskia and chance her waking up alone in the apartment again. After their first night together, he liked to think he'd learned his lesson. He knew he could leave her a note and hope she accepted intent behind the gesture, but he thought he might have a better idea.

"Are you free now?" he asked Corinne.

"Well, yes, but that doesn't do me much good if your fiancée is sleeping. I mean, I like her, but the unconscious tend to be lousy conversationalists."

"I'd really appreciate it if you could do me a favor," he said. "I have to go out for a little while, but we promised each other a few days ago that we wouldn't disappear without letting the other one know where we were going. If Sass wakes up while I'm gone, I'd feel terrible. Especially after what she went through this morning."

As he'd hoped, the woman audibly bristled at the idea that her friend had faced some sort of trauma. "What do you mean, 'after what she went through'?"

Nic felt a surge of satisfaction. "She got a visit from her father this morning and it really upset her. She wasn't expecting him, and he didn't exactly come by just to make sure I was keeping her happy."

"Well, what the hell did he say to her?"

"It's a long story," he neatly evaded the question. "Anyway, it would be doing me a huge favor if you would agree to come by and just hang out here to look out for Sass and make sure she doesn't wake up alone, wondering where I am. Would you do that?"

"I'll be there in half an hour."

The line went dead in his ear, and Nic smiled. Now, he thought, he could get back to business. Quietly he reentered the bedroom and headed for his closet. Time to gear up for the meeting with his father. He hoped he hadn't left his suit of armor at the cleaner's.

Eight

"Well, good morning, Glory. Or should I say good evening?"

Saskia opened her eyes and blinked in confusion. "Corinne?"

Her friend popped up from the sofa in the sitting area and set aside the notebook she'd been scribbling in. "In the flesh. How are you feeling? You slept longer than I thought you would."

"What time is it?"

"A little after two, I think."

"Two in the afternoon?"

"Well, sure. You're not that lazy. Nic said you went down about quarter after twelve, so you got about two hours. Feel any better?"

"Just . . . confused. Where's Nicolas?"

"He had to go out, which is why he asked me to come over and stay with you." Saskia pushed herself into a sitting position as Corinne hurried toward the bed, grinning when her friend had to grab the sheets to keep them from tumbling to her waist and flashing her company. "Careful there. It looks like someone forgot to put on their jammies."

Color stained Saskia's cheeks. She'd forgotten a

lot of things the last time she'd been awake. Like her own name. Those little details escaped her when her mate touched her. "Where did he go?"

"He said to tell you he went to have a talk with his father, but that you shouldn't worry," Corinne recited, and perched on the edge of the bed. "He said, and I quote, 'Tell Sassy that there won't be any trouble. I'm just going to go in, tell him to mind his own business, and leave.'"

"And when did he go out?"

"About an hour ago."

Saskia's brows drew together in a frown. "Sounds like he forgot about the leaving part of that plan."

Corinne laughed. "Well, he looked like he had a few things he needed to get off his chest. I'd give him a little leeway before you start wondering why he's not back yet."

"I'm not feeling particularly generous right now."

"Probably because you slept through lunch. You hungry?"

She thought about it for a second, then nodded sheepishly. "Starving."

"Good, because I've been dying to raid that kitchen. It looks like the back of a professional restaurant in there." The reporter bounced up from the bed and headed toward the door. "Get up and get some clothes on. Your man strikes me as the possessive type. I wouldn't want to make him jealous."

She hurried down the hall, and Saskia rolled her eyes. She also rolled out of bed, though, and after using the bathroom pulled out a pair of black yoga pants, and topped them with a pale blue sweatshirt with a slight V-neck and a rolled hem. Normally, she wouldn't wear the outfit for any reason other than working out, but she felt lazy and a little boneless at the moment. Likely the by-product of amazing sex.

Trailing her friend into the kitchen, Saskia looked around and spotted her half-buried in the enormous fridge. "Doing a little spelunking?" she teased.

"Dude, I totally could!" Corinne laughed and emerged with a loaf of bread and a platter of meat and cheese. "I think there might be people living in there. An entire city of very small polar bears, with their own postal service and everything. One of them tried to fight me for the roast beef. Sandwich sound good?"

"Perfect."

Corinne spread out the fixings while Saskia retrieved plates, glasses, and silverware from the cabinets.

"So, since you already know I'm nosy, I won't pretend I'm not dying of curiosity," Corinne said as she piled meat and cheese on thick slices of sourdough. "What happened with your dad? Nic told me he came over here this morning and really upset you. Did you want to talk about it?"

"You call him Nic now?" she asked, instead of answering the question.

"Sure; that's how he introduced himself. He also apparently calls you 'Sassy.' Fair warning, but I'm totally using that."

Saskia scowled but found she really didn't mind. She'd almost gotten used to the nickname over the last few days with her mate. He always said it affectionately, so it rarely occurred to her to protest.

"Does the fact that you're not answering mean you really don't want to talk about it?" Corinne prodded gently. "I don't mind being told to butt the hell out. I hear that from a lot of people, both personally and professionally."

Pulling out a stool, Saskia sat down with her sandwich and shook her head. "No, it's okay. I mean, it's not okay; it's a mess. But it's complicated, and I wouldn't feel right dragging you into it."

"You can't drag the willing. Believe me, I wouldn't ask if I didn't want to know. I also wouldn't be me. I *always* want to know. Curiosity is the besetting sin of the reporter."

"Fine. Just don't say I didn't warn you."

It took her entire sandwich to draw her friend the whole picture, from the current unrest in Tiguri society, to Saskia's visit from her father, to the plan hatched by Gregor and Stefan. Explaining Nic's reaction took slightly less time but was challenging due to her inherent discomfort with foul language. She'd been brought up to be a lady.

"Holy shit." Corinne whistled, not bothered by the same restraints. "No wonder he looked ready to chop wood with his face when he left here. Damn. I'm glad I've never pissed the man off."

"It isn't pleasant. But that's why I'm worried that he hasn't come back yet. The only reason to be away this long is because he's really having it out with his father. Or because he decided to go after mine, as well."

Corinne looked uneasy for a moment, then offered a reassuring smile. "I'm sure it's nothing like that. His father is a busy man, right? He probably had to wait for him to get out of a meeting or something. Or maybe they decided to go out for lunch to talk. Men always talk better over food and a martini. It's like their version of side-by-side pedicure chairs."

She sounded less than convincing, but Saskia didn't argue. She was too busy worrying.

After they tidied up the kitchen, Corinne took one look at her friend's face and proclaimed that a distraction was in order. "How about a movie? With the size of that TV I noticed in the den, I'm guessing there's a DVD library the size of Guam in one of those cabinets."

They did find several drawers full of discs, including a handful of recordings by stand-up comedians, but even Eddie Izzard couldn't keep Saskia's attention from straying toward the clock or her ears from straining to hear the sound of Nic's key in the front door. Halfway through *Dress to Kill*, Corinne stopped the film and threw up her hands.

"Okay, that's it. I can't take it anymore," she declared, using the remote to flick off the television and dragging Saskia off the sofa. "You're driving me crazy. We have to get out of here."

"What? What are you talking about? I can't leave," Saskia protested, and her friend grasped her wrist and began hauling her toward the door. "I have to be here when Nicolas gets back."

"Honey, if you're still here when Nic gets back, you're going to be ready for a padded room. You're already losing your mind, and frankly, you're taking me along for the ride. We'll leave Nic a note. I told him that if he was delayed I might have to leave. He knew I already had plans for later tonight that I couldn't cancel."

Saskia got as far as the living room before she dug in her heels. "Well, if you have other plans feel free to go. I'm going to stay here and wait for my mate."

"Sass, don't be an idiot. If you stay here alone, you really *will* wind up in Bellevue before the end of the night. I warned Nic about my plans, but I also told him that if I had to leave, I'd take you with me. He knows that, and when he sees the note he'll know where to find us. If you want, you can call his cell phone and leave a message. But it's getting close to five, and I really have somewhere I need to be."

"I can't interrupt your plans. You go ahead, and I'll just—"

"You'll just get your shoes and come with me," Corinne insisted. "Tonight's plans are of the 'the more the merrier' variety. Now, go on. Get your shoes and your purse. Let's go."

"Exactly what kind of plans did you have for to-night, Corinne?"

"I'm on Baby Watch."

"Actually it's more like BELLY WATCH. In capital letters, of course. And if this were a television station, there would be a news ticker scrolling across the bottom of the screen."

For a woman who looked about as pregnant as it was possible to get, Missy Winters sounded awfully cheerful as she explained Corinne's joke to Saskia forty minutes later.

"At this point, it's like the official New York pastime to sit around and watch to see if I pop. Since I feel like a blimp, I can sort of understand the fascination."

Corinne had hustled Saskia out of her apartment and marched her along the crowded uptown sidewalks to the Upper East Side, turning her down a quiet, tree-lined street to a pair of gorgeous old town houses in the eighteenth-century tradition. They had climbed the steps to the northern half of the pair, knocked on a beautiful set of carved doors, and been greeted by the wife of the senior-most werewolf in New York. The second of the two buildings, Saskia had learned, housed the famous Vircolac club and the chambers of the Council of Others.

"Don't worry," Missy had assured them as she waved her guests inside. "They're not in session at the moment. The club's generally pretty quiet this time of day."

Empty or not, Saskia didn't want to think about what might or might not be happening in the house next door, which Missy had mentioned was connected to this one by several doors, albeit well-secured ones. Instead, Saskia concentrated on her immediate surroundings, which consisted of a cozy sitting room furnished with a mix of surprisingly comfortable antiques and a few overstuffed modern pieces that blended well with the original moldings and high plastered ceilings of the historic home.

"Usually, I sit in the kitchen. It's like my space," Missy said from her perch on an old settee upholstered in burgundy velvet. "But the stools and hard chairs in there are just way too uncomfortable at the moment. I'm like Goldilocks this week. The kitchen chairs are too hard; the sofa you're sitting on is too soft." She made a face. "At the moment, this thing is working as my just right, but give me five minutes. I'm sure that will change."

In spite of her grousing, the Silverback Luna glowed with happiness. Clearly, although she felt uncomfortable so close to her due date, she adored the baby she carried. Her palm rested over her swollen belly as she spoke, and every time the conversation turned to her pregnancy she patted it with obvious affection.

Saskia wondered what it would feel like to carry her own child in her womb. She felt a surprising rush of longing. Clearing her throat, she blamed it on hormones.

"So, are you having a boy or a girl?" she asked.

"I wouldn't let them tell me."

"The betting pool is currently favoring a boy," Corinne said with a grin. "Last time I checked the odds were five-to-nine. Want in?"

Missy laughed. "Don't get suckered. I'll tell you right now it's a boy. A soccer player. Nothing else explains this level of kicking."

"Graham said she could be a future Rockette." Corinne wriggled her eyebrows.

"That's just him trying to be funny. It's a boy. Besides, can you picture Graham with a daughter? He'd convert to Catholicism before her third birthday just so he could lock her in a convent the minute she discovered boys."

Saskia couldn't help smiling, especially when she considered her own mate's reaction to a growing daughter. She bet she'd find herself attending mass pretty quickly herself.

"Anyway, Graham and I were sorry we couldn't attend your party last weekend," Missy said, focusing her attention on Saskia. With her ash-blonde hair, sweetly round face, and wide brown eyes, the human woman was as transparent as glass, and she clearly did regret their absence. "Graham will barely let me get out of bed at the moment, let alone let me leave the house. If he'd had his way, he would have checked me into the hospital the minute I started showing."

"Don't apologize," Saskia dismissed, finding Missy as irresistible as Corinne had predicted. The woman just radiated warmth and kindness. "We completely understand. Your health is more important than parties."

"Besides, if you'd gone into labor on the dance floor, it would have totally captured the spotlight," Corinne joked. "You can't do that to a sister, Miss. Total faux pas."

Missy shuddered. "God, can you just picture it? What a nightmare." She turned back to Saskia. "I really wanted to go, though. I was dying to meet you and your fiancé, so I'm just tickled that Corinne was able to convince you to come see me tonight. I just wish Nicolas were with you."

Corinne rolled her eyes. "Don't we all."

"Uh-oh. Do I detect a story?"

Saskia shook her head. "A long one. Very long."

"Don't worry, Sassy. I'll fill her in. You just lie back and think of England."

The only thing Saskia *could* think about was Nicolas. He should have returned to their apartment hours ago. The sun had begun to set when she and Corinne arrived at Missy's house. By now, it was full dark. What could have happened to keep her mate out so long? Unless the confrontations with her father or his had taken an unexpected turn.

She shifted nervously in her seat while Corinne filled her friend in on the situation with the Tiguri and Nic's and Saskia's fathers. Tactfully the reporter left out any mention of Nicolas's recent run-in with the Council of Others, since Missy's husband happened to sit on said Council.

"Oh, my goodness, that's horrible," Missy breathed when Corinne finished the story with Nic's departure from the apartment and the women's decision to come for a visit. "You poor thing! No wonder you look like you're a bundle of nerves. It must be driving you crazy that your fiancé hasn't even had the courtesy to call and give you an update on what's keeping him. If I were you, I'd be positively livid!"

"Careful, Miss Busybody," Corinne cautioned. "As far as I can tell, these two have not needed any prodding to raise their tempers with each other. They need help keeping them cool."

"Oh, I'm sorry. I just can't help imagining how I'd feel if I were in your position, Sass. I'm a worrier by nature, so I wouldn't be able to stand myself until I had heard from Graham. Of course he would be fine, just like I'm sure Nicolas is fine, but that wouldn't stop me from worrying."

Saskia cracked a smile. "I *am* a little tense."

"Right. We need to get your mind off your problem and keep you occupied," Missy decreed. "Corinne, it's time for Scrabble. Go get the box from the den."

Corinne groaned, but she was smiling as she pushed to her feet. "Just resign yourself, Sass. Missy doesn't take no for an answer. Plus, she's a teacher, so she thinks Scrabble is the answer to everything. She even has a Scrabble-based plan for lasting peace in the Middle East."

"It would work, too," Missy called after her friend, her voice full of laughter. "Just think of all the amazing new opportunities to use that stupid *Q*!"

And that was how Saskia—though since even Missy was now calling her Sass, she figured she might as well give up on her actual name—found herself playing Scrabble (her second game) when she heard the front door of Missy's house open and the sound of masculine voices on the threshold. Instinctively she stood and moved toward the door, but it wasn't her mate she saw in the front hall. It was Rafael De Santos, battered and bloody and carried carefully by two other men she knew she had never met before.

"Oh, my God! What happened?" Missy's voice rang with shock as she waddled as fast as she could toward the men. "How badly is he hurt?"

"Bad enough," one of the men said, and by focusing on his scent Saskia could match it to the traces she'd already picked up around the house. This was Graham Winters. "He's lost a lot of blood. We're going to need a Feline donor. I told Sam to ask around next door and start spreading the word if no one was immediately available. It would be a hell of a lot easier if the bastard were Lupine."

"If he were Lupine, he would likely be dead," the second man said, his rough, aristocratic face like a medieval knight wearing a veneer of civilization. "You can see the size of the claw marks. Whoever did this outweighed him by at least one or two hundred pounds."

"Fucking tiger," Graham bit out, making his wife gasp.

"Watch your mouth, wolf boy," the Luna snapped.

Saskia held up a hand to stop her. "Don't worry about it, Missy. He's just upset, and I can understand why. He has every right to be."

The Alpha's head snapped in her direction, and she saw his eyes narrow. Oh, yes, Graham Winters recognized her, probably from the photos of her and Nic that had been all over the papers this weekend. Notoriety made everything so much more convenient.

"What the hell is she doing h—" Graham snarled half the question, then stopped himself. "No, you know what? I don't want to know. Just keep her here. Misha and I need to get Rafe upstairs and make sure all the bleeding is stopped. After that's done, I'll come back down and then I want to talk to our *guest*."

Saskia remained silent and stood in the hall while the werewolf and the vampire—Misha could be no one other than Dmitri Vidâme—carried their awkward burden up the stairs. She got a better look at the unconscious man as they maneuvered him past her, and her stomach clenched at the sight. The handsome werejaguar looked a mess, more blood than skin visible to the naked eye. Huge ragged slices cut across his chest and abdomen, shredding his clothing into ragged strips. She saw puncture wounds in his arms and shoulders, likely bite marks, and she thought she could see bone poking out through the raw, bloody wound on his right leg. Whoever had attacked Rafael De Santos had clearly intended to kill him, and this time he had almost succeeded.

She jerked when Missy laid a hand on her shoulder. She had nearly forgotten the other women were there.

"I apologize for my husband," Missy murmured, her eyes soft and wide with concern. "He and Rafe are very close. I know it doesn't excuse his behavior, but you were right in thinking this has upset him."

Saskia shook her head. "No, it's fine. I understand. I'm upset, too, just seeing it. But I want you to know, Nicolas is *not* responsible for that. He couldn't be."

She repeated the same thing half an hour later when Graham and Misha strode grimly into the sitting room.

"Your mate had officially worn out his welcome in this city, Ms. Arcos," the werewolf growled, his lips drawn back to show the barest hint of fang.

Saskia made no mistake he intended her to feel the threat. "My pack and I will be escorting him out. Tonight."

"On a rail?" his wife shot back, planting her fists on her hips and glaring up at him. "What happened to gathering all the evidence against someone before we go throwing accusations in their direction? Do you have any proof that Nicolas Preda is the one who attacked Rafael?"

"What kind of proof do you want, woman?" Graham bellowed. "You saw him! You saw what was done to him! I say that's your proof!"

"Oh, so he signed his work, did he?"

Dmitri Vidâme stepped forward, a hard, dark presence that seethed where Graham raged. The contrast did little to reassure Saskia.

"The injuries tell their own story, Melissa," the vampire said quietly. Implacably. "They were undoubtedly inflicted by a Feline shifter, one considerably larger than Rafe. Since he possesses unusual size for a jaguar, that rules out nearly every other species we know of. The only possibilities are lion and tiger. You know as well as I do that there is no Leo pride within five hundred miles of this city. It had to have been Tiguri."

Melissa crossed her arms over her chest and rested them on her stomach, not backing down an inch from the intimidating bloodsucker. "And Nicolas Preda is the only Tiguri shifter in the city, is he? That's news to me."

Graham snorted. "What, are you suggesting she did it? Impossible. At best, she'd equal Rafe in size, and he's male. He'd still have the advantage in strength. If she had attacked him like that, she'd be looking just as bad, if not worse."

"No, I'm not suggesting Sass attacked Rafe. I'm suggesting we *don't know* who attacked Rafe. Did he say it was Nicolas?"

"He's fucking unconscious! He can't say anything."

"Don't you swear at me, Graham Winters!"

"Then don't be an idiot, Melissa!"

"Please! Enough!" Saskia shouted, taking her life in her hands by stepping between the quarreling mates. "Enough," she repeated at a more civilized volume when everyone turned to glare at her. "There's no point in fighting. I'm perfectly aware that you believe my mate already attacked your friend once, Mr. Winters, but I can assure you he did not. Nor did he do it this time. He couldn't have."

"You're wrong, Ms. Arcos," Dmitri told her, his dark eyes hard and unreadable. "Graham was one of the few Council members who did not immediately assume your mate's guilt after Friday's incident. He said then that proof was required before stones could be cast, and I can assure you, he risked his reputation by taking that stance. So, you'll understand if he finds this latest attack doubly troubling."

"I'm troubled by it, too, Mr. Vidâme, believe me. As is my mate. No one has wanted to find out who was behind the first attack on Mr. De Santos more than Nicolas and I. We even retained a private investigator to help us locate the culprit. Believe me when I tell you, Nicolas is not a killer."

Graham rolled his eyes. "Of course he's a killer, sweetheart. He's a predator. We all are. Killing comes naturally to us."

Saskia inclined her head tightly and struggled to hold back a scream. She needed to make these people understand that Nicolas was not guilty of these crimes, and throwing a fit would not help her cause.

"A fair point," she acknowledged. "Let me rephrase myself. Nicolas may have the capacity to kill, but he does not have the capacity to ambush another man and attempt to kill him out of spite or malice."

"You're sure of that."

"Perfectly." She lifted her chin and met the Lupine's stare. "I know my mate, Mr. Winters, and he is not the man you're looking for."

Graham stared at her. After a moment, he growled and raked an impatient hand over his hair. "This is ridiculous. Do you expect us to just take your word for it? Of course you don't want to believe your mate would do something like this, but as far as I know, there are only five Tiguri in the city. You and your mother aren't strong enough to have taken Rafe down, and you father and Preda's father are too old. Your mate is the only one who *could* have done this."

"Are you a hundred percent sure of that?" Corinne asked. When four sets of eyes turned her way, she clarified. "Are you a hundred percent sure that Saskia, her parents, Nic, and Mr. Preda are the only five Tiguri in the city?"

"Of course we are," Dmitri dismissed her. "They are the only Tiguri to have settled in the city in centuries."

"Okay." Corinne nodded and pursed her lips. "And I suppose it's impossible that a Tiguri could come visit the city? Or even stay here and neglect to mention that to the really suspicious and hostile locals? I suppose there's no way that could ever happen?"

For a moment, the two men looked shocked at the idea. Something like that would clearly never occur to them.

"The odds of that are extremely unlikely," Dmitri said, his eyes narrowing.

"But not impossible?" Missy pressed. She saw the chink in the armor and she aimed straight for it. "We do have these newfangled inventions called airplanes, you know. I hear it's possible for someone to fly in them and visit places halfway across the world at a moment's notice."

"Sarcasm doesn't suit you, Melissa," Graham growled.

"Really? I've always thought it brings out my eyes."

"No one is saying that is the definitive answer," Saskia said, seizing the opportunity, "but you have to account for the possibility. You also have to admit that you are probably right that both attacks were perpetrated by the same person."

"Right. Your husband." Graham glared at her.

"Wrong," she insisted. "If both attacks were made by the same individual, then I know for an absolute fact that Nicolas was innocent, and so does half of New York. That attack happened the night of our engagement dinner. Five hundred guests saw and spoke with Nicolas that night and can vouch for the fact that he did not leave the ballroom from seven in the evening until shortly after midnight. At that time, I walked with him to our waiting car and accompanied him to our apartment. He wasn't out of my sight for more than twenty minutes until we got the call that the Council required him to answer their questions sometime around two in the morning."

"Twenty minutes is a long time for someone who moves like a tiger," Dmitri pointed out, but some of the ice had melted from his eyes.

"It is, but regardless of the time, I know Nicolas never left the apartment. We had just gotten engaged, and that was our first night together. I knew where he was the entire time. Before you ask, I was nervous. I listened. I could hear him moving around, and I would have heard if he'd left."

"Again, you expect us to take your word for it?" Graham sneered, but the taunt lacked a certain heat.

"You don't have to take my word for it." She extended her hand to him, her fingers steady. "Scent me. You're Lupine; you should be able to smell if I'm lying. Taste me if you have to. I'm telling the truth."

Silence descended, enveloping the occupants of the room for several tense moments. Then Graham swore.

"I echo the sentiment," Dmitri said. "I must admit, our path seemed much clearer when we believed we knew the source of our troubles."

"I'm sure Torquemada thought his path was clear, too," Corinne offered, falling silent when Dmitri aimed a raised eyebrow in her direction.

"As I was saying, this leaves us with a bit of a dilemma. If we rule out the involvement of your mate, then we're left with the question of where to turn our attention."

This time, Corinne raised her hand before she spoke and Dmitri rolled his eyes. "Yes, Corinne?"

The reporter flashed him a cheeky grin. "Easy answer. You ask Mac."

"Mac?" he echoed.

"As in 'McIntyre Callahan'?" Graham asked.

"Yup. Sass wasn't pulling your leg when she said she and Nic had hired an investigator to look into this mess. Luckily, they had the good sense to go with Mac."

Dmitri looked to Saskia. "Is this true?"

She nodded. "It is, but we haven't heard anything from him yet. We only spoke to him the first time on Sunday. I think Nicolas mentioned he would give us his first report on Friday."

"That's tomorrow," Missy pointed out.

"So it is." The vampire rubbed the back of his finger along his jaw and sized Saskia up. "I would be very interested to learn what Callahan has managed to uncover, Ms. Arcos, as, I imagine, would the Council. Do you think your fiancé might consent to receiving this report while we listened in?"

Oh, yeah. Right after he salaamed each and every one of them and declared them all Grand High Poo-bahs of Righteousness.

She choked back a laugh. "I don't think that's likely, Mr. Vidâme. The Council doesn't rate very highly in my mate's estimation at the moment."

"Perfectly understandable. Do you think you might

be able to persuade him to allow only myself, Graham, and Rafael to be present?"

Saskia hesitated. She didn't think Rafe would be a tough sell, since he clearly had the most at stake in this entire mess—his life. She figured Nicolas would balk at the other two men, however, both Council members and neither what anyone would call a friend.

"I can ask him," she finally said, doubt coloring her voice, "but I can't promise anything. He's been under a great deal of stress lately, and he's not always in the best of moods."

"Also understandable. All we ask is that you try, Ms. Arcos. It would make everything much simpler. For all of us."

Saskia didn't doubt that. What she doubted was her own sanity for even agreeing to make the attempt. She could practically hear Nicolas's denial already.

Nine

"Absolutely not."

"But—"

"No. It's out of the question."

"Nicolas—"

"Saskia, this is not open for debate. The answer is no."

She frowned at her mate as he climbed out of bed and headed for the bathroom. "I think you're being unreasonable."

He turned to glare at her. "Unreasonable? Believe me, little tigress, I would be happy to show you unreasonable. In fact, I wanted very much to show you unreasonable last night when you finally walked in the door hours after I myself had returned to our home and found it empty."

"We left you a note! And a voice mail," she pointed out. "And Corinne said she told you we might have to go out if you were late."

"Yes, she did, which is why I controlled myself so *reasonably* last night. But I'm afraid I've used up my allotment for the week. You'll have to survive me being unreasonable until at least Monday."

She stuck her tongue out at the bathroom door when it snapped shut behind him.

Flopping back on the pillows, she contemplated the ceiling as she heard the water turn on in the shower. She had to admit he had behaved with remarkable restraint last night when she returned to their apartment shortly before ten. She had seen his impatience in the way he pounced on her the minute she stepped over the threshold, sweeping her into his arms and crushing her to his chest. She'd also tasted it on his lips and felt it when he carried her to the floor and mounted her on the parquet of the entry, unwilling to wait as long as it would take to move the dozen steps to the living room and their favorite chenille sofa.

He hadn't asked her a single question until he rolled his weight off her and pulled her against his sweat-dampened chest. She hadn't answered any until she'd caught her breath five or six minutes after that. The interrogation had lasted at least another sixty. They had discussed Corinne at first, whom Nic liked; then Saskia had explained to him how they had adjourned to the house of another friend, a woman named Missy Winters.

Nicolas was an intelligent man. He remembered the connection immediately, and that was when he'd stopped liking Saskia's friends. He had especially not liked hearing about the accusations hurled in his absence by the Silverback Alpha and the Russian vampire, nor had he liked that his mate had been forced to defend him. The fact that the two men had eventually come to see that he was not De Santos's mysterious attacker failed to even the scales in his eyes. He had immediately rejected the idea of allowing anyone to be present when he received Mac's report, and he apparently didn't like the idea any better in the light of day.

Saskia, though, wasn't done persuading.

She rolled out of bed and crossed the room naked, slipping into the bathroom and joining her mate under the pulsing jets of the shower. The space, with its tiled walls and multiple heads, could easily have held six, but Saskia didn't let that keep her from pressing close against Nicolas's back and wrapping her arms around his chest. He ducked his head to rinse away his shampoo, then shook off the excess water.

"This isn't going to make me change my mind," he rumbled, sounding almost amused.

Amused was a good sign.

"Who's trying to change your mind?" she asked, pressing a kiss to the skin between his shoulder blades. "I'm just trying to get clean. I feel like I've been very dirty lately."

Nicolas laughed outright and turned to take her in his arms. "In that case, hand me the soap, and I'll see what I can do about cleaning you right up."

As it turned out, her mate's idea of washing her focused on a very few specific spots and left her feeling more invigorated than truly clean. She discovered a handy way to expend her excess energy, though, by washing her mate in turn, paying similarly close attention to a few of her favorite spots along the way. By the time they emerged from the bathroom, thoroughly relaxed and squeaky clean, Saskia felt ready to launch her next sortie.

She began in the kitchen, reasoning that a beast with a full belly always felt more receptive to suggestions.

"You know, your way is probably better," she said, toying with her toast while she snuck glances at her mate's face, half-concealed behind his morning copy of the *Times*. "This way, there won't be any chance of a messy confrontation between you and anyone on the Council."

"Sass," he warned, eyeing her over the fold.

"No, I mean it," she persisted, donning a mask of earnest innocence perfected after years of practice. "If you let De Santos, or Vidâme, or anyone sit in on the meeting with Mac, there's a chance he might make a scene, no matter what Mac has to tell us. It's much better if we meet with Mac alone. Then I can be the neutral party and meet with the others alone to give them the information."

"Over my dead body." He slammed his paper down on the counter with a snarl.

Saskia stiffened her spine and pushed aside the urge to back down. "It's the logical solution. They've already eliminated me as a suspect, and they know I won't lie to them because they could easily check back with Mac to verify what was in his report. This way, they get to feel like we weren't deliberately insulting them and you don't have to risk a direct confrontation. It works for everyone."

"It does not work for me."

"Why not?" she demanded.

His eyes snapped at her. "Because aside from the fact that I already told you this subject was not open to discussion, this subject is *not open for discussion*! I will not have my mate act as my emissary as if I'm not strong enough to carry my own messages, and I will not pander to those idiots on the Council by giving them the slightest indication that I care whether they think I'm guilty or not."

"Of course you care! Nicolas, the Council has the authority to have you banished from the city, or even killed! We can't afford not to care about them."

"Yes, we can." He set his jaw. "If we have to, we'll relocate, but I will not play some ridiculous game and act as if they ever had any justification for accusing me of seeking to undermine their authority in any way. They set this in motion by acting on old prejudice and assuming I was guilty because of the lay of my stripes. Now they know they were wrong, but I'm not going to help them repair their public image by handing them the real culprit on a silver platter."

"So this is about your pride?" she asked quietly.

"Damn it, Sass, don't put it like that!" He pushed back from the counter and paced restlessly around the kitchen island. "This is about more than wounded pride. Yes, they stung me by accusing me of having such little honor that I would attack a man from ambush and attempt to kill him before he even got a look at my face. But they also threatened my mate when I wasn't around to protect her, and that's something I'm not willing to let go."

Saskia sat back, momentarily stunned. "Threatened me? Nicolas, no one ever threatened me. What are you talking about?"

"You were a guest in the Lupines' home, and Winters accused you of lying to protect me. Worse than that, he growled at you and raised his voice to you and showed you disrespect because you had no one to protect you." His hands clenched at his sides and his eyes burned with pain and fury. "I should have been there to protect you, Saskia, and instead I was off on a wild-goose chase that led nowhere. I couldn't find either of our fathers, and I couldn't defend you from that dog. I will not let you make yourself vulnerable to them again."

Heart aching, she slid off her stool and hurried to him, wrapping her arms around his rigid frame. "Oh, Nicolas, I was never in any danger. Not for one second. And I did have you to protect me." She tilted her head back to meet his gaze, fixing him with an earnest stare. "You're always with me, my mate. I carry your strength inside me. That's what gave me the courage to stand up to the men accusing you and make them listen to the facts. I felt you standing beside me the whole time, no matter where you thought you were."

She felt him shudder an instant before his arms closed around her like metal bands, crushing her against his chest. He lowered his head and buried his face in her hair to breathe deeply.

"I can't stand it," he growled roughly, his voice muffled. "Just the thought of anyone harming you, or threatening you, or even upsetting you when I'm not there to protect you . . . it drives me crazy, Sassy. I can't stand it. You're becoming too important to me."

"And you're becoming too important to me," she told him, pulling back just far enough to look up into his face. A lump formed in her throat at the mixture of tenderness and fear and pain she read there. "Nicolas, you're my mate. You're the center of my world now. You say you want to protect me, but I feel the same way about you. The thought of anyone accusing you of such horrible crimes, let alone trying to actually place the blame on your shoulders, makes *me* crazy. I can't let anyone get away with that, especially not when I know it's so blatantly untrue. I have to defend you, love, just as you have to defend me. I have no choice."

She knew her words hadn't entirely won him over, but she could see the softening of his expression, the lessening of the fear as he tamped it back and reached for some sense of calm. When the corner of his mouth ticked upward, she felt a tight knot unravel in her belly.

"Is this another one of those areas where we're going to have to compromise?" he asked.

Saskia chuckled. "It really, really is."

"I'll do my best, but I can't make any promises," he said, unconsciously echoing her own words from last night.

She laid a hand against his cheek and leaned up to kiss him. "That's all I ask."

When the phone rang and shattered the moment, they laid their foreheads together and laughed softly.

"I hate telephones," he groaned against her cheek.

"Me, too. Alexander Graham Bell should be shot."

"Probably make more of an impact if he weren't already dead."

"Don't nitpick."

"Sorry." Nic sighed and reached for the receiver on the wall behind her. "Hello?"

"Nic, listen, it's Mac Callahan."

Her acute Tiguri hearing allowed Saskia to hear the greeting almost as clearly as her mate.

"Speak of the devil," she murmured.

"Mac, I wasn't expecting to hear from you. I thought you were going to come—"

"Yeah, the plan has changed. "You're going to have to come to me. There's something I need to show you."

Saskia watched her mate stiffen.

"What have you found?"

"It's better if I show you. Can you meet me in one hour? I'll give you the address." He rattled off the information, and Saskia immediately jotted it down on the message pad beside the phone. Nic nodded his thanks.

"I can be there, but I'd like to know what's going on."

"Sorry, I haven't got time," Mac dismissed him. "I've still got other phone calls to make. It's only fair to warn you, you're not the only one who needs to see this."

"What's that supposed to—"

Saskia heard the muffled click and realized the

investigator had already hung up. She also realized
that something very unpleasant had resulted from his
digging.

Nicolas cursed. "I do not like the sound of this,"
he growled as he replaced the receiver. "That changeling is up to something."

"His eyeteeth, by the sounds of it," Saskia agreed.
"What do you think he meant by that last warning of
his?"

She already knew what she believed, but she
wanted to hear Nicolas's take on the cryptic statement.

"I think he means that the bloodsucker and the
lunatic are going to have their way after all."

Saskia winced at the politically incorrect labels.
"Bloodsucker" might be an accurate description of a
vampire, but the myth about Lupines being controlled by the phases of the moon had been disproven
ages ago. The insults did have a certain ring to them,
though, and she figured that's what he'd been going
for. Still, she hoped he wouldn't repeat them once the
two men in question were present.

"I agree. I think Mac is going to have Vidâme and
Winters—and De Santos, if he's able—meet him at
that same address he just gave us. I'm assuming that
means that whatever he found is significant enough
that he only wants to repeat it once." She clasped
Nicolas's hand in hers and squeezed. "On the bright
side, it might be the information we need to find out
who really did this so we can get everyone off your
back once and for all."

Nicolas grunted, but he didn't pull his hand away. He glared off into the distance, clearly not appreciating the last-minute change in plans. Saskia had begun to discover that her mate didn't like being surprised. She'd have to remember that when his birthday rolled around.

She tugged at his hand to get his attention and brushed her lips over his when he looked down at her. "Hey, don't worry," she reassured him. "I'm sure they'll be more interested in finding out what Mac has discovered than in making trouble with us. And if I'm wrong and any of them tries anything, I'll knock him into next week."

Nicolas didn't appear to appreciate her teasing. "You're not going."

She bit back a sigh. Damn it, hadn't they already discussed this?

"Yes, I am."

"No, you're not. Saskia, we already discussed this. I am not comfortable putting you in danger, and this meeting with so many hostile Others definitely counts as danger. You'll stay here, and I will tell you everything Mac has to say just as soon as I get back."

"Nicolas, I won't be in any danger," she said, struggling for patience.

Sometimes talking to him resembled talking to a mountain—both were large, obdurate, and immovable—but she couldn't just give in and let him run roughshod over her. It would mean giving up all the progress she'd worked for over the last few days.

"First of all, it's the middle of the day, and we'll be meeting somewhere in the city, which means there is absolutely no chance that there won't be other people around." She ticked off points on the fingers of her free hand. "Second, Mac will be there as a neutral third party. Or fourth, or seventh, for that matter. I sincerely doubt the Others would be stupid enough to try to harm either of us in the presence of a witness. And third, I will be standing right by your side. If you're there to protect me, I can't possibly be in any danger."

"Your faith in me is flattering, but I'm one man against three, if Vidâme, Winters, and De Santos all show up," he said tightly. "The odds aren't particularly in my favor."

"One against two. Remember, I saw how De Santos looked last night. Even if he's recovered enough to come to this meeting, there's no way he's up to fighting weight."

"Still," Nicolas growled.

Saskia sighed. "Nicolas, I understand your concern; really I do. I appreciate that you feel protective of me and want to keep me out of harm's way, but you can't tuck me away in the closet whenever you leave for fear of my getting hurt. A) it would drive me insane and make me hate you, and B) . . . I'm a big girl. I have fangs and claws of my own. I can take care of myself."

"But you shouldn't have to."

"And you shouldn't have to work so hard to clear your name when anyone who knows you knows that you would never do something so despicable as to attack an enemy from behind. I don't think 'shouldn't' means a whole lot right now."

"It means something to me."

"I know." She lifted his hand to his lips and pressed a kiss against his palm. "And this means something to me, being able to stand by your side when you're facing an unpleasant situation. I'm your mate, Nicolas. That is where I'm supposed to be. Besides, I have a third point you haven't let me get to yet."

"Oh?"

"Yes. Third, if what Mac has for us to see is really as important as he seems to think it is, you should have as many eyes looking at it as possible. This could be a key to this whole big mess, but what if you miss something? What if there's some angle of the evidence you just don't catch? Two heads are better than one, right?"

She could see he wanted to protest and found herself holding her breath. This was important to her, for more than one reason. Not only did she need Nicolas to become accustomed to having her at his side as his mate and his built-in support system, he also needed to accept that she had more to offer their relationship than just her body. She had been raised to understand all the nuances of Tiguri politics, to observe people and behavior, to perceive motives, and to uncover clues hidden in small details of word, action, or setting. She could really help him in this. He needed to know that, and she needed to know that he knew.

He stared down at her for several minutes, not blinking, just watching her with troubled jade eyes. "You're not going to budge on this, are you?"

She shook her head. "It's your turn to compromise."

"How did I know you were going to say that?"

Less than a week after his engagement and Nic barely recognized himself, he thought in disgust. What had happened to the man with the well-ordered life? The man who ran his family's company with a steady hand and his streak with a powerful paw?

Right. The woman sitting next to him had happened.

Nic steered the car through city traffic, his eyes on the road and his gaze turned inward. What on earth had made him think that Saskia would make a quiet, comfortable mate? Clearly, he'd been under some sort of delusion. Maybe it was those distracting blue eyes, or the classic purity of her features. Hell, maybe it was the fact that they hadn't exchanged more than a couple of dozen words with each other before binding themselves together. Whatever the explanation, Nic had found himself decidedly *un*-comfortable for most of the last five days.

What really disturbed him, though, was that he could no longer imagine his life without the sweet, stubborn tigress by his side. That knowledge threatened to cut him off at the knees.

Saskia had been right in all the points she had made during her argument to come along—two heads were better than one, especially when he had no doubt that the second head belonged to someone firmly on his side. His mate looked so sweet and feminine and fragile that at times he forgot how intelligent she was, how observant and well-informed. Not to mention how stubborn. He could well imagine that she might see something that he overlooked, or that she might be able to lend a new interpretation to evidence that he hadn't thought of. That knowledge filled him with pride, even as he struggled with the desire to wrap her up in cotton batting and store her someplace safe where she'd never be in a moment's danger. Already, she had become too important to him to lose. He hadn't planned for this.

"Are you sure we're headed to the right place?" Saskia asked, gazing out the window at a graffiti-painted storefront, the windows obliterated and the space clearly abandoned. "This neighborhood is looking a little . . . dodgy."

If by "dodgy" she meant "like a war zone."

Nic glanced at the street signs and pressed his lips together. "This is the right place. The address Mac gave us should be coming up on the left."

Nic now regretted not using a driver to ferry them to the location. When they had left the apartment, he'd just wanted as few people involved in this situation as he could manage, since it felt as if that decision had already been taken out of his hands; but seeing their destination, he decided it couldn't have hurt to have brought another male along to keep an eye on Saskia. Or rather, on anyone who dared lay an eye on Saskia.

Pulling the car to a stop, Nic looked around, then eased toward the curb, almost sorry to see a parking space magically waiting for them. He would have preferred the excuse not to stay in this neighborhood, let alone to leave the sleek Mercedes here unattended.

"Well, I'll give Mac one thing," Saskia said, blowing out a long breath. "He certainly knows how to keep things interesting."

"In the Chinese sense of the word."

Nic thought they might be in for a very interesting time indeed.

"Stay close to me," he ordered as he reached for the door latch. "Not only do I not like you being here; now I don't like you being *here*. You get more than eighteen inches away from me and it's going to make me cranky. Okay?"

"Okay."

Her immediate agreement told Nic that his mate didn't feel any better about this outing than he did. If he hadn't already spotted Mac waiting for them near the mouth of an alley, Nic would have turned the car around and headed back home. Where he could keep his tigress safe.

Saskia actually reached out and took his hand as they moved down the sidewalk toward the private investigator. Luckily, none of the three had dressed up for the meeting, but the very fact that they all wore clean, neat, obviously well-made clothing was enough to have them standing out like sore thumbs in the poverty-ravaged area. Nic felt a small measure of reassurance in seeing that Mac, though positioned casually leaning on the wall of the closest building, watched their surroundings with wary eyes, clearly alert to any danger.

At least he wasn't a complete idiot.

"Jesus, Callahan, what the hell are we doing here?" Nic demanded, halting in front of the other man. "Is there a reason we had to have this meeting in the fifth circle of hell?"

Mac pushed away from his wall and extended his hand. "Unfortunately, there is. I'm glad you managed to find the place." He looked around him and grimaced. "It's not exactly on any of the local tourism maps."

"That's because the only map it belongs on is the kind that's color coded according to the homicide statistics." Nic set his jaw and shifted closer to his mate. "I don't like being here, and I really don't like Sass being here, so let's make this quick, shall we?"

"As soon as the others get here, we'll get started."

Saskia stepped in before he could blast that idea out of the water. "Can you at least tell us why we're here while we're waiting?"

"Because this is where Rafe nearly got himself torn to pieces last night."

Nic jerked back at that revelation. "Here? Christ, why would De Santos be wandering around this shithole after dark? Is that what he does in his spare time? Go slumming?"

"As a matter of fact, I was looking for information to help your ungrateful ass," a voice growled behind them.

Nic half-turned to see two of his least favorite people in the world stroll toward them. Well, Graham Winters strolled. Rafe De Santos barely managed a limping echo of his normal graceful glide.

Sympathy drew a reflexive wince from Nic. Sass had described the Felix's injuries to him, but she hadn't gotten a good look before the Others had whisked De Santos upstairs. If this was how he appeared the next day, even with the advantages of a shifter's healing abilities, Nic was amazed the jaguar was still breathing.

Curiously, even given De Santos's obvious, if temporary, handicaps, not a single one of the watchful, greedy presences scattered here and there along the street made any move to approach the men to demand money or valuables, or just to have the satisfaction of making someone else's day just a little more miserable. Or maybe it wasn't curious. Any creature blessed with the slightest hint of intelligence or perception would be able to recognize the predator in the two men. It covered them like a shadow, a dark air of danger even a human would have a hard time ignoring.

"Where's Dmitri?" Mac asked quickly. "I know it's daylight, but he said he'd figure out a way to make it."

"He's here," Graham said. "We recognized the address, so Rafe told him exactly where the attack happened. He'll meet us there. He's just taking the darker way around."

"Fair enough. In that case, let's go."

They followed the changeling into the alley. Nic had to concentrate hard to block out the fetid odors of urine, garbage, vomit, and traces of old blood, not to mention the underlying stink of poverty and despair. Out of the corner of his eye he saw his mate swallow hard, and he squeezed her hand reassuringly.

Three-quarters of the way down the dark, dead-end space, Mac headed for a doorway only half-covered by a broken green door. The cheap plywood bled through the thin layer of colored stain, and whoever had reinforced the flimsy barrier with a z-shaped configuration of two-by-fours nailed over it hadn't even bothered to try staining those. They had weathered to a sick, silvery gray color, except where rain and other unidentifiable liquids had caused the green color to bleed into the porous wood.

Bolted to the brick, a metal latch flapped uselessly. The other half that secured on to the door itself was missing, perhaps still attached to the equally missing section of plywood from the door's center edge. The damage had happened so long ago that the ragged, splintered edges of the hole had also bleached gray and sickly.

Graham made a noise of disgust as Mac pushed the door open on a pitch-black space inside the brick shell. "Christ, Rafe. You went in here willingly? What the hell were you thinking?"

De Santos snarled but didn't bother to answer.

Nic tugged Saskia close to his side, keeping her shielded behind his big body as he followed Mac through the doorway. His spine itched to have the two Others he didn't entirely trust at his back, but he calculated them to be less dangerous to his mate than whatever could potentially be waiting inside the dark building.

Eyes designed to hunt in darkness quickly adjusted themselves to the interior space. Only two small, high windows on the near wall existed to let in any light, since this room had been created from the interior of the building. Those openings had been painted over, so only a few feeble rays managed to sneak their way into the room, doing little to provide illumination. Not that there was much to see.

Four metal pillars appeared to be the only erect structures in the room, and probably the only things that managed to keep the ceiling of the dilapidated building from collapsing on their heads. Graffiti of the least original kind decorated the walls, spray-painted suggestions of anatomically impossible acts and faithless tributes to a darker power the artist clearly didn't understand. Surprisingly little trash covered the floors—a few empty bottles and dented cans, some loose newspapers and a couple of discarded condoms, though how anyone could bring themselves to have sex in a place like this eluded Nic. In one corner at the far side of the room, a pile of cloth bunched up, probably contributing to the smell of the place. That odor closely resembled the one in the alley outside, with the prominent addition of dust and that musty smell of some place people used to live but had long ago deserted.

"A charming little spot," a new voice commented dryly. Looking up from his survey of the room, Nic got his first look at Dmitri Vidâme, vampire. The slight accent in his words allowed for no question about his identity.

Tall, powerfully built, and hard as stone, the vampire wore an exquisitely tailored suit, minus the tie, and carried an expensive pair of sunglasses in one lean, long-fingered hand. A watch that likely cost

more than the average inhabitant of this neighborhood made in a year clasped one thick wrist, and a
heavy platinum band encircled his left ring finger. Yet
even with all that temptation, Nic doubted this man
had faced any trouble on the street, either. Again, the
man looked like a predator, all steely strength and
quick reflexes, ruthless purpose and finely honed instinct.

In other circumstances, Nic realized with surprise,
all of these men were ones with whom he could see
himself forming friendships. They were men like
him. He understood them. Unfortunately, at the moment, they all thought of him as a brutal coward.

So much for the meet-and-greet portion of the
entertainment.

"Okay, so what are we looking at here?" Winters
demanded, scanning the room impatiently.

"Nothing yet. It's in through there."

Gesturing toward another door, this one on the far
side of the room, Mac led the way deeper into the
building. When the second door opened, Nic could
smell the difference instantly. The odor of blood was
fresh here, and he could smell more of it. A lot more.
He could see the others noticing it, as well, and followed his mate's wide-eyed gaze to the wall at the
front of the building.

The interior walls in this room still bore large
patches of plaster that hadn't yet flaked or been
pounded off the surfaces. The one Saskia was staring
at also bore large smears of thick, dark blood.

"Yours?" Dmitri asked quietly, arching a brow at
De Santos.

"Most of it. I like to think I got a swipe or two in."

Graham whistled. "Wow, no wonder you looked like so much ground beef when we found you. How big did you say this thing was?"

The jaguar scowled. "Big. Five or six hundred pounds, easily. In my other form, I weigh more like four, on a good day."

"Relax, Garfield. No one is questioning your manhood. Er, cathood."

"Listen, Fido—"

"Gentlemen," the vampire cut in, his voice even, if slightly amused. "Let us save the squabbles for another time. We came here so Mac could show us something important."

"Right." The changeling stepped forward to the edge of the pool of blood that had gathered on the floor beneath the other stains. "So, you know that Nic here hired me to look into the original attack on Rafe. Nic knew that since he hadn't done it, there was someone else out there with a grudge against Rafe, but he was afraid that the Council wouldn't look very hard at the other possibilities because of the general bad blood between the Tiguri and other shifters."

Rafe stiffened and glared at Nic. "I can assure you, Preda, that I have no interest in heaping blame on an innocent man. If you were not responsible—"

"I wasn't."

"He wasn't," Saskia echoed, stepping forward and gripping his hand tightly. The glare she shot at De Santos dripped with venom.

"Gentlemen," Vidâme said again, his voice less

amused this time. "And lady. Please, let Mac continue."

The changeling hurried to do so. "Anyway, justified or not, Nic felt that the best way to clear his name would be to find who was responsible for the attack and bring that person to justice. I thought the logical place would be to start digging into who might have some sort of grudge against Rafe."

Graham snorted. "Christ, don't you want to have time for, you know, breathing?"

Mac's mouth quirked. "Yeah, I might have been a little naive there. Who would have thought a guy known for his diplomatic skills and his way with the ladies would have so many enemies."

Rafe shrugged. "As head of the Council, I am occasionally forced to make some unpopular decisions. It comes with the territory."

"Hm, seems like an awful lot of territory to me, but whatever you say, pal. Anyway, when I realized that would be a dead end unless I hired like a thousand assistants and set aside all my other cases for the rest of my life . . ."

Rafe glared, but Mac just grinned.

". . . I decided to take another tactic. I decided to treat it like a mugging and handle it the way the police would. I canvassed the scene of the crime and tried to dig up some witnesses."

"Were there any?" The Felix looked doubtful.

"Just one. A human. Which, of course, made the whole thing that much more difficult."

Nic understood what Mac meant. One of the reasons that the Others had managed to keep their existence a secret from humans for the last millennium or two had been by hiding in plain sight and taking advantage of a happy little talent of the human brain. Humans, as it turned out, had a very convenient inability to see things that did not fit in with their beliefs about the universe. For instance, if a human didn't believe in ghosts, the chances were, he or she would never see one. Likewise, if a human didn't believe in werewolves or Feline shifters, he wouldn't see one of those, either. This occasionally—and humorously—resulted in human witnesses to Other events reporting things like, "This clown—really, this guy in clown makeup, red nose, painted-on red smile, the works—he was trying to give the guy mouth-to-mouth, but it must not have worked. The paramedics said the guy was dead when they got there. But the guy in the clown suit should get a medal." In reality, the speaker had just seen a rogue vampire, his face stained with the blood of his victim, leave the dead human in an alley and go on his way. But since vampires didn't exist, the human's mind had made up a more "plausible" explanation for what the eyes had observed.

"I don't see how that does us any good," Graham said with a snort. "You can't believe anything a human says about seeing one of us. According to them, the population of werewolves in the city is accounted for by an exceptionally high concentration of Labradors of an Unusual Size."

"You can't take them at face value," Mac agreed,

"but that doesn't mean they can't be useful. The human I talked to remembered seeing someone following Rafe as he left the hotel on Friday night."

"And that helps how?"

"It helps us because the witness remembered noticing the tail because she thought it was interesting that the person following Rafe seemed significantly smaller than him. In fact, the witness thought it might even have been a woman."

Ten

Saskia felt the moment when every eye in the room turned on her. She didn't see it, though, because the second it happened Nicolas grabbed her arms and shifted her to place his body between her and the other four males.

"Forget it," he roared, the fierce sound booming off the walls around them. "She is not involved in this, and I will gut the first one of you to point a finger at her."

She could see by their expressions that not a single one of the others doubted him. Considering the tone of his voice, she didn't, either.

"Calm down," Dmitri said, slowly raising his hands and holding them palms out in a gesture of peaceful intentions. "No one has accused anyone of anything."

"Is that right?" Nicolas sneered, revealing lengthening fangs. "I have to tell you, what you all consider 'not accusing' someone feels a lot like it to the person in question, and I say that from personal experience."

"No one has been accused," the vampire repeated. "Mac has not even demonstrated to us that a Tiguri is definitely to blame."

"Actually, that's why I asked you all to meet me here," Mac said, shifting uncomfortably. He reached into his pocket for a pair of tweezers and plucked something up off the floor. "I was going to get to this part in a little bit, but when I first came here this morning I found samples of hair mixed in with the blood. I took some of it to a contact of mine at the zoo and asked him to identify it for me. He found a mix of black, gold, and orange hairs. The gold and some of the black came from a jaguar—that's Rafe—but the rest of the black and all of the orange, that's tiger fur."

Saskia felt her mate's arm snug around her waist and knew she had about five seconds before he swept her up bodily and carried her out of the building and away from her accusers. Only, she knew the reaction was totally unnecessary.

"Wait," she said, raising her voice to be sure Nicolas heard her over his own snarling and what she figured had to be the blinding rage cluttering up his head. "If that's true, about the fur, I can prove in the next thirty seconds that I could not have been the Tiguri who attacked Mr. De Santos."

The Others looked at her with interest. Her mate's arm tightened around her, but he let her keep her feet on the floor. She considered that a win.

"You are Tiguri, right?" Mac asked. "How can you eliminate yourself as a suspect here and now?"

"She is *not* a suspect," Nic snarled.

She laid her hand on the arm around her waist and patted reassuringly. "It's okay. Really. Just let me do this so we can eliminate the slightest doubt and move on."

Before her mate could protest, Saskia shifted her weight away from him and slipped out from under his arm. Taking two small steps away, she looked straight at the private investigator and calmly slipped her skin.

It took no time at all for her tigress to break free. The excitement of being newly mated and the surging hormones of her first heat had kept the beast close to the surface for days now. A couple of blinks, a couple of careful stretches, one quick shift of power and Saskia the woman had disappeared. In her place crouched Saskia the tigress.

The men around her all gasped, including her mate.

As predicted, her tiger form outweighed Rafe the jaguar's by at least a hundred pounds, maybe a little more, but not an ounce of fat marred the sleek, muscular lines of her body. Her wide blue eyes had taken on an exotic slant and stared out from a feline face of exceptional beauty. A delicate fringe of a mane framed her features, softening the rounded tips of her ears with a creamy fuzz. The most striking feature she possessed, however, was her unusual striped coat.

"I've never seen anything like that," Mac said, fascination thick in his tone. "I didn't even know it was possible."

"It's very unusual," she heard her mate explain, pride and awe filling his voice. "I've seen photos before, but never the real thing. It's called golden tabby, though some still refer to it as the strawberry tiger."

Gracefully Saskia the tigress stretched and stood,

her tail swinging gently behind her. She padded across the dusty cement floor to twine around her mate's legs, rubbing against him with rough affection. In this form, Saskia's thoughts weren't quite as clear, but her instincts cried out sharply. Instinct told her she wanted to touch this man, wanted to stay close to him and draw in his scent, so that's what she did. She felt his hand drop to her head, and she butted against it until he dug his fingers into her fur and scratched at the base of her ears, eliciting a rumbling purr.

In her tiger form, Saskia possessed none of the black fur of an average striped tiger and had paler fur all around. Her belly, neck, paws, and lower legs sported fur the color of rich cream, with pale blond markings. As the fur grew up her sides and head and over her back, it darkened into a color remarkably similar to her human hair, a muted reddish gold often referred to as strawberry blonde. Instead of the traditional markings, her stripes appeared as slashes of darker red against the pale background. The effect was unusual and breathtaking and put paid to any idea that Saskia could have been involved in Rafe's attack.

"Are you satisfied?" Nic asked, and his voice drifted down to her full of challenge and possessiveness. His fingers in her fur also spoke of ownership, and Saskia the tigress relished the show of power and jealousy. She sat on her haunches at his feet and wrapped her tail around his ankles to show that she owned him as well.

"I think it's clear that Saskia could not have been

involved in the attack," Dmitri said, carefully polite. "Her demonstration of the reasons was, er, most effective."

"But it doesn't rule out the other Tiguri," Graham pointed out, and Saskia could feel her mate stiffen with anger and pride. "In fact, it looks like it rules the other Tiguri in."

"Is there any way your contact can test the hair?" Rafe asked Mac, finally tearing his gaze from the beautiful tigress in the room and earning a hostile glare from her mate. "Extract DNA so we can positively identify who it came from?"

"Sure, it can be done," Mac conceded, but his tone of voice made sure they knew there was a catch. "But according to him, that would take a minimum of three to four weeks."

"Unacceptable," Nic bit out. "I will not have this hanging over the heads of my people for another month."

"I think we can rule out you as well," Rafe said, eyeing Nicolas warily. "If the witness is to be believed at all, you clearly don't fit the profile. We're roughly the same size, and I can't imagine a blind idiot mistaking you for a woman."

Saskia the tigress purred her agreement.

"That still gets us nowhere. Even with Sass and me eliminated, I'm not going to agree that anyone in our families was involved, either."

"I've started looking around to see if I can find any other Tiguri who may be in the city at the moment," Mac offered, "but it's slow going. You're not the most open bunch of so-and-sos I've ever run across. Plus customs doesn't exactly have a 'check your species' box on the entry forms."

"Then all of this has been an exercise in futility." Nic waved his hand around the abandoned building in disgust. Saskia pressed against his leg, offering the comfort of her presence.

"Not futility." Dmitri shook his head and watched them with an expression of careful consideration. "We have confirmed that there is a Tiguri connection to the events, and that gives us a starting point to dig deeper."

Graham rolled his eyes. "Come on. We all knew the tigers were involved. I don't see how any of this has helped, except to rule out two of them."

Saskia narrowed her eyes at the Lupine and crouched low, hissing in displeasure.

"Careful, friend," the vampire warned. "Your prejudice is going to get you into trouble one of these days. Besides, I don't agree that we've learned nothing new. Before we had only suspicions and bad blood. Now we have facts. First, a Tiguri was involved; and second, we should be looking at a smaller man or perhaps even a woman. That is more than we knew a few hours ago."

"It's still not enough. Especially not for me," Rafe said. "After all, I'm the one who's been attacked twice in the past week. I'd prefer not to prove the old adage that trouble comes in threes."

"Actually, if you'd all let me finish a thought, I'd share the rest of my news with you." Mac stood and dusted his hands off on his jeans.

Graham shot him a bad-tempered look. "If you

have more to say, say it. We're all waiting to be astounded by your brilliance."

"Sadly, honesty forces me to admit it's only partly my brilliance. The rest came from the reporter we all know and love."

Dmitri groaned. "Corinne? How is Corinne involved in this?"

"She's not really involved; she just happens to have taken a shine to Saskia." Mac nodded to where Saskia sat on her haunches at Nic's feet and frowned. "You know, she's made her point. She can turn back into a person now. That way, she'll be able to contribute to the discussion."

Saskia chuffed in amusement and felt her mate's fingers tighten in her fur.

"No. She can't."

"But—"

"Do not push him, my friend," Rafe said, his eyes glinting with amusement. "While I, too, would like nothing more than to look on the beautiful Saskia's human form again, her mate would prefer to deny us the sight. Apparently, tigers are selfish creatures."

Graham rolled his eyes. "Don't you push, either, Rafe. She can't turn back to her human form, Mac. Are you forgetting she no longer has any clothes? The power of her shift would have incinerated them. You need to spend more time around shifters if you're forgetting details like that."

Mac cleared his throat. "Right. Sorry."

Nic accepted the apology with a baring of his teeth.

"Anyway, like I was saying, I got the idea from

Corinne," the investigator continued, studiously looking away from the tigress and her mate. "She came over to pick up Danice the other day for some girl thing or another, and she mentioned that Saskia had had an interesting idea. It seems that when she thought about the fact that whoever was behind the attacks had to have a grudge against Rafe, she wondered if they were using the Council's prejudice against the Tiguri as a kind of smoke screen. By striking now, when the Tiguri are new in town and there's already a lot of suspicion aimed against them, the real culprit could deflect everyone's attention away from his actual motives and watch while we in the Other community all turned against the Tiguri."

The men in the room thought about that for a long moment. Saskia could practically feel the wheels of her mate's mind turning.

"Okay, I see a certain logic in that," Graham said, breaking the silence, "but I don't see where that gets us. We already knew Rafe was the target, and so many of the Others distrust the Tiguri that saying the attacker is using that for his own ends doesn't really narrow it down much."

"But that's where my brilliance took over," Mac said, grinning. "That was when it occurred to me. Saskia was on the right track, but she didn't take the thought far enough. The key to the whole mess isn't actually Rafe; it's the Council."

Dmitri's eye narrowed. "Clarify, please. How did you come to make that leap?"

"I went over the details of the first attack," Mac explained. "On Friday night, Rafe wasn't actually hurt. Oh, maybe a little bruised, but the attacker didn't get much on him; he couldn't. The attacker followed Rafe from the hotel, yes, but if he really wanted to kill, he would have waited to strike until Rafe reached some place a lot less crowded. Unless, of course, the attacker wanted the attack to be witnessed."

"You're saying this tiger is a nutcase who wants to get caught?"

Mac shook his head at Graham. "No, I'm saying he wanted to be *witnessed*. He made sure he had enough cover so no one could really describe what they'd seen, but he clearly wanted people to know about the attack right away. He wanted that news to get out."

"Why?"

"To get the Council involved."

"What purpose does that serve?" Rafe demanded. "And why the elaborate ruse? The Council gets involved with any crimes committed by an Other. Of course we would look into an attack, witnesses or not."

"But the attacker didn't just want the Council to be aware and watchful; he wanted them stirred up and crying for blood. That, I think, is why Rafe became the target. No better way to piss off an organization than to attack the head of it, especially at a time when they're already stirred up over something else."

"The Tiguri," Dmitri mused thoughtfully. "The Council had already begun to discuss the implications of having tigers move into the city. The membership was split. Several Council members expressed an unwillingness to let go of old prejudices, but there were a few of us who preferred to judge the situation on its merits, and the merits of those involved, rather than on the basis of old and potentially inaccurate beliefs. The attack just drove a deeper wedge between the sides. Those who had already denounced the Tiguri began to demand their blood."

"Well, then it makes no sense for a Tiguri to be behind the attack." Graham threw up his hands in exasperation. "Not even a Feline species could be dumb enough not to realize that if the Council is all ready to blame you for the slightest wrongdoing, then actually doing something wrong is only going to make things worse. They'll watch more closely, and come down harder in the end. You'd practically be inviting the Council to persecute you."

"True," Dmitri said. "In fact, one could say you would have turned yourself into a martyr."

"And there's nothing a group likes better than to rally around its martyrs," Rafe said, his expression grim.

Saskia tried to wrap her Feline brain around the human logic and shook it in confusion. She was missing something, but she felt the tension race through her mate and knew he had followed the logic on to the next step.

"If a Tiguri is truly behind this, then he is not motivated by a simple desire to kill De Santos." Nic sounded so angry and shaken that Saskia stood and wove herself around his legs making comforting chuffing noises. "He is trying to start a war between the Tiguri and the Council of Others."

"And the second attack on Rafe was truly the first missile strike," Dmitri agreed. "Take out the head of the Council before the original Tiguri suspect has been cleared and the Council will no longer care about gathering evidence. They would strike back immediately to punish Nic as the suspected killer."

Rafe nodded. "And by the time they realized their mistake, it would be too late. The war would have already begun and Nic would truly be a Tiguri martyr. All the tiger shifters in the world would rally behind his name."

"At the very least, they would be able to bring the Council down." Mac finished the chain of logic with grim certainty. "Even non-Tiguri would have trouble stomaching the council's having blamed an innocent man. The Council would lose all support and tumble like a house of cards."

Graham blew out a breath, shaking his head in disbelief. "That's positively *diabolical*. Who the hell has a mind that works like that? I could barely follow along with it, let alone dream it up. Whoever hatched that plan is the definition of an evil genius. So how are we supposed to find him?"

Dmitri's mouth curved in a smile that made Saskia's whiskers twitch. "I believe I may have an idea."

They decided to discuss the plan somewhere that didn't smell quite so foul or suffer from quite the same lack of creature comforts. Nic's resistance was quickly overruled, and all six of them made their way toward the Vircolac club with only minor grumbles.

In the end, it was decided the club might be a bit too public, so they detoured next door, where they found Winters's mate waiting along with another woman Nic hadn't met.

Saskia entered first, padding into the foyer on all fours to two admiring feminine gasps.

"Sass, you're positively gorgeous!" Missy Winters cried as she waddled her very pregnant form forward. "Oh, I've never seen a coat like that. It's amazing."

Saskia the tigress preened and lifted a paw to groom her face.

"She needs clothes," Nicolas said. "I hate to impose, but is there any way—"

"Oh, don't be silly," the Luna dismissed easily. "We'll fix her right up. I always keep extra clothes on hand in different sizes for emergencies. We'll find something. Come on."

Nic watched uneasily as his mate followed the Lupine's female up the stairs and out of his sight. The other woman stayed behind and offered him a smile.

"Don't worry. She'll be fine. Missy's been mothering people since way before she got pregnant. She'll take good care of your mate." She held out a pale, slender hand. "I recognized you from the papers, Mr. Preda. I'm Regina Vidâme."

Nic grasped her fingers, feeling the coolness of her skin, and noticed her lack of scent. She was a vampire, and her introduction named her as Dmitri's wife. She was a little thing, especially in comparison to her husband, with lush curves and deeply auburn hair worn long and waving down her back. Her expression appeared sweetly open, and she spoke of the Alpha's mate with genuine affection.

"A pleasure to meet you," Nic murmured, but he couldn't keep his gaze from straying back to the stairs.

Regina laughed. "Ah, to be newly mated again."

Dmitri wrapped a strong arm around her waist and tugged her firmly against his side. He grinned down at her wickedly. "Do you fear the spark is gone from our love, *dushka*? Perhaps I must spend more time demonstrating my passion for you."

He bent to her lips, but she slapped her hand against his chest to hold him away playfully. "Thanks, but I like being able to walk, sweetheart. You're doing just fine as it is."

Graham Winters stepped around them and rolled his eyes. "Ignore them. They're always like that. It's diabetes on the hoof. Let's all sit down so we can hammer this thing out."

The werewolf led the way into a comfortable living room with a huge fireplace and plenty of seating. Logs already crackled in the hearth, but he took up a poker and jabbed at them before settling his shoulder against the mantel and waving everyone into seats. Nic sank into one of two oversize armchairs facing the fire. Rafe eased himself into the other while Dmitri settled himself on the end of a sofa perpendicular to the chairs and tucked his wife firmly against his side. Another sofa sat directly opposite, completing a u shape, and Mac took the end closest to the fire.

Nic found himself glancing back toward the stairs.

Graham noticed. "I give you my word your mate will come to no harm under my roof," he said stiffly. "My Luna will care for her as if she were a member of our pack."

Nic recognized the gesture. Lupine law decreed that an Alpha was responsible for the welfare of every member of his pack. By making his statement, Winters had taken a vow to keep Saskia safe. But that didn't mean Nic had to like him.

Nic inclined his head stiffly. "Thank you."

Mac snorted. "And here I thought the cold war was over." Wolf and tiger both turned narrowed eyes on him. He threw up his hands and laughed. "Sorry. Sheesh."

This time Graham glanced toward the stairs and frowned when no women appeared on them. He looked back at his guests and seemed to remember himself. "Ah, can I offer anyone a drink while we wait? *Bratok?* A glass of wine?"

"I would not say no." Dmitri nodded.

Regina smiled. "I'll just have a sip of his."

"Nothing for me," Mac said.

"Whiskey." Rafe shifted in his chair and winced. "Neat. Please."

Nic nodded. "I'll have the same." It would give him something to do with his hands, and frankly, he deserved the treat just now.

By the time the Lupine had poured and distributed, the soft sound of footsteps whispered on the stairs. Nic turned to see his mate and the Luna wolf descending to join them. Heavily pregnant and apparently human, Missy Winters made the bulk of the noise, his mate gliding along barefoot wearing a pair of black athletic pants with white stripes on the outsides of the legs and a long-sleeved red T-shirt that proclaimed: "Namaste, mofo."

Saskia tugged at it self-consciously as she halted beside his chair. "Missy said the people who donate the extra clothes tend to do it with a sense of humor."

His mouth tipped upward. "I can see that."

She took the hand he extended and let him tug her down and settle her in his lap. There was plenty of room in the chair, and his mate didn't take up much space. In fact, she fit perfectly tucked under his chin against his heart.

Graham had hurried to his wife and guided her to the sofa where Dmitri and Regina sat, lowering her carefully to the opposite corner and positioning a pillow behind her for comfort. "Okay?" he asked in a low murmur, and Nic saw Missy smile up at the gruff werewolf with obvious love.

"Perfect."

The Alpha pressed a tender kiss to her forehead before straightening and retrieving a glass of cold milk from the small refrigerator under the bar. He handed it to her, then turned to face the rest of the room. "Okay, now we can get started."

Nic heard Saskia muffle a giggle and sighed. Damn it, he'd gotten very comfortable with hating the Lupine. Why did the man have to go and ruin his image as a complete asshole by taking such tender care of his mate?

"I think Dmitri was going to tell us about his grand plan," Rafe prompted.

" 'Grand' might be a slight exaggeration. 'Workable' is perhaps more accurate."

"Then give us something to work with."

The vampire nodded. "Very well. I believe Graham earlier characterized our villain as a diabolical genius. In my experience, men of that sort always have the same weakness: arrogance. They believe they are significantly more intelligent than their opposition. Not only that, but they tend to hold the rest of the world in such low regard that hubris leads them to commit their worst mistakes. I believe that we can use this villain's ego to draw him into a trap."

"What kind of trap?"

"It will require the cooperation of several key parties. First, we'll need several members of the Council, preferably of the Inner Circle. Ones we can trust, obviously."

Rafe tilted his head back to think. "We can use Adele Berry, most likely. She's a tough old bird and she believes herself to be superior to, well, everyone, but she dislikes prejudice against minority shifters. She might agree to help out of sympathy for the Tiguri."

Dmitri nodded. "Who else?"

The Felix suggested two more names and Graham added another. Together they came up with another shifter, a brownie, and a half giant. Mac joked that the last two balanced each other out.

"So what do we need them to do?" Rafe asked.

"Before I get to that, we'll need more assistance."

The vampire turned his gaze to Nic. "I'm afraid that for this to work, you will be asked to make some difficult decisions, Nicolas Preda. The question is, how badly do you want to know the truth? And what will you do when you find it?"

Saskia followed her subdued mate into their apartment shortly after eight that night, a little more than eleven hours after they had left. It felt more like eleven years.

The short drive from the Winters house had been accomplished in silence. When Dmitri Vidâme had first proposed his plan that afternoon, Nic had had plenty to say, much of it at volume, but since they had left the house nothing. Saskia felt desperate to know what he was thinking but couldn't decide how to push without shoving too hard against what she knew had to be open wounds. She still hadn't figured it out, but she knew she couldn't wait any longer. He had to talk before he wore himself out inside.

"You asked Dmitri to give you until morning to think things through," she said softly, trailing him into their bedroom and perching on the foot of the bed while he calmly emptied his pockets at his dresser. "Do you want me to help you sort it out?"

He shook his head but didn't look at her. "What is there to sort? The plan makes sense and appears to have every chance of working. We should do it. But . . . the bastard behind all this is Tiguri. Every Tiguri in the city is a member of my family, one way or another. No matter what I decide, I will have to watch one of my own people suffer."

"You'll be suffering with them," she said. "You already are."

He said nothing.

"Nicolas." She rose and crossed to him, wrapping him up in her arms. "You have to remember that you are not responsible for this. You did not make this happen. The Tiguri who is responsible brought this on himself. Or herself. You have done nothing wrong."

He stood stiffly, not looking at her. "I didn't prevent it."

Saskia tilted her head back to look into his face. "Are you serious? You're worried that you didn't prevent it? What could you have prevented? You can't prevent insanity, or a thirst for power. You can just deal with it when you find it."

She felt him shudder, and his arms came around her. He crushed her to his chest, burying his face in her hair.

"I can't stand it," he growled, shaking. "I can't stand the thought that my own father might have done something like this, been willing to sacrifice lives just to bring down the thing he hates. Willing to sacrifice *me*, his own son. To make me some kind of sick martyr. And the idea that it might be your father is even worse. How can I let him hurt you that way?"

Saskia understood his fears, and she shared his pain. She didn't want to think her father could be responsible, either. She didn't want to think she could have lived her whole life loving a man who could think any cause would justify the chaos recent events had caused. Because of the actions of one Tiguri, the Council of Others could fall and the population of New York divide into two camps: the tiger shifters and the Others who hated them.

And that was when it hit her. She nearly staggered as the room seemed to tilt beneath her.

"Oh, my God," she breathed, then choked on the next inhalation. "Oh, my *God*!"

Nicolas gripped her arms and looked down at her in alarm. "Sass! What is it? What's the matter?"

Her knees buckled and her mate had to lift her into his arms to keep her from falling.

"Sassy, tell me what's wrong, baby. What hurts? What's happening?" He swept her to the bed and set her down, crouching beside her to place his face level with hers. His gaze drilled into her, looking for the source of her distress.

Saskia could only shake her head and struggle to breathe. She pressed her fingers between her breasts to massage the tightness in her chest, but it refused to budge.

"It's not that," she gasped. "I'm fine. I'm fine. But I finally realized what this is all about—why someone would want to bring down the Council and start a war between the Others and the Tiguri. God, it's just . . . crazy."

Nicolas gripped her hands in his and squeezed gently. "Tell me," he ordered, his voice slightly calmer and infinitely more commanding than it had been when she'd first scared him with her outburst. "Tell me what's going on."

"It *is* the Tiguri. I mean, it is *all* about the Tiguri."

She met his gaze, sure hers was stormy with the turbulent mix of emotions roiling inside her. She felt anger and shock and grief and incredulity and a sick sort of understanding. And overlaying it all was the knowledge that she was about to break her mate's heart, just as her own had broken when she had realized the truth.

"Explain it to me," he urged. "Tell me what you know, little tigress."

"Nic, do you remember the conversation I had with my father yesterday? The one that upset me so badly?"

He nodded impatiently. "Of course, but what does that have to do wit—"

"Think," she urged. "My father was so anxious to know if I was pregnant because he and Stefan needed to unite our streaks behind a leader all of the old families could follow. Our parents believe that unless our mating is proven successful and you step forward as leader of the old families, the new guard is going to rebel and go their own way with disastrous results for our people. What better way to unite the old families, to unite *all* the Tiguri, than to start a war that pits us against the world of Others? Rafe was right when he said every tiger shifter on the planet would unite to fight a war they believed was about the future of our species."

She saw her mate go pale and hated every word she knew had to come out of her mouth now. Hated them on his behalf and on hers.

"Nicolas, it's not your father, and it's not my father. It's *both* of our fathers working together, with every one of the other old families probably helping them out."

Saskia knew her mate had to feel like a knife had just been plunged into his chest, because she felt the same. She ached with the pain of betrayal, but she knew that only the two of them had a chance of stopping this mad plan.

Nicolas was shaking his head. "Sassy, that's just . . . I mean . . . that's—"

"It's crazy, I know, but it makes sense. It makes so much sense. The plan was too elaborate to just be about the Council, especially when our people have never cared about the Council of Others. This is about what the Tiguri consider important, and that's tradition. The traditions of the old families."

"But my father knows I have no desire to unite the Tiguri. I don't want to lead an entire people. I have enough trouble leading my streak and my mate."

She hugged him. "I think he knows that, but he doesn't want to believe it. I think he was hoping that being placed under a cloud of suspicion by the Council and having to deal with all the questions and insinuations would make you angry enough that when his plan reached the point of Rafe's murder and the Council declaring war on the Tiguri you would give in and take charge out of a sense of righteous fury. And if you didn't . . ."

Saskia couldn't bring herself to say it, but she didn't have to. He said it for her.

"If I didn't, then he had a backup plan. Watch me die, and then use my memory like a bloody banner of the Holy Cross to lead our people to victory."

His bitterness carved little slices in her heart. She didn't know what to say. She could tell him she understood, but the words felt hollow. She could say that her own father was part of the plan and that she felt dirtied and tainted by the association, but this moment wasn't about her. She could validate his feelings by telling him his pain, and anger, and sense of betrayal were completely justified and completely natural, but that wouldn't change anything.

Instead, she just drew him to her and cradled his head to her chest. All she knew to do was hold him, so that was what she did.

He leaned into her for a few minutes, his breathing ragged. No tears dripped from his eyes, but she could feel the way he fought for control, fought to make sense of a world that had fundamentally shifted. It seemed to take hours for the trembling to ease.

When it did, he stood, drawing Saskia up with him and keeping her cradled against him. He reached for the phone on the bedside table and punched in a number.

"Hello?" she heard on the other end of the line.

"It's Nic," he said. "Let's get this thing rolling."

Eleven

Saskia had never expected to set foot in the chambers of the Council of Others. Why would she? No Tiguri sat on the Council, and none of her people had ever accepted the authority of the European Council, let alone their American counterparts. Of course, she also had never expected that she would end up mated and living in New York, or that her father would participate in a malevolent plot for power.

It just went to show that life had a way of taking a person along for the ride.

The chambers themselves turned out to be a revelation. They appeared to have been designed and decorated by whoever had built the stage sets for the 1931 version of *Dracula*, the one with Bela Lugosi and the "children of the night." The walls looked like the interior of a medieval castle, specifically the dungeon, all rough-hewn stone with not a window to be found. Since the Council met in the basement of the Vircolac club, that wasn't surprising, but the fact that the rooms and passages were lit with torches rather than electric lights was. A fire roared in a huge hearth, driving away the damp chill that seemed to

seep through the stones and further illuminating the
faces of the figures gathered for Dmitri's plan.

The vampire had decreed that they would use the
Inner Circle's meeting chamber for that ring of veri-
similitude. The large room with its heavy carved
door and high vaulted ceiling opened just a few
doors down from the main Council chamber but occupied less than half of the space.

About twenty feet by thirty feet square, the room
contained little in the way of furniture. At one end
of the room, a huge antique sideboard squatted
against the wall, its surface elaborately carved with
hunting scenes that Saskia's undergraduate studies
dated to the sixteenth century. Only instead of the
usual hounds and men on horseback chasing a stag
or a wolf, in these scenes the wolves chased the rid-
ers and brought them to a bloody end on the face of
the right-hand cabinet door. As decorative elements
went, that one made a statement.

In the center of the room, two enormous rectangu-
lar tables had been pushed together to create a roughly
square seating area surrounded by thirteen wooden
carvers. Each of the huge chairs showcased a tall
back topped with fancy finials and skilled carvings
along the mahogany frames. The seats and backs had
been covered with velvet upholstery the color of fresh
blood. The decorator had been either a gothic mad-
man or an Other with a wicked sense of humor.

Someone had pulled in a hard wooden bench
from somewhere and shoved it into the shadows to
the left of the hearth, but even that appeared to have
been made well before the industrial revolution and

kept lovingly polished until the wood nearly glowed in the firelight. Her mate had instructed her to sit on it until the show began, but she found herself wishing for a sketch pad so she could capture its rough lines and angular beauty. Not that she would have the time.

The supporting cast in Dmitri's carefully plotted drama had already arrived and begun to take their places at the center table. Not all of the seats would be filled, since not all of the members of the Inner Circle had been trusted to participate in this well-laid trap, but enough Others had been included to lend an official and serious air to the room.

Saskia recognized no one, but she listened carefully to any greetings and idle chatter and used her training, research, and excellent memory to make the connections.

Adele Berry was the first Circle member she identified and the only one to surprise her. With a reputation that preceded her, the grand dame of New York's Other society turned out to be much smaller than Saskia had expected. The woman made up for it, though, in sheer presence. She wore her gray hair sleeked back in a bun, a la Audrey Hepburn, and made no effort to disguise the lines and wrinkles carving her face; in fact, she wore them like medals of valor. She was dressed elegantly, in the kind of clothing Saskia knew cost the earth but would last until the end of it. She clutched a silver-topped cane in her frail, soft hands, but her eyes sparked with energy and cunning. Saskia had a feeling she did not want to be on the woman's bad side.

Saskia recognized the brownie and the half giant immediately. With the soil-colored skin and diminutive size of the first and the impressive height and wide shoulders of the second, they didn't require much guesswork. The shifter she identified by process of elimination. The roomful of people made picking up the man's scent difficult, but Saskia guessed based on appearance and demeanor that he might belong to one of the small species—ferret, maybe, or rat.

With Dmitri and Graham rounding out their numbers, six of the members of the Inner Circle had agreed to assist with the plan. Rafe, of course, was present as well, but concealed behind a service door in the corner. For the plan to work, he could not be present at the start of the meeting. Mac also remained absent, waiting patiently in the chamber next door.

Everyone was in place for a rousing drama. Now they only needed to wait for the main characters.

Dmitri had arranged for cars to pick up Stefan and the Arcoses at their homes on behalf of the Council. No one wanted to take chances on the guests of honor not showing, and Rafe had argued that since the Council had sent an escort for Stefan the last time, the move would not appear out of the ordinary. According to the slim watch clasped around Saskia's wrist, they should arrive any minute.

The chamber grew quiet and thick with anticipation. The crackle of burning logs and occasional low murmurs from one of the Council members sounded almost muffled by the atmosphere. Tension crept up Saskia's spine until she thought she would go mad.

Before a scream of frustration could build up in her throat, she picked up the sound of footsteps in the stone corridor and stood, stepping close to her mate's side. According to her role, she kept slightly behind him as if subservient, like a traditional Tiguri mate, but she needed to feel his steady presence calming and supporting her. It reminded her that he possessed the strength to get through this and so did she.

The footsteps halted outside the door before the heavy panel swung inward and three figures stepped forward. A fourth, a club employee, hung back.

"Thank you, Thomas," Dmitri said, nodding at the servant. "You can go. And please make certain we're not disturbed."

"Nicolas. I see you've been subjected to this ridiculous exercise once again," Stefan Preda said as he glanced around the room. When he caught sight of Saskia standing just behind his son, the muscles in Stefan's jaw tightened visibly. "Was it necessary to bring your fiancée? I'm certain the stress of something like this won't help her to conceive."

Saskia felt the ripple of anger move through her mate, but he betrayed not a flicker of emotion.

"She asked to accompany me, and given the nature of the questions I was asked here the last time, I thought it might speed things along to have her verify certain details of my schedule."

Stefan looked less than pleased with the answer, but he said nothing. To protest further would seem odd given Victoria Arcos also stood behind her mate.

Saskia's father looked around the chamber and frowned. "Where is De Santos? I was promised this wouldn't take up my whole evening. Don't tell me we're going to have to wait for him?"

Surreptitiously Saskia watched both her father and her soi-disant father-in-law's expressions. The confusion on Gregor's face appeared genuine, but she could read nothing behind Stefan's irritated mask.

Dmitri waved the Tiguri to five empty chairs arranged along one side of the table. "I'm afraid Rafael has met with an unfortunate accident. I will be overseeing these proceedings and serving as interim head of the Council."

Nic carefully placed Saskia in a chair at one end of the table, ensuring she sat closest to the door. He claimed the spot beside her for himself, placing his body between her and his father. Stefan automatically chose the middle seat as the position of power, and the Arcoses settled into the two remaining spaces.

"How long will this interim be?" Stefan asked, the question just bad tempered enough to seem idle, but it made Saskia's skin crawl.

"That has yet to be determined."

Gregor flexed his shoulders and stretched his arms out along the arms of his chair, a gesture Saskia recognized from childhood. He always did that when sitting down to a business meeting or for an important discussion. He called it settling into his space.

"Eh, he's a shifter, isn't he?" her father dismissed. "Whatever's got him under the weather won't take long to clear up. Me, I almost sliced my own finger off in the kitchen once. Managed to leave a thread holding it on, but that was enough for my body to set it back to rights. A week later, I could barely find the scar."

"I'm afraid Rafael was not quite so lucky," Dmitri said gravely. "There was another attack on him two nights ago. This time, he appears to have been completely unprepared. His attacker got the better of him. It was not a pretty sight."

Gregor blanched. "Are you saying De Santos was killed?"

Nicolas swore explosively and played his part to perfection. He shoved away from the table with a show of furious disgust, looking for all the world like a man convinced he was about to be blamed for a murder. He began to prowl the room restlessly, all the while making himself mobile in case something unexpected happened.

"Is that why we've been dragged here again?" Stefan demanded, scoffing. "For more ridiculous questions? Obviously, whoever failed to kill De Santos the first time went back to do a proper job, and since you know we all had alibis for the night of the first attack, it makes absolutely no sense that you would think we were behind the second one. You people wouldn't know how to investigate a disturbance if it came with a map and a crime scene analyst."

He shoved to his feet with a great show of indignation. "Let me tell you something, vampire, I've had enough of this sideshow you're running. I will not stand by and listen to you throw more accusations at my son's head, nor will I listen while you try to pin it on any other Tiguri. Every one of us here has provided you with an account of our whereabouts the night of the first attack, and I won't be insulted by being asked to provide another one for another night just because you can't figure out who's after the jungle cat. My people have faced nothing but ridicule and insults, hostility and slander, since we arrived in this city, and I—"

Dmitri cut off the tirade with nothing more than a raised eyebrow. "To be frank, Mr. Preda, it has come to our attention after further review that not all of your alibis for the night of the first attack are necessarily . . . adequate."

"What the hell is that supposed to mean?"

"It means that all of you either show gaps of time during which your whereabouts were not fully accounted for or have provided us with nothing more than the word of a family member as verification of those whereabouts. I'm afraid that means we have more questions to ask you."

With impeccable timing, a brisk knock sounded at the door. Dmitri wore a ferocious scowl as he turned to face the entry. Thomas, the servant who had escorted the Tiguri in earlier, hurried to apologize.

"I'm so sorry, sir. I know you said you didn't want to be disturbed, but—"

"You need to hear this." Mac shouldered his way past Thomas and into the chamber, a piece of folded paper held in his hand. "My contact at the DNA lab just got the results. He faxed them to me a few minutes ago. We got it."

"Got what? What are you talking about?" Stefan

blustered. "Vidâme, who the hell is this and what is he blathering about? I will not stand by for this sort of interruption, especially not when it's an insult for me to be here in the first place."

Dmitri took the folded paper from Mac but didn't glance at it. His gaze remained locked on Stefan's face. "Mr. Preda, meet McIntyre Callahan. Mac is a private investigator often retained by the Council to look into matters we deem important. He is here because of the very matter I was about to discuss with you. After the Council realized there were gaps in the alibis you all gave us for Friday night, the night of the first attack on Mr. De Santos, we asked Mac to go back to the scene of the attack to see if there might have been any evidence left at the scene that might have been overlooked earlier."

He nodded to Mac, who picked up the thread of the script.

"I interviewed a witness to the attack, but it turned out she was human and didn't get a very good look at the attack in the first place, so she wasn't much help. But she did point me to the exact spot where she witnessed the two figures struggling. I examined the area very carefully and was able to find a few strands of hair caught in the brickwork of the building outside of which Mr. De Santos was attacked. The color told me they didn't belong to him, so I took the chance and sent them to a friend of mine at a DNA lab. Like me, he's a changeling. Half sphinx. Frighteningly brilliant, and familiar with DNA processing on both human and Other samples. He was able to determine not only the species of the person who left that hair at the scene of the attack—definitely Tiguri, by the way—but also that person's sex, race, and ethnic makeup. All we need to do is provide a reference sample and he can match it to the exact individual." He paused to grin. "Science is just so *cool*."

The rush of movement came from a completely unexpected quarter. In a desperate rush, Victoria Arcos leapt across the table and snatched the paper from Dmitri's hand, flinging it into the fire. Then she stood before the hearth, panting, to watch it burn.

Nic, grim faced and silent, stalked toward her. Clearly, he hadn't expected this, either, but he kept with their plan and paced himself close in case the guilty party tried to run.

"Mother?" Saskia choked on the question.

Of all the scenarios they had discussed while planning the dummy "DNA report" they would use to flush out the attacker, none of them had considered this.

She pushed out of her chair and began to cross behind the other Tiguri to join Victoria near the fire. "That's impossible. You're not big enough or powerful enough to have attacked Rafe the second time. I saw his wounds. He was torn apart."

Victoria lifted her face, ashen pale, and her gaze darted toward her daughter. Only she didn't meet Saskia's eyes and it took the space of a heartbeat for Saskia to realize her mother wasn't looking at her but at the man in front of her.

The man responsible for the second attack.

Stefan Preda.

Saskia had just passed behind the chair of the would-be killer.

With a roar of rage, the elder Preda spun and snatched at his son's fiancée, wrapping one arm around her neck and hauling her in front of him like a shield.

"You stupid bitch!" he spat in Saskia's ear, and it took her a moment to realize he was talking to her mother. Or rather, screaming at her. "All you had to do was sit down and shut up, but could you do it? Of course not! You're a woman! A stupid, worthless, useless woman! You've ruined everything!"

Saskia tore at the arm imprisoning her, but for all his advanced age, Stefan Preda was frighteningly strong. His forearm felt like a steel band pressed against her throat and he was beginning to compromise her ability to breathe.

"Let. Her. Go," something snarled, something huge and feral and enraged, and Saskia shifted her gaze to see her mate half-crouched near the fire eyeing his father through the cold, hard eyes of a predator.

"Why? She's just as useless as her bitch of a mother. She was supposed to serve two purposes: to keep you distracted while I set my plan in motion and to breed your cub to unite the streaks and provide a future for all the Tiguri to rally behind. But she's failed at both. She's worth nothing now."

"Let. Her. Go."

"Stefan, this has gone far enough," Gregor said, rising to his feet to face the man who held his daughter's life in his hands. "I agreed with you that we

needed the old families to come together and put
down those upstart newcomers, but I never agreed to
murder. At least Victoria didn't actually hurt De
Santos, but you went ahead and killed him? That's
too much. That's crazy. This stops now."

"This stops when I say it stops," Stefan hissed.
Saskia had to struggle for air, but she could smell
the bitter, cloying scents of rage and madness pouring off him in waves. He truly believed even now
that he could make everything come out the way he
had planned, and she wasn't certain he wouldn't kill
her to accomplish it.

In front of the fire, Nicolas roared a final warning, and Saskia knew she couldn't live with being
responsible for her mate killing his own father. She
had to get free.

Mustering a surge of strength, she forced the
power through her limbs and shifted just one part of
her body, the hardest trick a shifter could perform. It
took intense concentration and massive amounts of
power, but in the space of a couple of heartbeats her
hand became a paw adorned with sharp, curving
claws and reached back to swipe hard against her
captor's face.

He shrieked and struck out even as he released
her. The blow caught her on the side of the head,
stunning her, and Saskia collapsed to the floor like a
bag of bones.

Everything seemed to happen at once.

She heard her mate roar until it felt as if the very
stones of the floor and walls vibrated with his fury.
Several people shouted. Chairs crashed to the floor.

Doors slammed against walls as security forces from the Silverback Clan rushed into the room from the hall outside and Rafe sprang out of concealment from his hiding spot in the service hall.

A woman screamed, and Saskia recognized the voice as her mother's. Saskia tried to raise her head, but her muscles wouldn't cooperate. She was still stunned.

Large hands grasped Saskia under the arms and dragged her across the floor away from the melee. She was aware of a large presence crouched beside her and her senses told her it wasn't her mate, but her brain couldn't quite function well enough to identify who it was. She lay in a daze for several more moments before the world began to fall back into place and she tried to sit up. The same hands that had dragged her to safety helped her up and then propped her back against the wall.

Graham Winters frowned down at her and held up a hand. "How many fingers am I holding up?"

She blinked. "Two."

He grunted and shifted, placing himself slightly in front of her so that anyone approaching would have to go through him. No one approached.

The fighting was over.

Saskia tried to make out what had happened, but overturned furniture blocked her view of some of the room. The Council members had all been rushed outside by the Lupine guards, though she could see the brownie and the shifter craning their necks to look inside.

In the corner between the sideboard and the

hearth, her mother crouched on the floor weeping
while her husband gazed dully into the flames. Dmitri and a member of the Lupine pack stood in front
of them, clearly on guard.

The sight that shook Saskia, though, played out in
the middle of the floor in front of the fire, where the
Council tables had been shoved away and chairs
flung to the walls.

Stefan Preda lay on his back on the cold stone,
bloody but defiant. The old man's face bore three
sharp grooves where Saskia's claws had caught his
flesh, but already the blood had slowed to a trickle
and the wounds had begun to draw together. Shifters
were hard to kill. Stefan stared up at the shape above
him and hissed and spat in furious madness.

Nic crouched over his father in full tiger form,
over seven hundred pounds of muscle and teeth and
claws. His green eyes looked hard and vicious, and
he had one huge paw pressed against the older man's
chest, his claws flexing rhythmically as if testing the
resilience of the flesh beneath them.

Saskia gave a mewl of distress and tried to rise, to
go to Nic, but Graham stopped her with a growl and
a firm shove. That was all it took to send her slump-
ing back to the floor. Her eyes remained on the scene
before the fire, though, and fear and pain warred in
her belly. Fear of what might happen and pain for
the decision her mate tried to make.

Graham shifted, giving Saskia a more complete
view of the hearth, and she saw that Rafe crouched
there, too, facing Nic over his father's body. The head
of the Council had retained his human form, but he

watched the Tiguri with the golden eyes of a predator.

"Think before you act, my friend," Rafe spoke, his quiet voice seeming loud in the calm that followed the storm. "Actions are not like words; they can never be taken back."

Nicolas snarled.

"I understand your fury," the Felix continued. "Believe me, I feel the burn of it, too. Your father tried to take my life. The beast in me says that can only be avenged by taking his. And the man in me is furious that I was nearly bested by an old cat twice my age. But I can decide not to be controlled by my beast. I can make the decision to let him live and continue to suffer the consequences of his actions."

A half roar, muted but angry, filled the air. The tiger looked at his sire, then lifted his head and looked across the room to his mate. Saskia stared back, trying to pour love and comfort and reassurance across the room.

The tiger snarled again and bared his fangs at the man under his paw.

"I know," Rafe spoke again. He didn't move, but he kept talking to the tiger, searching for a connection with the man within. "This man harmed your mate. I would want to kill him, too, if he'd laid a hand on mine. It doubles the weight of his betrayal, that he tried to use you for his own ends and that when his plans began to crumble he raised a hand against your woman even as he hid behind her. But that doesn't make him worthy of your fury. It makes him worthy of your contempt."

Saskia silently urged the Felix to keep talking. He seemed to understand the thoughts going through Nic's only partially human mind, but he kept forcing the Tiguri to cling to that human reason. She prayed Rafe's strategy would work, because she didn't know if her mate could live with himself if he killed his own father.

"Nicolas, look at your mate," Rafe urged, nodding his head at where Saskia sat, leaning against the rough stone wall. "She is here and she is healthy. She doesn't need to be avenged; she needs you."

God, yes. The man was absolutely right.

Slowly, Nic lifted his paw from his father's chest. Shifting his weight, he sat back on his haunches and stared down at the seething old man. At a nod from Rafe, three more Lupines stepped into the room to surround Stefan and ensure he made no further attempts to escape.

With fluid grace, the tiger pushed to his feet and wove between the legs of the werewolves to pad across the floor to his mate. Graham stepped aside as he approached, giving the couple room.

Saskia held her breath as Nicolas stopped just a few inches away and watched her with those fathomless green eyes. Hesitant, she waited until he lowered his head and chuffed, leaning forward to nuzzle her chest.

Crying softly, she wrapped her arms around his massive head, buried her face in his thick fur, and wept. After a second, she felt human arms slip around her and the fur beneath her cheek became smooth, bare skin. She only held on tighter.

"God, I love you, Nicolas. I love you so much," she gasped against his skin, and felt his embrace tighten.

"I love you, too, Sassy girl," he murmured against her hair. "I love you, too."

Gently Nicolas scooped his mate into his arms and began to carry her toward the door, oblivious to his nudity.

"What a pitiful display."

The bitter tones of Stefan's pronouncement echoed under the vaulted ceiling and earned a warning growl from several throats, but the old man was too caught up in his bitterness to care.

"It's too bad I didn't build my plan around killing you myself," he spat. "Now I have to go to my grave knowing my own son turned out to be such a disappointment to me."

Nicolas never paused, and he never looked back.

"No, you don't," he said as the crowd at the door parted before him. "I don't have a father."

Epilogue

The mess turned out to be more easily cleaned up than anyone had suspected.

With Nic's blessing, Dmitri contacted the Tiguri *theri* in Europe to discuss the situation. Acting as their leader and representative, Milan Voros pronounced judgment over the Arcoses. While Gregor and Victoria had acted more as pawns in Stefan's master plan than as true co-conspirators, they could not be allowed to benefit from their crimes, nor could they go unpunished. Accordingly, the Arcos clan was stripped of its identity as an independent streak and the couple was given provisional membership in the Voros clan. Milan would personally oversee their behavior, which would not be difficult, as they had been assigned to live in a small farmhouse on the *ther*'s vast estate near the border between Russia and Georgia.

Feeling magnanimous after all of that, Voros also agreed to allow the Others to assist in arranging for the punishment of Stefan Preda. Dmitri himself made a few phone calls and arranged for the man to be incarcerated for the remainder of his life in an inescapable fortress prison designed and most often used for vampires convicted of unforgivable crimes.

Nicolas was not told of the prison's location, and he did not care. As far as he was concerned, his family, and his new streak, consisted of him, his wife, and any cubs they might conceive together. He considered that more than enough to make him happy.

It did not make him quite as happy to have to offer his thanks to not only the resourceful vampire but also the head of the Council of Others and the Alpha of the Silverback Clan. With only a slight prod from his mate, he did it anyway. After all, De Santos had kept him from committing an act that might have changed him forever, and Winters had protected Nic's mate when he had been unable to do it himself. Maybe they had a few redeeming features between them.

He did, however take great delight in vocally turning down Rafe's offer of a seat on the Council of Others. As Nic told the Felix, he'd rather serve on the Council of Digging Out His Own Eyeballs with a Rusty Spoon. Rafe had decided not to press the issue. Especially not when Nic had offered him another option. Nic still refused to serve on the Council, but he was happy to offer his recommendation for another Tiguri to fill the position. Saskia, after all, made a much better politician than he ever would.

She, after all, had been the one to fully grasp the motives behind his father's plan, to see the implications of the attacks, the scheming, and the attempted murder. She had realized what Stefan was after with a clarity Nic didn't think he himself would ever have achieved on his own. Saskia understood people, she understood what drove them and consequently what could drive them over the edge. What better qualifications for a seat on the Council of Others could a tiger have?

Of course, Nic had felt compelled to warn the werejaguar that if the other man so much as looked at Nic's mate the wrong way—meaning other than straight in the eye and for more than any three consecutive seconds—the Tiguri would be happy to turn him into cat chow. Saskia deserved recognition for her unique talents, but that didn't make her any less Nic's mate, and he was one Tiguri who had finished catting around. Permanently.

And so, less than a week after the execution of the plan, Nic found himself waking up in his own bed to the very pleasant memory of his mate's last official night in heat. At this point, her ovulation window had closed and it would be at least another month before Nicolas was able to stimulate her into another cycle.

He sighed. He supposed he'd just have to be patient, although a few weeks of only having sex twice a day might turn into a nice change of pace.

Grinning to himself, Nic opened his eyes and discovered his bed was empty. For a change, Saskia had managed to wake before him and sneak out of the bedroom without disturbing him. Or maybe she saw it as making her escape. With her heat over, she might be feeling more than a little relief at the idea of taking a short break from the sexual marathon they'd been running recently.

He swung out of bed all but whistling a jaunty tune. Tugging a pair of sweatpants out of his closet, he pulled them on for the sake of decency before following his nose into the kitchen.

Actually, it was more so that his morning erection wouldn't send his mate running for the hills. There were some things over which a man had very little control.

He found Saskia in front of the stove with a bright red apron tied around her waist. Nic sighed in disappointment that it wasn't the only thing she wore. So much for his masculine fantasies. Under the apron, he spied a pair of crisp cotton pajamas in virginal white. At least she hadn't tried to wear them to bed, he consoled himself.

His mate turned when she saw him and waved at him with an upraised spatula. "About time you got up, lazybones. Breakfast is almost ready."

He grinned. "It wasn't my fault. I needed my rest. Some insatiable woman kept me up all night attending to her lustful needs. I'm exhausted."

"That's funny." She winked at him. "I woke up feeling positively energized. I could run a marathon. But I decided to make pancakes instead. I hope you're hungry."

"Starved. I worked up one hell of an appetite."

She blushed, and he laughed. He loved that he could do that to her so easily.

He stepped up behind her and wrapped his arms around her waist, snuggling her back against his chest. Dipping his face to her shoulder, he buried his nose against her neck and inhaled deeply.

"Mm, strawberry jam," he murmured appreciatively. "How did you know I liked that on my pancakes? Smells fresh, too. Did you run out to the farmer's market before you started cooking?"

Saskia laughed and craned her head to give him a look like he was crazy. "What on earth are you talking about? We don't even have any strawberry jam. We'll eat our pancakes with maple syrup like civilized people."

Nic made a face to show his disappointment, and again the scent of fresh strawberry jam drifted up to him. His eyes ran over his mate's slender form from the tips of her toes to the top of her strawberry blonde head.

He froze.

Strawberries.

His eyes widened, and his gaze shot to hers. His mouth opened, then closed, then opened again. Saskia stared at him for a moment, clearly puzzled. Then she read something in his expression and recognition dawned.

Strawberry tiger. Ripe, *fertile* strawberry tiger.

The grin that widened his mouth started at his toes and lit up half the city by the time it settled on his face. Reaching out, he placed a hand over his mate's still-flat belly and purred.

He loved strawberries.